SHALLOW SUBMISSION

MASTERS OF MARQUIS
BOOK 6

GOLDEN ANGEL

For Blake, the original Persian Excursion, whose self-given nickname clearly stuck in my head.

Also for every woman who loves doing her hair and makeup, who enjoys dressing up, who is naturally graceful, who has big boobs, and who usually only gets to see herself as the 'bad woman' in romance.

This time, you get to be the heroine.

CONTENTS

PROLOGUE

3 Years Earlier

Morgan

What's a safe word?

Who knew that one little question would blow up her entire life? Though perhaps she should have expected it. It wasn't the first time her whole life had changed without warning. This time was more physically painful than emotional, which was new.

"Ow, ow, ow," she whimpered as the gurney she was on was jostled.

"Sorry, hun," the EMT said sympathetically.

"It's okay, Morgan, they've got you," Naomi, the very nice submissive who had inadvertently exploded Morgan's life, said. She climbed into the ambulance, leaving her husband, Drew, hovering worriedly outside. Naomi looked back at him as she took Morgan's hand. "Meet me at the hospital."

"You don't have to come with me— Ow." Morgan winced. The stabbing pain in her right side wasn't going away, even though she'd stopped moving. Her stomach had been hurting all day, though not consistently until about an hour into the play party when it had become difficult to stand, much less walk.

Master Richard had been very annoyed at her.

"Of course, I'm coming with you. Unless you'd rather have someone else?" Naomi's dark eyes were full of sympathy and worry, and she didn't seem mad at the idea. But that wasn't what Morgan had meant.

"I don't have anyone except Master Richard." She sucked in a breath, trying to breathe through the pain and not make too much noise.

Naomi's lips pressed in a thin line, and the EMT who was attaching something to Morgan's arm paused.

"Just call him Richard for now, honey, okay?" Naomi said. "And I'm coming with you. You aren't going to the hospital alone. Not on my watch." She made a little huffing noise.

Morgan didn't understand, but she nodded, partly because Naomi seemed very determined but mostly because it was becoming painful to talk. She breathed short, shallow breaths, trying to keep her chest and stomach from expanding, and that helped a little.

The doors to the ambulance slammed shut, then the vehicle started to move a moment later. Morgan whimpered. Even that little bit of movement hurt. She was starting to worry something was seriously wrong. Master Richard had accused her of being overly dramatic, but she really wasn't trying to be.

It just hurt so bad.

"What happened?" one of the EMTs asked as they worked on her.

Morgan couldn't find the breath to answer, but it didn't matter because Naomi started answering for her. She couldn't help but be both amazed and grateful in the midst of her confusion. She knew Naomi was submissive, but she wasn't acting like it right now.

"She's been holding her right side for the past hour and seemed to be in pain. Her... boyfriend,"—the way Naomi said the word made it sound like something bad, her tone sour—"was ignoring it, but I could tell it was getting worse. When she collapsed, we called for an ambulance. I think it might be her appendix."

Naomi didn't mention that she'd been the one to catch Morgan or that Master Richard had yelled at Morgan for falling and at Naomi for daring to touch his sub. She also didn't mention that her husband, Drew, had put himself physically between Master Richard and the two women because he'd been so enraged.

And Morgan hadn't been able to do anything because it had hurt too much.

Master Richard was going to punish her severely, but she really hadn't been able to get up. And she hadn't been able to stop them from escorting him out the door. Or from calling the ambulance.

Once he was gone, the only one giving her any directions was Naomi. Even though she was a submissive, Morgan had listened because no one else was telling her what she should be doing.

Morgan moaned as the road turned a little bumpy. She wanted to push down on the spot that hurt, but even the lightest touch made her hurt worse.

"It's okay, sweetie. I've got you." Naomi's grip on Morgan's hand tightened.

She wasn't acting at all like Master Richard said other submissives would. He'd always said other submissives would hate her because women usually didn't get along with each other, especially submissives. They were always trying to steal each other's Masters, even if they already had their own, which was why she always needed to be on her guard against them. He'd also said the black submissives were the worst about it.

But Naomi was black and a submissive, and she didn't want anything to do with Master Richard.

She seemed genuinely concerned about Morgan.

It felt... odd.

She tried to remember the last time anyone had held her hand while she wasn't feeling well.

It hadn't been Master Richard. When she was sick, she was supposed to take care of herself so as not to interfere with his daily activities. And to get better as quickly as possible, so he didn't need to find a new submissive to replace her. Well aware of how much she owed him, she'd done her best, and thankfully, she'd always been quite healthy. Her parents hadn't had much patience for illness, either. If either of them had ever held her hand while she was sick, she couldn't remember it.

Naomi held Morgan's hand all the way to the hospital until she was forced to let go. For the first time in years, Morgan cried when the other submissive promised she would be there when Morgan woke up. She wasn't crying because she was scared of the surgery—although she was—she was crying because she hadn't wanted to let go of Naomi's hand, even though she didn't fully understand why.

But when she woke up, Naomi was there again, holding her hand, and the pain was magically gone. Morgan's face felt odd, though. She reached up with her free hand and touched her lips. They were curved up.

She was smiling.

Morgan giggled.

"Hey there, how are you feeling?"

"Good. I feel *good*." She didn't think she'd ever truly felt good. Not until this moment.

"Good. They had to remove your appendix. How much do you remember?"

Trying to catch her thoughts was like trying to catch fog. They slipped through her mind, too incoherent and too quick to be sensible. She blinked rapidly, trying to get a handle on herself. Master Richard would be so angry if she took this long to answer him.

"Richard isn't here. You take as long as you need," Naomi said firmly, squeezing Morgan's hand.

"Oh, good." The words slipped past Morgan's lips before she could stop them, and both of her hands flew up to her mouth to cover it, yanking her fingers away from Naomi. The other woman sat back in surprise, blinking at Morgan as if she couldn't believe what she'd just heard. "I'm sorry! I'm sorry, please don't tell him, please don't tell him I said that! I'm sorry, I'm so sorry—"

"Honey, honey, no." Naomi reached forward to take Morgan's trembling hands, lowering them to her lap. "Trust me. I am not telling that... that *man* anything. He's not going to be allowed to get anywhere near you ever again. Not if I have anything to say about it."

Relief and fear flooded Morgan in equal measure. She didn't particularly like Master Richard. She never had. She'd cried when Master Jason had sold her to him. But he was also all she'd known for the past five years. And it wasn't so bad, as long as she was a good girl and did what he wanted. Sometimes, it felt good. His rules were much easier to understand than her parents had been.

"I don't know what that means," she said.

"It means you don't have to go back to him. You can make a choice. My husband and I can help you. I know you don't know us, but you can talk to the others you know at the play party, and they'll tell you."

Morgan didn't know anyone else at the play party. Master Richard didn't like her talking to anyone. The other Doms all wanted to steal her away, and the other submissives wanted to seduce him and replace her. She wasn't sure why he liked to go to them, other than sometimes he liked to be watched. She didn't care about being watched, not that it mattered what she wanted.

That wasn't the point that she got stuck on, though.

"Your husband would be my new master? Master Richard threatens to sell me again sometimes, but I didn't think he meant it." Morgan frowned. The loopy feeling was making it hard for her to think, but Naomi had been so nice. Much nicer than she'd ever thought another woman could be. "I wonder if he'll think you stole me. You should go. I don't want you to get in trouble."

An odd expression had crept over Naomi's face.

"Sweetie, why don't you tell me about Master Richard and how you came to live with him?"

Under other circumstances, without the fuzzy happy feeling bouncing through her, Morgan would never have spoken so freely. After she'd told Naomi everything, she learned why she should never tell anyone else the full story of her life.

1

Asad

Asad was feeling oddly nervous about meeting his soon-to-be fake girlfriend for a real date. Though Asad didn't like to think of it as a date so much as a prep meeting. He and Morgan were going to have to sell themselves as a couple to his parents and extended family for a whole week.

Granted, most of the focus was going to be on his brother, Cyrus, and Cyrus' bride, so it shouldn't be too hard. Asad fully expected to fly under the radar, even though he was bringing a girlfriend home with him. In fact, the whole reason for bringing Morgan was so his mom didn't spend the entire week trying to fix him up.

He didn't need her help to get a date, dammit.

Considering his mom never hovered over him when he was a kid, it was damned annoying when she'd suddenly decided to once he was an adult, as if trying to make up for lost time. Like getting him married off would solve everything.

If anything, he needed help keeping anyone from getting too invested in him as a romantic partner, which was why he liked BDSM. Everything was nice and neat, and expectations were clearly laid out.

Bringing a woman home to a family event was going to muddy that, even though it was a fake relationship.

Walking into Marquis' restaurant, Asad looked around. The place was already busy, with most of the tables full and the bar both loud and packed. He glanced around, and it only took him a moment to spot Morgan's red hair among the tables. She was sitting perfectly still, hands folded neatly on her lap, staring at her menu.

He happened to know she had the menu memorized since she occasionally worked on the second floor of Marquis.

Maybe she was nervous, though she hadn't seemed so when the owner of the kink club they both belonged to had suggested her as the perfect solution for Asad's dilemma. Patrick's submissive, Lexie, seemed to think it would help Morgan out as well, which Asad privately agreed with. She had a traumatic past, it was true, but the Stronghold and Marquis Doms had gone a little overboard trying to protect her from what he could see.

Getting away from all the Doms breathing down her neck for a week was supposed to be good for her. And Asad got a fake girlfriend who was gorgeous, happy to be there, and not looking for a relationship.

The only thing that sucked for him was the 'no sex' rule, which even Lexie had supported. He and Morgan had scened together before at the clubs, but Lexie had pointed out that having sex while on a trip to meet his family could cause some emotional entanglements. Asad wasn't worried about that for himself, but Morgan...

So far, she hadn't fully latched on to any of the Doms, but that was partly because they'd all gently rejected her the first go-around when she'd been like a lost little baby bird, trying to find a place to land. Once she'd realized she didn't need to do that, she'd changed. But it would be better not to muddy the waters, so Asad had agreed.

No sex.

Which really was too bad, he thought, as he waved to the hostess and made his way past her to the table where Morgan was waiting for him. The scenes they'd had together had been hot as hell, and she was gorgeous. Keeping his hands to himself wasn't exactly his natural state, but it was only for a week.

As he approached the table, Morgan looked up and met his gaze. Her face relaxed into a smile. Fuck, she really was gorgeous. Her makeup was flawless, as usual. He knew enough about women and makeup to know that looking so natural took a lot of effort.

"Hello," she said, still smiling. The color on her full lips made them look like a delicious pout. "You're late."

"I am. I'm sorry," he said cheerfully. He was only a minute or two late, but anyone who spent time with Morgan knew that wasn't an argument they would win. She wasn't saying it to be censorious, the way his mother would have. She was just stating a fact. "You look lovely."

As always, Morgan preened at a compliment.

"Thank you." She paused for a moment. "You look very handsome."

"Thank you." Asad sat down across from her, smoothing his hands over the button-down shirt he was wearing. He hadn't wanted to dress up too much, but on the other hand, he hadn't wanted to appear slovenly next to Morgan, who always looked incredible. The dark purple dress she was wearing tonight dipped low in front and made her skin appear even creamier than normal, and her auburn hair glowed where the curls spilled over her shoulders and down to her breasts.

Sometimes, he wondered how her hair would look straight, but she never wore it that way.

"How was your day?" he asked, glancing down at the menu.

"It was good. Yours?"

"Exhausting." He flashed a grin at her. "But looking up now."

Morgan frowned for a moment, then her expression cleared with understanding.

"Your day is better because you're seeing me?" She sounded pleased, and Asad nodded.

Sometimes, his efforts to be charming with Morgan backfired. She took things very literally and often seemed surprised anyone would put in the effort to compliment her. That was why Asad made it a point to do so as often as he could—not that he was being insincere. He always kept his compliments legitimate.

A moment later, the server arrived with a glass of water for him, and they both put in their orders. Asad hadn't needed to look at the menu any more than Morgan did—Marquis was his favorite place to eat or hang out at the bar, even when he wasn't heading up to the second floor where all the kinky stuff was.

"So, what did you want to talk about tonight?" Morgan asked, placing her hands on the table, one atop the other, her head tilting to the side in curiosity.

"I figured we should try to get a little more natural about being a couple. Talk about things that might come up with my family, and well, everything that we didn't really talk about before."

The night that Patrick and Lexie had suggested Morgan as his date, he and Morgan had agreed to a few things—namely that she would go with him, and he would pay for everything. He'd given her a bit of information about his various family members, but that had been it, other than agreeing to meet and talk again.

"Like what?"

"Well, for starters, I don't really want to tell them that we met at a kink club," he said with a grin. "As funny as it might be at the moment, the longer-lasting repercussions would be a lot less amusing."

"I see." Morgan pressed her lips together, her eyes unfocusing. "We could say friends introduced us. It's true."

"That's what I was thinking, too. And that we spent some time together just hanging out, and we hit it off... it was casual and has only gotten more serious lately."

"Like when you asked me to come with you to the wedding?"

"Exactly." He chuckled. "I thought we should also probably know more about each other. We've scened together, but we haven't really had a whole lot of conversation, at least not the kind that people who are spending time together would."

"Oh. What do you think we need to know?"

This was where it was going to get a little tricky, thanks to Morgan's past, but Asad figured he'd better prepare her. On the off-chance his parents decided to actually pay attention to him and Morgan, there might be some nosy questions. He wanted to know if there was anything that would be particularly upsetting to her or that he would need to protect her from.

No, stepping in to shield someone else wasn't his norm, but he was going to be responsible for her for a whole week. Thankfully, no longer than that, but for that week, he would take the responsibility seriously, even if it made him uncomfortable.

"Well, for one, I told you that my brother is the one getting married, but I didn't tell you that Cyrus had childhood leukemia, which is something a girlfriend would probably know." There was a heavy feeling in his chest, remnants of the fear he'd felt growing up, far too aware he could lose his little brother any day.

"Oh, I'm so sorry. That must have been hard."

"It was." In so many ways. "There's a good chance my family will ask me about your family as well."

Understanding flashed in Morgan's hazel eyes, then she shook her head.

"I'm no-contact with them."

"I know," Asad reminded her gently. He also knew that was the line she'd been told to use when people asked. "It's possible they'll try to pry, which I want to prepare you for. If there's anything specifically you want me to say or that you think you might say, so we're on the same page."

Morgan

Master Asad's—no, just Asad since they were in a restaurant, not at a club—statement made sense. She'd seen a lot of television shows and movies with nosy parents. She just didn't have any firsthand experience since she'd never been allowed to date, then she'd been with Master Jason—who definitely hadn't introduced her to his parents—then with Master Richard, whose parents had already passed away.

She didn't like the idea of having to talk about her past with people who were meeting her for the first time. Even though she would be Asad's fake girlfriend, she still wanted to make a good impression. She didn't want to be treated as an oddity or breakable.

Part of the appeal of going away for a week was to be around people who knew nothing about her or her past. To see what it would be like to be around people who knew nothing. That was why she'd always liked scening with Master Asad. Rather than treating her like she was made of glass or like she didn't know her limits, he seemed to trust her to tell him what she wanted and didn't want.

Most people accepted that she was no-contact with her parents, and if they did press, she brushed them off with "I don't talk about that."

It might be harder to brush off her fake boyfriend's parents.

"We can tell them my parents were very religious and kicked me out at sixteen when they caught me with a boy." The words came out in a rush, and Asad froze for a moment, his gaze jerking up to meet hers. She could feel her heart pounding in her chest. She suddenly realized she was smoothing her hands over her napkin, over and over, feeling the silky material against her palms. Immediately, she pulled her hands away, dropping them to her lap and folding her fingers to clasp them tightly.

That was a little detail she hadn't mentioned at the time she'd been interviewed by Master Patrick and Lexie. Naomi and her husband knew, but she'd asked them not to share it with anyone. With everyone she'd met, she'd shared a little less of her past, and things had gone better for her. Mostly.

She wasn't going to tell Asad that Master Jason had been no boy. He'd been twenty-five and her piano teacher, which had made her parents even angrier. Not with him, with her. The evil seductress who had tempted a good man into sin. She knew now that had hardly been the case, but back then, she'd truly thought she'd done something wrong.

"I'm very sorry about that," Asad said, sympathy filling his dark eyes.

Morgan frowned. She didn't want him to change how he saw her. This was why she didn't tell people things.

"It's fine. I have come to the conclusion that I am better off without them." Especially after the one attempt she'd made to get back in contact with them last year. It had reaffirmed her decision to focus on her current life and not on her past.

"Well, I'm sorry about that, too. My parents might be a pain in my ass, but they love me." There was something odd in his voice as he said the words, and he seemed almost relieved when the server reappeared at their table with their drinks.

Morgan was relieved, too. Once the server stepped away, she decided to see if she could move the conversation to a different topic.

"What else do you think your parents might ask about?"

"Probably when you want to get married and have babies." Asad grinned at the expression on her face.

She could feel the horror practically emanating from her. Asad would make beautiful babies. He was a beautiful man, but Morgan wasn't sure she wanted kids, much less marriage.

"Looks like we're on the same page for that question, but maybe try not to make that exact face when they ask. A simple 'we're nowhere near that point' will do, and if they push, tell them they should talk to me."

He said 'when' they asked, not 'if,' so it sounded like it was a foregone conclusion that they would. Morgan would try not to make the face.

"Are we getting more serious?" she asked. "You are taking me to a family wedding." Her understanding was that it only happened in serious relationships. Something she had no experience with. It was probably going to be fun to pretend and good practice for her.

She now understood what she'd had with Master Richard wasn't at all normal, even within the kink community. Morgan was looking forward to playing 'boyfriend and girlfriend,' especially because it wouldn't really matter if she messed something up since she and

Asad weren't together, anyway. Though, of course, she was going to do her best because she didn't want to embarrass him in front of his family.

"More serious, but nowhere near living together. In fact, you living with Brian is something that will drive that home, so make sure you bring it up." He grinned at her. "If that's okay."

"That's fine." She had never intended to lie about her living arrangements. "So, we are seeing each other more often but not living together and definitely not talking about children or marriage. And your brother had childhood leukemia. Is there anything else I should know about him? Or his bride... Anna, right?"

"Anna." He nodded. "I've only met her a few times, so it makes sense you wouldn't know much about her. Cyrus and I aren't really close, either. He went into accounting and works at my dad's firm, whereas I rebelled, got my GED, then went to school to become an engineer. Which makes me the black sheep of the family."

"You're a black sheep because you're an engineer?" Morgan was confused. Her friend Carolyn had told her that Asad had a really good job that made him a lot of money, something Carolyn held in high esteem.

"Maybe not a black sheep exactly, but my parents were disappointed I didn't follow the family line." He shrugged with one shoulder. "They were also really disappointed about me not walking across the stage for graduation, but I wasn't sad to miss it."

"I never graduated, either," she suddenly felt compelled to share. "I got my GED, too." She'd gotten hers last year, something else she didn't share with many people.

"So, we have that in common." Asad winked at her.

Something inside her fizzed with happiness in response. She liked having things in common with him. Everyone liked Asad. He was impossible not to like, and he was really good at focusing on a person and making them feel special.

Morgan liked feeling special in a good way.

"The wedding is right outside Pittsburgh, right?" she asked. There was a club there she wanted to visit called the Outlands. Naomi had told her about it. That was where she and Drew had settled after he'd left the service and they went on occasion. Morgan liked the idea of trying out another club again, somewhere not everyone would immediately know who she was. Though, because of that, she wouldn't feel comfortable scening with anyone but Asad, but that was okay since he was going to be her fake boyfriend for the week.

"Yup, and we've got a whole week of activities."

Their food arrived, and Morgan listened happily as Asad described the schedule his mom had sent him for the week. It sounded like an interesting combination of his culture's wedding traditions and the bride's. She was looking forward to all of it. Especially because she'd never attended a wedding before. This one sounded even more interesting than the ones she'd seen in movies.

2

When Morgan opened the front door, Brian pounced.

"How was it? Did everything go okay?" Brian shot the questions at her from where he was standing behind the kitchen counter before she'd even closed the door. His house, in which she rented a room, was set up with a huge entertaining space in the main room, which meant there were clear sight lines from the kitchen to the dining room to the living area where the front door was.

It reminded her a little of her parents, except the questions would have been very different and asked in a different tone of voice. She did her best not to chafe. Friends cared enough to ask—that's what Amy had told her. Brian wasn't trying to control her; he was just making sure she was okay.

"It was fine. Everything went well. We talked about what the week is going to be like and got our stories straight for his family."

"Good. And you're still feeling good about going?"

There it was again, that little stir of annoyance in the pit of her stomach. This was why she needed to get away for a bit. She didn't want to be annoyed with Brian. He'd been nothing but generous to her, and it would make living together awkward if they were fighting, but she didn't like how he questioned everything she did, multiple times.

"Very good. I think I'm going to enjoy having a practice boyfriend. Asad is very kind, and the wedding sounds like it's going to be fun. I've never been to a wedding." Morgan debated going to her room to end the conversation, but she'd learned when she first moved in that going to her room tended to distress him as he thought it meant she was hiding something.

To be fair, sometimes she was.

Leaning on the counter with his elbows, Brian lifted one hand.

"Cookie?"

That decided it. She'd rather have a cookie than end the conversation.

"Yes, please." Taking out her phone before hanging her purse on the hook, Morgan went to sit on the bar side of the counter, happily accepting a plate with two cookies. Turning back into the kitchen, Brian opened the fridge to get out the milk and pour them both a glass. As he did so, he hummed under his breath.

"What are you happy about?" Morgan asked. Brian only hummed under his breath when he was particularly happy about something. She also liked the idea of getting his attention off her.

"Nothing."

But he didn't stop humming. Morgan eyed him as he slid the glass of milk in front of her. Should she say something about how he expected her to answer his questions, but he wasn't answering hers truthfully?

She didn't want to make him angry.

It also didn't seem fair.

She was saved by her phone chiming with a text message before she had to make a decision. Tapping on her phone, she saw it was one of the group text messages she was in. She was in several, which could become overwhelming at times.

This one was with Amy, Sam, Noelle, Marissa, and Carolyn—her 'group' at Stronghold and Marquis. Even though the clubs welcomed everyone, Morgan had noticed people sorted themselves into groups within the larger group. She was happy to be a part of one. It was the first time she'd ever been a part of a group.

Even at their church, her parents hadn't liked her spending time with the other kids too much, not even the other little girls, unless they were learning something. It was hard to make friends when you weren't supposed to talk to each other.

> Amy: How was the date with Asad? Are you still there?

The phone chimed again.

> Noelle: Tell us everything!

"Now, what are you so happy about?" Brian asked teasingly.

Morgan couldn't help but grin at him.

"Having friends." People who cared. She might still be learning the rules about what friends could and couldn't do, but she knew she liked having them. And thankfully, her friends were patient when she messed up.

Not everyone was.

"Friends are definitely good." Polishing off his cookie while Morgan typed out a response, Brian came around the counter to give her a kiss on top of her head before ambling off to the couch and turning on the television.

> It was good. I have a lot of events I need to pack for, though. Can anyone come over next weekend to help? We leave on Monday.

A moment later, her phone was chiming incessantly from the flurry of responses as everyone joined in to say when they were free. Morgan texted that she had a wedding she was doing makeup for on Saturday afternoon, but other than that, she was free, then let the others work it out for themselves. It didn't take long for them to come to the conclusion that Sunday afternoon was the only time that worked for everyone.

That was one worry taken care of.

The first time she and Asad had talked about the wedding, he'd told her there were a lot of events, but this time, they'd gone more in depth into what the events were. He hadn't had much of an idea of what she was supposed to wear to any of them, though.

"A dress is fine" wasn't much direction.

Hopefully, the others would be able to tell her. She was also going to look up Persian weddings online. Brian kept telling her she needed to stop relying on movies and television for her societal knowledge, but there was a lot of really useful information online. At the very least, she bet there were videos of weddings she could watch.

It sounded like the wedding week was going to be a mix of two cultures celebrating the union. She was looking forward to it.

Hopefully, this week would go by fast.

A*SAD*

"Yes, Mom, Morgan is very excited to meet you, too." Walking into his friend Law's house, Asad rubbed his forehead. His mom was giving him a headache, which was nothing new. "We're going to drive up on Monday, then we'll leave after the *Mādarzan Salām* next Sunday."

There were a lot of traditions being combined for the week, and the traditional greeting to Cyrus' new mother-in-law was going to be part of the morning-after brunch his bride's family was throwing. Asad wasn't going to promise how long he'd stay after the exchange because he had a feeling he'd be ready to run by then. If he could have gotten out of the brunch entirely, he would have, but it would look bad for the groom's brother and best man to totally skip it. It would also draw attention his way from his family, which was the last thing he wanted.

Asad wanted to get in, get out, and go home as quickly and painlessly as possible.

"We're going to have dinner Monday night after you get here," his mom said. "Just our immediate family, so we can meet Morgan."

Ah, fuck. Asad barely held in his groan as he walked into Law's kitchen. It looked like he was the first one to show up. Law was the only one there, standing behind the counter and getting some kind of food ready. His girlfriend, Iris, who also lived here, was nowhere to be seen. Asad gave his friend a little wave and Law nodded his head in greeting before refocusing on what he was doing.

"She's kind of shy, Mom."

"Which is why it will be better for her to meet your immediate family first, so she doesn't feel like she's being thrown into a group of strangers," his mom retorted. "This way, at least she'll know me and Anna when you have duties to attend to."

Crap. His mom had a good point.

"Yeah, okay."

"You could try to sound a little grateful, you know. It's not like adding in something extra to this already packed week was easy," his mom chided him.

It didn't matter that Asad hadn't asked her to add a dinner, that he didn't even want her to add a dinner. Nope, he was supposed to be grateful. Biting back the reply he really wanted to make, he cleared his throat. It was easier to go along with his mother than argue with her.

"Thank you, Mom."

"You're welcome." Her voice softened. "I can't wait to see you, sweetheart. It's been too long."

Something inside his chest tugged uncomfortably, and he suddenly felt very aware of Law's presence. Turning away, so he was facing the hallway rather than the open kitchen, Asad rubbed his hand over his collarbone, where the inner pressure was pushing the hardest.

"Looking forward to seeing you, too." It was the truth, even if it wasn't the whole truth. Family visits were always uncomfortable for him, but he did love his family and knew they loved him. At least he had that.

He was even more grateful for it this week after his conversation with Morgan last Saturday.

"I love you. See you Monday."

"Love you too, Mom. See you Monday." Only two days away. A day and a half, really, since Saturday was already half over.

Hanging up the phone, Asad cleared his throat as he turned around to face Law again. The other man was still standing behind the counter, cutting something, and seemingly entirely focused on his work, which Asad didn't trust at all.

"Hey, man, sorry about that."

"No problem. You ready for the wedding?" Law asked. Asad's friends knew a little about his complicated family dynamics, enough to understand why visits home could be difficult for him.

"Oh, sure, a whole week centered around Prince Cyrus. I'm so ready." He fist-pumped through the sarcasm, and Law shook his bald head, a smile hovering on his lips. Filipino-American, his skin was several shades darker than Asad's, and he had some grey threaded through his goatee and mustache. That grey was exactly why Asad didn't have facial hair... but then, he still had hair on top of his head. Something he took great pleasure in teasing Law and their other friend Q—whose real name was Quinton—about.

Before Law could comment on his snarky response, the sound of the door opening and Q's voice filled the air.

"Sam gave it to me. Of course, I'm going to wear it." Q walked into the kitchen, Connor following behind him with a bemused expression on his face—easy to see because, as tall as Q was, Connor was even taller, a giant teddy bear of a man. Asad guessed the topic of conversation was the t-shirt Q was wearing, which his girlfriend must have given him.

It's Not a Bald Spot
It's a Solar Panel for
A Sex Machine

The bold print stood out starkly on the black shirt. It only took Law and Asad a moment to read it, then they both cracked up. Q grinned sheepishly, running his hand over his very bald head. He'd shaved it recently from its closely-cropped cut when he'd noticed a bald spot forming on the top.

Connor shook his head. He was the shyest out of the four of them. Asad couldn't imagine him wearing a shirt that said anything like that. Or a shirt that said anything at all. Shirts with funny sayings were definitely not his style. They weren't really Asad's either, but he still had a few to whip out when the occasion warranted it.

"It's not like you can understand," Asad joked, looking up at Connor. "The only way anyone could ever know if you have a bald spot is if you sit down... but you can see everyone else's."

"That's true." Connor shrugged.

"Well, Sam and Iris will be coming back eventually, so you can tell her yourself that you don't approve," Q teased, and Connor frowned at him.

"It's not that I don't approve. I'm just saying... You know what, never mind." He shook his head again, sighing as he sat down at the counter. He was tall enough that, even sitting on the barstool, if he had a bald spot on top of his head, the only one who might be able to see it was Q.

"It's okay, big guy. We would never get you a shirt that says anything like this," Q said, patting Connor's shoulder as he sat down next to him. "We know you prefer to be a secret sex machine rather than announcing it to the world."

Groaning, Connor rubbed his hands over his face.

"Anyone want something to drink?" Law asked. As a recovered alcoholic, Law didn't keep alcohol in the house, so they all asked for either water or soda. Law insisted he didn't mind if they drank, but for the most part, they all still tried not to around him, especially not in his own home.

"Did you hear that Nick and Avery got engaged?" Q asked, taking his root beer from Law.

"No, when did that happen?" Asad settled on the other side of Connor, leaving Law on the opposite side of the counter alone, which was how he liked it.

Lifting the veggie and dip tray he'd been preparing, Law slid it in front of them.

"Last night."

"Then how were we supposed to hear about it?" Connor asked.

"I knew," Law said. "Avery called Iris."

"And Nick told Luke, who told Olivia, who told Angel, who told me this morning." Q lifted his root beer in a kind of salute, chuckling while the others shook their heads.

The Stronghold gossip train was something to behold. Asad had used it for his benefit when he'd put out the word he needed a fake girlfriend for his brother's wedding, but he was also wary of falling prey to it. Taking Morgan as his fake girlfriend was putting him in a bit of the spotlight, but since everything was out of town, he hoped it wouldn't be too bad.

"Seems like there's something in the water," Q said, looking pointedly at Law. "Lots of people getting engaged."

"Wait, is there something we should know?" Asad asked, his head gaze whipping back and forth between Law and Q. The grin on Q's face seemed to say so, but Law looked completely unamused and unperturbed.

"Not anytime soon for me and Iris. Maybe you should ask Q about him and Sam."

"You've been together longer."

"You've known Sam longer."

"Hmm. Good point." Q stroked his chin, causing all three of his friends to turn and look at him with surprise. He laughed. "No, we're not there yet, either, but that's definitely where we're headed. For now, we're having a good time living in sin."

"As are Iris and I," Law said pointedly. There was a little smile on his normally grumpy face, and Asad couldn't help but think that maybe things were a little farther along there than Law was willing to admit.

3

———————

Asad

Hanging out with his friends the Saturday before his trip was exactly what Asad had needed. He didn't like to admit that he was nervous about his plan to bring Morgan home as his fake girlfriend, but now that the time was almost upon him, he was feeling his nerves. Far more than he'd expected.

Maybe some of it also came from having to spend a week with his family, something he hadn't voluntarily done since he was a teenager. A few days was usually his limit.

Normally, he would think Morgan was a delightful distraction, but with Patrick and Lexie's edicts that there was to be no sexual contact, that had gone up in the air. At least he would still be distracted by making sure she was okay, and at the end of it, he'd be able to come home to his friends.

Relaxing on Law's back porch and shooting the shit was the perfect way to spend his last afternoon... at least, it was for most of the afternoon.

"So, what's going on with you and Morgan?" Q asked, as though he'd picked up on Asad's thoughts.

"Nothing." Asad shrugged. "She'll go up to Pennsylvania with me for the week, then we'll come home."

"And she understands this is just for the week?"

"Yes. We talked about it last weekend and had a whole dinner to go over things. I think she's excited to go someplace where everyone won't be watching her every move." He gave Q a pointed look. Though Q wasn't the worst of the bunch who kept an eye on Morgan, his girlfriend Sam was friends with her, so Q was a little more invested than some of the other Doms. "She's not stupid."

"No, but she is naïve about a lot of things." Q arched his eyebrow at Asad, as if daring him to argue, but of course Asad couldn't.

He remembered what Morgan had said about her parents. Though she hadn't explicitly asked him not to tell anyone, he'd gotten the sense she hadn't told many people about her family. So, he held his tongue and didn't say that he probably had a better sense of how naïve she was than Q did.

Any parents who were willing to kick their daughter out of the house at sixteen because they'd caught her with a boy... well, there were a lot of assumptions that could be made. He also couldn't be one hundred percent sure his assumptions were correct, so better to just stay quiet.

"She is, but not about this." He shook his head. "Patrick and Lexie already gave me the 'don't sleep with her so things don't get confused' talk."

"Oh, good," Law chimed in. "With you pretending to be boyfriend and girlfriend, sex would likely only confuse things... at least while you're away from the club, and there's no one to help explain things to her if she gets the wrong idea."

Ouch. That hurt, even though he knew Law didn't mean it to. Asad tried not to take it personally. When it came to Morgan, pretty much all the Doms at the club were incredibly protective. *Over*-protective. It was no wonder she wanted to get away for a bit with someone who didn't tiptoe around her. Asad wasn't a bad Dom, but he wasn't one of the Doms subbies in need went to. He wasn't the kind of Dom anyone wanted to lean on, and he liked it that way.

A hot scene, a few orgasms, and a bit of aftercare, and he could send a happy subbie on their way. If they needed someone to coddle them, they could go to Connor or one of the other Service Doms or Daddy Doms. That wasn't him.

And he was starting to think that was exactly what Morgan needed.

It wasn't as if his reputation was unknown. That was why he called himself the Persian Excursion. He'd deliberately named himself as a ride, a short trip, not a place to settle down and stay.

"Did I just hear you say that Asad shouldn't have sex with someone?"

All the men jumped as Iris opened the back door, coming out onto the porch, followed by Sam. They'd been so quiet, the men hadn't heard them come in—and with the windows open for the warm air, they would have been able to hear everything that was being said.

"Hey, beautiful," Law said, his expression mellowing. He reached out his arm, and Iris went to him, flipping her long brown hair off her shoulder as she settled onto his lap. Considering what a grump Law was, and how bright and sunny Iris was, it was amazing the two had managed to get together, but somehow, they fit perfectly.

"Move over," Sam said to Q, making everyone laugh. He *was* taking up the entirety of a two-seat swing.

"As you wish," he replied cheerfully, scooting over. He and Sam had an interesting relationship because they were both switches rather than Dom and sub. The power exchange between them was in constant flux. It looked like Sam was feeling a little bossier today, and Q was feeling a little more subbie.

"Oh my God, that feels good," she said as she sat down with a huge sigh of relief.

Blonde and curvy, she and Q were pretty close to the same height, which made her a little taller than Asad. Not that it had stopped him from scening with her before she and Q had gotten together, though they'd never had sex. He'd never had sex with Iris, either. Thankfully.

He was sure it would have been enjoyable, but not worth it now that they were dating his friends.

"I'd forgotten how exhausting shopping can be," Sam said with a loud sigh.

Without a word, Q reached down to pull her legs onto his lap, turning her in the seat as he did so. Popping off her shoes, he started massaging her feet, and Sam groaned, leaning her head against the back of the seat.

"Hey," Iris said, sitting up straight in Law's lap and frowning down at him. "Why didn't you offer me a foot massage?"

"Because I didn't know you wanted one." Rather than reaching for her feet, Law sat perfectly still, his gaze steady on Iris' face as she pouted at him. After a moment, she huffed.

"Please, Sir, would you rub my feet?" She managed to make the request with complete sincerity, kicking her sandals off and lifting the feet in question up as she wriggled back to make the position more conducive to a foot rub. Asad and Connor exchanged an amused look as Law started to rub Iris' feet.

A year ago, Asad would have said he didn't think Law would ever let himself have another relationship, yet now here he was, happy and rubbing his submissive's feet. Life could be strange that way. Was there a little ache of envy in Asad's chest, watching his friends? Sure. But he also knew that wasn't what he really wanted.

Having to be responsible for a girlfriend would be bad enough, but once he'd realized he was kinky... well, a submissive was a responsibility. No, thank you.

Connor was watching the two couples as well, his expression stoic, yet Asad was sure his friend was feeling the same yearning. Most likely even more so. Unlike Asad, Connor had no problem stating that he wanted a relationship. That was part of why he'd gone through the classes at Marquis. Once he'd realized he was kinky, he'd been hoping to meet someone he connected with.

"So, what's this about Asad not having sex with someone? There aren't that many subs who haven't already hopped aboard the Persian Excursion," Iris said, leaning her head against Law's shoulder and smiling at Asad with true fondness. She found his nickname for himself particularly hilarious.

"Hey, you haven't taken a ride yet... unless you want to ask Law for a threesome for your birthday?" He winked at her as Law snorted in derision.

Yeah, Law was not the sharing type.

Iris laughed delightedly, turning to look at her boyfriend.

"Oh, are threesomes on the table for birthday presents? I had no idea." She grinned wickedly, poking Law in the side. "Maybe I need to get more creative with my wish list."

"We're talking about how Asad shouldn't have sex with Morgan this week while they're on their trip," Law said, ignoring Iris' teasing, which was really the only way to deter her most of the time. She was an epic brat and thrived on getting under Law's skin.

"Shouldn't that be Asad and Morgan's decision?" Sam asked, frowning. "I'm pretty sure that's not anyone else's business." Though her words were fairly mild, her tone wasn't. Mistress Samantha was in the house—or on the back porch, in this case.

"Yes, but there's also good reason for them not to," Q said, not pausing in the foot rub as he countered her statement. "They're going to be away from everyone and pretending to be a couple. Things get confusing. You can't tell me that's not the plot of at least a quarter of the romances you read. I know you love fake relationship romances."

He raised his eyebrows at her, his fingers deftly stroking over the soles of her feet. Sam made a face at him, but didn't argue.

"Ooh, what would we be in a romance?" Iris asked, turning to look at Sam.

"Age gap, grumpy-sunshine for sure," Sam replied, making Asad and Connor crack up at Law's expression.

"I'm not sure I like that," he grumbled.

"Of course you don't, grumpy." Iris poked him in the side again before leaning forward to kiss the top of his head. Asad wasn't able to see exactly what Law did, but she yelped a moment later. Poke a Dom often enough, and eventually, he was going to poke back.

Especially a big grump like Law.

"The point is, I don't want to be in a relationship," Asad interjected. "My life is not a romance novel."

"That's what they always say," Sam whispered.

He glared at her.

"She and I are going on a trip. We are not going to have sex. No one's feelings are going to get confused. But if hers do, I'll let her down easy. It's not like she doesn't have plenty of Doms who would be interested in starting something with her." Although no one had stepped up to the plate yet. It was probably intimidating as fuck, knowing everyone's eyes would be on them.

Morgan was gorgeous, funny, and sweet. She was a fantastic submissive. There was no reason a great Dom wouldn't snap her up the moment she made herself open to that.

"Do you think Morgan has a magic vagina?" Iris whispered to Sam, though he didn't know why she bothered since all of them could hear her.

"Maybe?" Sam whispered back, appearing uncertain.

Asad was not going to ask. He was so not going to ask.

"What's a magic vagina?" Connor asked.

Great. *Now* the big guy decided to talk.

"It's when a playboy hero, or a rake in historical romance, has had sex with hundreds of women—"

"I have not had sex with hundreds of women!" Granted, he hadn't been keeping count, but it wasn't *hundreds*. Surely. One hundred at most.

Sam kept explaining, ignoring Asad's outraged interjection.

"But then he finds that one woman where the sex is so good, he suddenly becomes monogamous, even if he didn't intend to start a relationship." Sam paused thoughtfully. "Though, usually, the magic vagina seems to belong to a virgin, and we all know Morgan isn't that."

"Great. I'm so glad to know I'm safe," he said sarcastically. "Stay away from virgins... good life advice."

It really was. Virgins were far more likely to read into things.

Especially at their age since there was usually a reason they were holding onto their virginity. Society built up losing it to be special.

Asad didn't want to be *anyone*'s special someone.

Sam and Iris exchanged another look he didn't like.

"Can we talk about something else?" he asked. "Literally, anything else?"

"Did you know there are magic penises, too?"

He groaned.

4

Morgan

Looking at the clothes spread out over her bed, dresser, and hanging from the closet doors, Morgan rubbed her hands together in front of her before realizing what she was doing and dropped them to her sides.

"You okay?" Amy asked from where she was sitting on Morgan's bed, several shirts heaped on her lap. Noelle and Marissa were in Morgan's closet, debating what else they might pull out for her to look at, Sam was sitting in Morgan's computer chair, and Carolyn was sifting through the things she'd brought over for Morgan to try on since they were about the same size.

"Yes, I'm fine," Morgan said automatically.

Even though she wasn't.

Her palms were sweaty, and her heart was beating faster than normal, and she... she was nervous. Even with her friends there to help her out, she felt like she was completely out of her depth. The last time she'd felt like this had been when Naomi and Drew had handed her off to Patrick, explaining he was Drew's cousin and he'd keep her safe while they dealt with Master Richard.

It had been a leap into the unknown, and part of her had been sure they'd just sold her, the same way Master Jason had. But Patrick had been just as kind and gentle as his cousin, then he'd introduced her to Lexie and Freddy and his friends, and everything had fallen into place from there.

This would, too.

At least, that's what she tried to tell herself, but it didn't seem to be doing anything to help settle her nerves. She wanted to pace and flutter her hands, and she couldn't. Not with all her friends there, watching. Taking a deep breath, she pushed down the emotions welling up inside her, the urge to move.

"It's going to be okay," Amy said soothingly, brushing the shirts off her lap and getting up to hug Morgan.

The secure weight of her arms around Morgan's body made her feel a little better. She hugged Amy back, releasing her breath and searching for the calm that had deserted her. Amy was right. It was going to be okay. She could do this. She had to do this. If she chickened out now, she could only imagine how everyone would react.

They'd be supportive, of course, but who knew when she would get another chance to get away from the protective cocoon she'd been wrapped in? She'd be doted on, sympathized with, and no one would really understand. Not even her friends.

So, she was going. It was going to be okay because it had to be.

"I'm just nervous. What if I wear the wrong thing?" That wasn't all she was nervous about, but it helped to focus on one thing. One fixable thing. Hopefully fixable, with her friends' help.

"You're not going to wear the wrong thing. We're going to send you with options for every event, whether it's dressy or more casual," Sam said sternly. "And you can ask Asad for help. I'm sure he'll be more helpful when presented individual questions and options."

For a moment, it seemed as though she was about to say something more, but instead she sat back in the chair, watching the others. Amy let go of Morgan and stepped away, sliding her hand down so she could hold Morgan's like a lifeline. Sometimes, Morgan didn't like to be touched, but right now, she wanted something to hold on to, and Amy was making herself available.

She also didn't want to hurt Amy's feelings by pushing her away.

"I don't want to look out of place."

"The key is to overdress rather than underdress if you're unsure of the dress code, and do it with confidence," Marissa said, emerging from the closet with another dress. One that Morgan hadn't picked out because she hadn't been sure what she'd wear it to. "That way, even if you stand out, it's in a good way."

"She's got a point. Plus, if you're overdressed, you can always take off some jewelry or something to help tone it down." Amy squeezed Morgan's hand. "There's not much you can do if you're underdressed."

"And you're always going to look amazing no matter what you wear, so you have that going for you," Sam added.

"Has anyone even seen Morgan without her makeup?" Noelle asked, teasing. Unlike Marissa, she came out of the closet empty handed.

"Nope, and if Morgan is smart, she'll keep it that way for Asad." Carolyn smirked. "Men don't want the real thing, anyway. They like the fantasy."

Asad and Morgan would be staying in the same hotel room to keep up appearances for his family. He had booked them one with a king-sized bed, which he'd said would be more than enough room for both of them, and Morgan agreed. She was used to sleeping on her full bed.

It would be interesting to sleep in a bed with someone else again. Master Jason had done that with her, but not Master Richard. She'd usually slept on the mattress he'd put in the corner for her or sometimes in the cage if she'd been bad. Sometimes, she'd fallen asleep on the couch or the mat in the Dungeon and stayed there. But never in his bed. He said it might give her ideas above her station. Morgan had never really understood what that meant, but she'd understood the rules about where to sleep clearly enough.

"Has Brian ever seen you without your makeup?" Noelle asked.

"A few times." But not often. The other women weren't wrong when they talked about Morgan wearing her makeup and hair done all the time. It had been a requirement of Master Richard's. She'd tried going without it while she recovered from having her appendix removed, but she'd found she preferred to wear makeup.

Putting it on soothed her, and seeing the results gave her a boost of confidence she often needed. Mistress Julie said that as long as she was doing it for herself, that she was making the choice, there was nothing wrong with it. She'd heard quite a few people saying she didn't 'have' to wear makeup or that they thought she'd be even prettier without it, but she wasn't wearing it for them.

She was wearing it for her and because she liked to do her makeup. Mistress Julie said there was nothing wrong with that. Since Mistress Julie was also Morgan's therapist, she trusted the Dominatrix's opinion more than most.

"Where is Brian today?" Noelle asked. "Is he going to be around?"

"He's out with friends," Morgan replied, standing still as Marissa held up the dress she'd found in front of her.

Marissa nodded. "You should definitely bring this one. You said there's an after-wedding brunch, right?"

"Yes," Morgan said, looking down at the bold green-and-white print. Made of flowy material, the waist cinched in, but otherwise, it was blousy, with a skirt that ruffled around her legs as she walked. "It's not too bold?"

Her understanding was that she wasn't supposed to take attention from the bride. Again, she didn't really understand what that meant, but it seemed to mean muted colors that weren't white and not dressing too sexy. This particular dress wasn't sexy, but it was very bright.

"It's perfect. Casual but classy, it's a total brunch dress," Marissa said definitively. "You're taking it."

Relief flooded Morgan. That was one more outfit decided. She had the Monday night family dinner, casual outfits for the week that could be dressed up with jewelry, a dress for the wedding, and a dress for the brunch.

"All we have left is the rehearsal dinner."

Which seemed to be the hardest to pick out.

"Maybe you should take two dresses for that," Sam suggested. "Then you can find out how dressy it's going to be after you're there."

"I'm going to guess cocktail dress," Carolyn mused, flipping through the clothes yet again, pulling out some of the more formal options. "The wedding is black tie, so the rehearsal will at least be cocktail."

"Cocktail or formal... but... you said the bride's family is throwing the rehearsal dinner?" Marissa frowned as she looked at the two dresses Carolyn held up in front of her, hands on her hips as she tried to decide.

"Yes. Asad said there was some back and forth about who was paying for what. Anna's family is hosting the rehearsal dinner, ceremony, and brunch, but his parents are hosting the reception." He'd sounded amused by it all, as if people arguing over who was going to pay for something was funny.

"Hmmm." Marissa made a considering noise, tapping her finger against her lips.

"What?" Amy asked her, squeezing Morgan's hand.

"I think it's possible the rehearsal dinner might be as big a deal as the reception for this one," Marissa said. "With American customs, the bride's family pays for the wedding and the groom's family pays for the rehearsal dinner. I'd be willing to bet money the rehearsal dinner is basically going to be another reception." She turned to look at Morgan. "Did Asad say how many people were invited to the rehearsal dinner."

Morgan shook her head.

"All he told me was that I needed a dress. I'll text him."

"Men," Carolyn muttered under her breath while Morgan sent the text. "They never understand how important the details are."

Giving Morgan's hand another squeeze, Amy let go, then started gathering up the more casual dresses and clothing that had been rejected. Realizing she was cleaning up, Morgan started helping.

"So... do you know when Brian is going to be back?" Noelle asked as she moved to pitch in, taking the dresses they were still looking at and moving them next to the headboard, so they didn't get mixed up.

"No." Morgan frowned. Was Noelle here to see her or Brian? "Did you need to talk to him?"

"Not need, no." Noelle smoothed her hands over the sundress she was wearing. She did look very pretty. No one else was wearing a dress. Morgan had just assumed she'd wanted to dress up a little today or that she'd come from somewhere that necessitated a dress. Now she wondered if Noelle had worn it for Brian. "But I was hoping to run into him."

"She's hoping to lock him down before he finds out that Master Damien and Rae broke up," Carolyn smirked as Noelle shot her an outraged look.

"That has nothing to do with it." Noelle lifted her chin, tossing her blonde hair as she did so. "I've always liked him and just thought it was time to make my move."

She'd always liked him? Morgan hadn't known that. She decided not to say anything, though. Picturing Noelle and Brian together... it didn't fit. Though Noelle seemed to prefer indulgent Doms, Morgan couldn't see Brian with her.

"I don't know when he'll be back, sorry. He told me it might be late." Morgan was relieved when her phone chimed with a text to distract her from the conversation. It wasn't Asad, though. "Oh, our food is here!"

"I'll go get it." Carolyn stepped away from the cleanup help and was already through the door before anyone else could say anything.

"I'll help!" Noelle dropped the clothes she'd started picking up onto the bed, hurrying after Carolyn.

After Noelle had left the room, Sam let out a huge sigh, causing all of them left to turn and look at her. She blushed a bright pink when she realized they were all wondering what the sigh had been for.

"Sorry, it's just... Noelle's driving me a little nuts today. The whole way over here she wouldn't stop asking questions about my day with Iris yesterday. She didn't mention Brian once. I just... I don't know what's going on with her." Sam rubbed her hands over her face. "Sorry, I probably shouldn't have said any of that."

Marissa shrugged. "It's okay. Carolyn drives me nuts sometimes, too, and we've been friends for years. It happens."

"Noelle's probably worried Iris is going to turn you against her. She seems very concerned about that," Amy said, trying to comfort Sam. "I'm sure she'll relax more when she sees that you're not going anywhere."

"I hope so. I keep trying to reassure her, and she says she totally understands, and she's fine with it, but then she keeps trying to... I don't know. I don't even know how to describe it. Maybe I'm just hangry."

"Good thing the food is here then," Morgan said, thankful she was finally able to contribute to the conversation. She didn't really know what to say. Noelle was... well, sometimes Morgan didn't like Noelle very much, but everyone else did. Noelle hadn't actually *done* anything to her, so there wasn't anything she could say about it.

"Yes. Let's go get something to eat, then hopefully, by then Asad will have texted Morgan back and we can pick out something for the rehearsal dinner," Amy said, going into the closet to hang up the clothes she was holding. Everyone else did the same, which cleared the bed of everything but the rehearsal dinner options and the clothing Carolyn had brought over.

"Thank you," Morgan said as they headed out into the hallway.

"Of course," Amy replied, linking her arm through Morgan's, a wide grin on her face. "This is exactly what friends are for. Plus... well, actually, let's wait till we're all downstairs."

Curious.

Especially when Amy didn't just wait until they were all downstairs. She waited until they were all gathered around the dining room table with their food. Then she got to her feet, holding a glass of wine in her hand.

"Since Morgan was kind enough to gather us all here today... well, I didn't want to steal focus until we'd gotten her squared away, but since we're basically done, I figured now would be a good time to ask—"

"Spit it out," Noelle called out. The grin on her face indicated she was teasing, and everyone laughed. Morgan did, too.

"Right." Amy cleared her throat. "I wanted to officially ask all of you to be my bridesmaids."

The deafening sound of excited squeals filled the room, and this time, Morgan's response was entirely genuine. She'd wanted to be a bridesmaid ever since she saw the movie *27 Dresses*, which definitely wasn't the point of the movie, but it had looked like fun. And she really wanted to help Amy have an amazing wedding.

"Who's going to be your maid of honor?" Carolyn asked when they were all done hugging and telling Amy, 'yes.'

"I'm not going to have one. You and Marissa have both been my friends for the same amount of time, and I could never choose between you," Amy said immediately—and very firmly. Carolyn made a face but quickly changed her expression to a more neutral one.

Morgan was just happy to be included. She'd have to pay close attention to the wedding this week to see what might be expected of her as a bridesmaid.

5

Asad

Things he hadn't thought about when he'd decided to take a fake girlfriend to his brother's wedding—the three-hour car ride to get there and the fact he'd never been in a car for this long with a woman he was attracted to but wasn't supposed to fuck.

Talk about hellish.

First, he had no idea what to talk about.

Second, Morgan was wearing a flirty little green sundress with white flowers, the hem landing about mid-thigh, and he couldn't stop thinking about what her reaction would be if he reached over and put his hand on her thigh, then slipped his fingers higher and higher...

She was a good sub, so she'd probably spread her thighs wider and let him do whatever he wanted.

Then, in a week, when they got home and Lexie or Patrick or anyone else at the club found out what he'd done, they'd cut his fingers off.

Unless...

Lexie had specifically said no sex. So had everyone else, for that matter.

Did a little bit of fingering count?

He had a feeling that would be considered following the letter of the law, not the spirit.

So, he kept both hands firmly on the steering wheel... but that didn't stop him from thinking about it.

It didn't help that Morgan was texting nonstop with her friends. He wasn't sure whether he had the right to ask, but eventually, the complete lack of conversation was too much for him, even with the radio on.

"Everything okay?" he asked, as her fingers furiously moved over her phone screen, swiping out a message.

"I'm not sure." From his peripheral vision, he could see her lift her head to look at him. "If you were getting married and your bride was gaining weight, would you care?"

What the fuck?

Asad was immediately sorry he'd asked. It sounded like there was some kind of drama going on with Morgan's friends—he would guess Amy since she was the only one engaged. Her fiancé had never come to the clubs. She scened platonically with a few Doms, mostly Master Zach, so Asad didn't know the guy at all.

"Is he worried she has a medical issue?" That was the only reason he could think of that wouldn't make the guy sound like a complete and total douche.

"Well, he's insisting she go to the doctor because she's been working out a lot and dieting, and she keeps gaining instead of losing." Morgan frowned, looking back down at her phone. She shook her head, then bent forward to slide it into her purse, focusing on him rather than the text conversation that was happening. The chiming notification kept going off, but she ignored it. "I'm worried about her. I don't think she'd be as upset about the weight gain if he wasn't putting so much pressure on her about it."

"Well, weddings can put on a lot of pressure." He wasn't exactly up to date on bride behavior, but trying to lose weight to fit into a dress seemed to be part of it, which he didn't entirely understand. Apparently, the weight she was at when she got the proposal wasn't the weight she wanted to be when she got married. "It might not be all him."

"It might not." Morgan was still frowning, though. She sighed. "Do you think it's a problem to accept the position of bridesmaid when you aren't sure you like the groom?"

"I think you're fine. There are a lot of weddings where not everyone approves of the relationship. It's more important that you're there to support your friend because she wants you there for her. That's the real role of the wedding party." Not that he was against his brother's wedding, but he wasn't going for Anna or because his parents wanted him to; he was going for Cyrus.

His little brother had asked him to be his best man, and even though they might not always have the best relationship, Asad would always be there for his brother, the way he had been his entire life. Thankfully, the burden wasn't as heavy as it had been when they were children. Now he just had to show up, play his role, and not do anything to embarrass the family or take attention away from Cyrus. He had a lifetime of practice at that last one, though admittedly, he'd done some rebelling in his late teens after Cyrus was in remission... which was why he was now the black sheep of the family.

This week, he was back in the role of supportive big brother and best man.

"Okay. I feel guilty because I feel like it's a little selfish to want Amy to get married just so I can be a bridesmaid." The guilt she felt was clear in her tone, and it wasn't just a little. Morgan was an inherently honest person, to the point of bluntness, which she was working on because sometimes the things she said came out in ways she didn't mean. Asad enjoyed her candor, though.

"I think Amy wants to get married, and she's going to be happy to have her friends there supporting her... even if her fiancé is a douche. Trust me, you do not want to get in the middle of someone else's relationship, even if you're right." He paused for a moment, thinking about it. "Especially if you're right, in fact. People need to make their own mistakes, and all we can do is to be there for them when things fall apart."

"Is that what you're doing for your brother?" she asked, seemingly curious now that he was talking about it.

Asad laughed. "No, if anything, Anna is too good for my brother, and I'll be sure to tell him that a lot this week." He grinned. "But I've watched a lot of relationships go wrong and a lot of relationships go right."

"Have you had a relationship go wrong?"

"No. I don't do relationships." Hey, it didn't hurt to remind her of that on the way up there. Not that he was arrogant enough to assume she might want one with him, but it was best to keep the fact they were fake boyfriend and girlfriend at the forefront of her mind.

"Why not?"

"Because I don't want anyone to rely on me like that." He was so distracted by driving and fighting back his desire to reach over and play with the flirty hem of her skirt, he answered without thinking. Maybe her honesty was rubbing off on him because that was not the answer he usually gave. He winced when he realized he'd answered a little too truthfully with something he hadn't even really known about himself.

Or, at least, hadn't been willing to face.

"You don't want anyone to rely on you?" Morgan's confusion was clear. "But you just said that's what friendship is about to you. And you have a lot of friends."

"It's different. Friendship is... my friends rely on me to be there for them when they need me, but it's not an all-the-time thing. A relationship, especially as a Dom, feels like more. It's a responsibility. It's someone relying on me all the time to be able to be there for them. They are always part of every consideration for any major decision in your life." He grinned, though he didn't really feel like smiling. "And now I'm the one who sounds selfish because I don't want that."

He glanced over to see her reaction, but she didn't look appalled as he might have expected. She looked thoughtful, and he wondered what was going through her head. He didn't have to wait long to find out.

"I don't want anyone to have to be responsible for me," she said after a few long moments, proving that Asad was putting way too much importance on himself. She hadn't been thinking about what a shitty person he was. She'd been thinking about how what he said applied to her own life. "I feel like I'm always someone's responsibility. First my parents, then Master Jason, then Master Richard, then Naomi and Drew, and now Brian and all the other Doms. Except you. You treat me like I'm just me."

"Because I don't want to be responsible for you, remember?" He winked at her, even as his gut twisted. He wasn't sure he liked what that said about him, but it was still the truth. "But we're friends. If you need me, you can always call on me."

Morgan was quiet for another long moment, her hands no longer resting quietly in her lap but fiddling with the hem of her skirt. Which, unfortunately, reminded Asad why he'd started the conversation in the first place. This was going to be a really long fucking drive if he couldn't get his mind out of the gutter—or out from between her legs, as it were.

"Thank you," she said finally. "And if you need me, you can always call on me."

"I already have," he teased, relief flooding through him. Hopefully, the uncomfortable part of the conversation was over. "That's how you ended up as my fake girlfriend, remember?"

Morgan laughed, and the atmosphere in the car lightened.

Unable to help himself, Asad reached over to take her hand, sliding his fingers through hers. Morgan jumped a little in surprise. It was more torture for him, his fingers now actually touching her thigh, but holding her hand would keep him from moving them higher. And at least this way, he was touching her a little...

"Speaking of being my fake girlfriend, we should probably get used to holding hands and things." He glanced at her. "If that's okay with you."

She was staring down at her lap as though she couldn't believe it.

"Um, yes, that's okay."

Even though he knew her past, sometimes it still caught him off guard that totally normal things were foreign to her. What Morgan had been through... he wanted to go pound someone's face in.

"So... you don't have to answer this if you don't want to, just say the word, and we'll talk about something else, but do you mind me asking what happened to your former... Doms?" He cringed calling them that, but he didn't know how else to refer to them. Calling them her former abusers seemed like it could be hurtful to her, and they definitely hadn't been boyfriends or anything like that. "Do you know?"

"It's fine. Master Patrick's cousin Drew is part of some kind of security firm. They keep an eye on both of my old... men." Either Morgan didn't want to call them Doms either, or she was catering to Asad's obvious distaste for doing so. "They both did some time in jail, but not much, and once they were out, Black Fox Elite started keeping an eye on them. Naomi reassured me they won't be welcome back into the community no matter where they go, and they won't be able to... to buy and sell another person ever again."

Even though she said it was fine, her flat and emotionless tone told a different story. Asad squeezed her hand.

"I'm glad to hear that, although pretty pissed they didn't get much jail time."

"I was surprised they got any at all. It was my word against theirs, and... well, I wasn't a very good witness, to be honest. I'm lucky Naomi and Drew were there for me. Mas— I mean, Richard was very wealthy and had donated a lot of money to the police. If it hadn't been for Naomi and Drew, I'm not sure anything would have happened to him."

Asad shook his head because he knew she was right. Money talked, and women who dared to have sex—especially kinky sex— tended to be looked at differently by people who weren't part of the community. If this Richard had claimed it was all consensual "Fifty Shades" kind of stuff, penniless, unconnected Morgan would have likely been brushed off.

He'd heard of Black Fox Elite. Drew was *definitely* connected if he was working there, and Patrick was connected to a lot of the major players in the kink community across the U.S. and even internationally.

"I'm fine," she said after another moment, and this time she squeezed Asad's hand, as if she was trying to comfort him. "I'm just happy to be where I am and know they can't hurt anyone else."

Yeah, that was important.

At least the conversation had finally gotten his mind off of his filthy imaginings.

"So, when is Amy getting married?" That was a much safer topic, especially since Morgan was excited about being a bridesmaid.

She lit up.

"Next May. Her colors are going to be ivory, sage green, and gold. She's letting us pick whatever dresses we want as long as they're sage green."

Which Morgan would look incredible in. Still holding her hand, Asad couldn't help but smile as he listened to her happily chatter about the wedding plans. It seemed his reassurance had helped her relax and enjoy being excited about it. And she was damn cute when she was excited.

6
———————

Morgan

"Do I look alright?" Morgan came out of the bathroom and spun around as Asad looked up.

She'd changed from the sundress she'd been wearing for the car ride to a more fitted but more modest eggplant dress. The keyhole in her neckline was small, only a couple inches tall, so it didn't show even a hint of cleavage. The skirt went down to about an inch above her knee and flared out just enough that it didn't need a slit for her to walk.

Her friends had claimed it was a great 'meet-the-parents' dress. She looked like she was trying to impress, but it was still casual enough that everyone else could be wearing jeans, and she'd only seemed a little overdressed. They'd assured her that, especially in that scenario, overdressed would be fine and probably seen as a compliment.

Asad blinked, his eyes sliding over her body while she stood before him with her hands held out to her sides, fingers spread. Nerves rattled through her, but she managed to hold her position.

It didn't hurt that he was giving her a lot to look at. Although he was wearing jeans, he was also in the process of putting on a crisp, white button-down shirt with long sleeves. Seeing what he was wearing did help her a little. She would look appropriately dressed next to him. He was doing the buttons, so the shirt hung open, showing off his muscled chest and stomach, which was a very nice distraction.

Her body stirred as the fact they were alone together in this hotel room hit home.

Since she'd had to go to the bathroom and touch up her makeup, it had just made sense to change in there, but now she kind of wished she'd put on her dress out in the main room. She'd missed a show. And missed giving him one.

That could have been fun.

On the other hand, she didn't want to make them late for dinner with his family, so maybe this was for the best. She could give him a show when they got back and didn't have any more plans for the evening.

Excitement thrummed through her.

Intellectually she'd known she was going to be alone with him for a week, and she'd been looking forward to it, but that didn't compare to how it *felt* to realize they really were alone in each other's company. No Doms looking over her shoulder and watching to make sure not one foot was stepped out of line.

No well-meaning friends hovering protectively, always watching.

She hadn't realized how much their anxiousness had added to her own until this moment when no one was watching.

It was incredibly relaxing.

"You look fantastic," Asad said after a long moment. He gave his head a little shake. "Way out of my league."

Morgan laughed, dropping her hands back to her sides. "I doubt it, but thank you."

He grinned at her, doing up the rest of his buttons and hiding the view. Morgan sighed inwardly. It wasn't like she hadn't seen it before, but it had been a while since they'd last scened together and—more importantly—the lack of anyone else in the room watching made everything feel different.

Sharper.

More exciting.

Anticipation fizzed and bubbled in her, but she pushed it back. Now wasn't the time.

Shrugging his shoulders to settle his shirt properly on his frame, Asad tugged on the bottom of his shirt, which he apparently wasn't tucking in. Morgan rather liked the look of something associated with formal wear worn casually. Her parents would have called it sloppy.

"Alright." Taking a deep breath, he moved over to her and put his hand on the small of her back.

Morgan felt her skin tingle, where she could feel his palm through the fabric of her dress. Yup, this was going to be a fun week.

Though, first, she had to get through meeting the parents as his fake girlfriend.

"Should we go over our story again?" she asked nervously as they headed to the car.

"Sure," Asad said easily, his hand moving slightly on her back as though he was rubbing it to reassure her.

She took a deep breath. Between her excitement that they were alone in the hotel room and her anxiousness over meeting his parents and pulling off being his fake girlfriend, she was feeling a little overstimulated. Every touch of his hand rasped along her skin, though not in an unpleasant way.

It was just a lot.

She was almost relieved when they got to the car, and he had to stop touching her to let her get in. But then, as soon as he got in, he took her hand again, the same way he had during the drive. It was just pretend, just practice for being in a fake relationship, but it still made her heart jump.

No one had ever held her hand. Not even Master Jason.

It's not a big deal. It doesn't mean anything.

She knew that, but there was a part of her that wanted to pretend it did. Just for a little while. To fall into the ruse and enjoy being in a fake relationship, a romantic relationship like she saw other people have. Even though, technically, she'd been in two sexual relationships previously, she had no idea what it was like to be in a romantic relationship. And wasn't that sad?

Mistress Julie would tell her it wasn't her fault, and she'd be right, but Morgan was still right that it was sad.

Did she want a relationship like the ones she saw her friends in?

Yes, but she wasn't sure she was capable. Not with a past like hers.

Sometimes, it seemed like even people who thought she'd been through something traumatic weren't any better at getting their personal lives together than she was. Brian was constantly worried about what she was doing and who she was doing it with. Meanwhile, he was pining over a woman who didn't want him. Mistress Julie had cackled when Morgan had made that observation during one of their sessions.

She knew Mistress Julie thought this week away would be good for her, but she wasn't sure what her therapist would say about actually pretending the relationship was real for the duration of it. Would she think that was healthy? Or that Morgan was delusional?

"Okay, so our mutual friend Patrick introduced us at a party, right?" Asad said, giving her hand a little squeeze as he maneuvered them out of the hotel parking lot. It took a moment to realize he was going over their story the way she'd requested, and she made herself focus.

She could call Mistress Julie later if she really wanted to talk through things.

"Right," she said.

They spent the rest of the drive going over their backstory. Asad winked at her several times, helping to ease her nerves as he made her laugh. It wasn't until they pulled up in front of a huge house with a perfectly manicured lawn and a half-circle driveway, she realized how tense *he* was.

The smile faded from his lips as he looked up at the house, and he didn't look all that excited to go in and see his family. He'd called himself the 'black sheep' and made jokes about it, but clearly, he was more affected by it than he'd been pretending. Now, it was Morgan's turn to squeeze his hand.

"We could pretend I got sick and can't go in," she offered.

Asad huffed a laugh.

"No, we're not going to do that." He shook his head. "Besides, I can guarantee my mom already knows we're here. Even if it wasn't for the security cameras, I bet she's peeking out one of the windows as we speak." Sighing, he gave her fingers a squeeze back, then let go so he could unbuckle his seatbelt. "We'll be spending all week with them. Might as well go ahead and get the party started."

Asad

"Mom, Dad, this is Morgan. Morgan, these are my parents, Lena and Darius."

"Hello." Despite the death grip Morgan had on his hand, her greeting was cheerful and warm.

His parents looked a little shell-shocked.

He wondered what kind of girl they'd been expecting him to bring. To be fair, the last girl they'd seen him with had been eight years ago, and Molly had been deep into the goth scene. She'd had spiked hair, black lipstick, and rarely wore anything that wasn't ripped to hell. They'd had a good time together, enjoying each other's company without ever getting serious, until she'd moved to New York. He hadn't formally introduced her to his parents, of course, but they'd seen him and Molly together out in public. His mom had done her best to cover her horror when she'd questioned him about the 'young lady' they'd seen him with, but she hadn't entirely managed it.

It had been funny as hell, and Molly had thoroughly enjoyed playing her part.

Now, his parents were staring at Morgan like they were waiting for her to explode.

"Hello, dear, it's *so* lovely to meet you." Seeming to have gotten over her trepidation, his mom stepped forward and wrapped Morgan in a big hug.

Only Asad knew that Morgan had rocked back for a moment before his mom got her arms around her. Giving him a glance, as if looking for approval, Morgan gingerly hugged his mom back, patting her shoulder with the hand he wasn't holding.

"Um, hi, Mrs. Khan."

"No, no, Lena, I insist." Was his mom blinking back tears as she pulled away?

Asad was acutely aware of how uncomfortable he felt under this parental scrutiny. He hadn't grown up with his parents much caring what he did. They hadn't needed to because he'd been a good kid, so they wouldn't have to worry about him *and* Cyrus, up until he'd hit his rebellious years, which his parents hadn't appreciated at all. This show of emotional approval from his mom was weirding him out.

"Come on in. Cyrus and Anna should be here any moment."

"Ah, the boy wonder is running late," Asad joked, earning himself a 'look' from his mother. His dad frowned at him. That was more like it. Now, they were back in his comfort zone.

"It is his wedding week. It's expected they're a little busy," his mom replied in a repressive tone. Criticizing the boy wonder was a no-no.

"Of course," he replied mildly.

"You have a beautiful home," Morgan said, interrupting what was sure to be a devolving conversation where Asad made general remarks and his parents leapt to his brother's defense. "Is that a family portrait?" She was looking up at the painting that hung in the back of the foyer, underneath the double staircase to the second floor.

His mom brightened. Turning so she was standing on Morgan's free side, she linked her arm through Morgan's, pulling her away from him.

His hand felt suddenly very empty.

"It is. We had it done when Asad was ten and Cyrus was eight. Aren't they adorable?"

What his mother wasn't saying was that they'd had it done when Cyrus had been going through a particularly bad period, and they hadn't been sure he was going to beat the cancer. The artist who had done the painting had taken a lot of artistic license when it came to Cyrus' appearance, working more from photos than from what Cyrus had actually looked like at that moment in time. Asad's gut tightened as he remembered how gaunt his brother had been, how unnaturally pale, with huge shadows under his eyes.

He'd spent every night terrified that he was going to wake up in the morning to the news that his brother was gone.

But Cyrus had pulled through. And now the boy wonder was getting married. It was the happily-ever-after all of them had hoped for.

Which was why the bitterness Asad tasted in his mouth was so hard to swallow. He didn't want to feel this way about his brother, but sometimes, it was hard to push the resentment down. Cyrus *had* gotten better, yet somehow, the family dynamic had never changed.

"Let me show you around," his mom said to Morgan before glancing over her shoulder. "Asad, dear, do you want to join us?"

That resentment buried in the pit of his stomach flared again, and he wasn't sure why. This was good. This was what he'd wanted.

Yup, for my mom to only approve of me once I brought a girl home, that's exactly what I wanted.

Asad squashed the thought. It wasn't as if he'd acted like he wanted his mom to approve of him otherwise. He'd hit a point in his life where he'd stopped being her good little boy and started doing the opposite of anything she and his father asked of him. Looking back, he realized that.

He just wasn't sure how to shake off the emotions surrounding it. So, he pushed them down and away instead.

"Coming, Ma." The casual 'ma' made her wince because she hated being called 'ma,' which was exactly why he did it. He hadn't even done it consciously; it was just what came out of his mouth. Behind him, his father sighed that deep-deep sigh of disappointment he was so good at.

Asad felt tension roll down his spine, but he shook it off again and sauntered after his mom and Morgan.

He might feel it, but he'd be damned if he let them see it.

7

———————

Morgan

There was something going on with Asad's family, though Morgan couldn't quite put her finger on it. She hadn't noticed at first, but as the evening went on, it became more and more obvious to her that he was very tense, and she couldn't understand why.

His mother was lovely and welcoming, his father was quiet but friendly, and his brother had bounded into the house with boisterous energy and a huge smile when he saw his brother. Anna was also very friendly, though clearly nervous and a little distracted. Asad had seemed glad to see Cyrus, they'd shared a huge hug, but during dinner, she'd realized he wasn't behaving like himself.

He wasn't behaving like the confident Master Asad she knew, with his flirtations and jokes. Did he still joke? Yes, but there was an edge to it, an undercurrent rather than the lighthearted jokester he often was. He was being more sarcastic than funny, and the laughter that followed was more uncomfortable than truly amused.

And she had no idea how to fix any of it.

"So, how did you two meet?" she asked Cyrus and Anna as they all started dessert. The baklava was very sweet, which Morgan wasn't usually a fan of, but she liked honey better than most sugars.

Combined with the nuts and pastry, it turned into something she liked rather than being too sugary for her palate. Conversation had hit another lull while everyone dug in, and she figured that at least should be something they'd enjoy talking about.

"Asad didn't tell you?" Cyrus raised his eyebrows and shrugged at the same time, hinting that maybe it wasn't as innocuous a point of conversation as she'd thought.

Asad shrugged as well, looking unconcerned as he leaned back in his chair and took another sip of wine.

"We spend more time talking about me than you, as unusual as that might seem." Asad smirked, turning the words into something teasing, but it didn't feel like a very nice tease. Then again, Morgan hadn't had siblings. It was her understanding that siblings did tease each other a lot. Maybe she just didn't understand the relationship because she didn't have any experience with it. It wouldn't be the first time.

"Afraid she'd be more interested in the better brother?" Cyrus puffed his chest out, grinning as he teased Asad back, at the same time that Lena frowned at her eldest son.

"Asad, be nice to your brother," she chided over the top of Cyrus' retort, which she didn't give any sign of hearing. At the other end of the table, Darius sighed. He seemed to do that a lot.

Morgan had absolutely no idea what to do, and she felt like she'd blundered into dangerous waters. Thankfully, Anna rescued her. The pretty blonde looked as uncomfortable as Morgan felt and as if she was relieved to have a topic to grab on to.

"Cyrus and I met in high school, though we were just friends back then." She glanced to her right and smiled at him. His gaze softened as he looked back at her, and the atmosphere around the table relaxed. Morgan could have sighed at how romantic it looked, like a moment straight out of a movie. "We met again a few years ago through mutual friends at a party, and... well, things just worked out."

"Yeah, it did." Cyrus leaned over to give her a kiss.

"Wow, that's wonderful. I didn't realize after Asad said he'd only met Anna a few times." It wasn't until after she'd said it that Morgan realized she maybe should have kept that to herself, even though he had said it.

"Yeah, well, Asad wasn't around much when I was in high school, so that's true," Cyrus said mildly.

"He went off to get his engineering degree," Lena added. "Which we were very proud of, even though it meant we didn't get to see him very much."

"I'm surprised you noticed," Asad said dryly as he glared at his plate, pushing the pieces of baklava around rather than eating it.

"Of course, we noticed." Lena pressed her lips together. Her eyes darted back and forth between Morgan and Anna, as if she wanted to say more but wasn't sure she should with them there. Morgan was already regretting asking her question. It might be better not to introduce any new topics of conversation during the rest of the week.

Darius cleared his throat.

"Morgan, you said you're a makeup artist?" he asked.

Asad's head snapped up, and he glared at his dad.

"Yes, and I also do ASMR videos," she said, setting down her fork and reaching out with her free hand to place it on Asad's leg. Something about the way his posture had shifted made her think of a predator about to pounce, and she really didn't want to be the cause of an argument in his family. She didn't mind talking about what she did. She loved her work.

"What's ASMR?" Anna's question was full of simple curiosity, and maybe because it was her asking and not one of Asad's family members, Morgan felt Asad relax. His hand covered hers.

She was only half finished with her baklava, but she kept holding his hand. She couldn't eat while she was talking, anyway.

"It stands for Autonomous Sensory Meridian Response, which is when something makes your scalp tingle—in a pleasant way—and the sensation can move down your neck and to the rest of your body. I've heard some people describe it as 'having their brain tickled.' Basically, I post videos on social media and video streaming sites of various techniques to create that sensation for people."

Everyone stared at her for a long moment, and Morgan smiled

proudly. Sam had helped her work on that description to explain what she did. Not everyone was familiar with ASMR, and Morgan had found herself frustrated when she tried to tell them what it was. Sam helped her make it sound impressive, which she was especially grateful for right now.

When Morgan had tried to explain it to people, somehow, they'd always gotten the impression that she didn't make much money or that she did make money but without doing much work. She made money, but it was a lot of work to keep up with. For this week, she'd let her followers know she wouldn't be going live, but she'd batched a lot of content for them on her various channels.

"Wow... that's pretty cool. Can we follow you?" Anna asked.

"Of course." Morgan gave them her handle. Asad squeezed her fingers, and when she looked at him, he smiled encouragingly. He seemed pleased and more relaxed than he had been before.

Talking about the kind of 'triggers' she used for her work—and explaining what a trigger was—took the rest of dessert, then it was time to go. Asad insisted they needed to go and rest up since they were tired from the drive earlier.

Morgan wasn't, but she understood that he was saying it because he wanted to leave, and it was more polite than baldly stating he wanted to go. She didn't mind leaving, ending the evening on a pleasant note rather than risking conversation going awry again.

When they got into the car, Asad let out a huge sigh of relief.

"Are you okay?" she asked, reaching over to put her hand on his thigh again as they pulled away from the house.

"Yeah, I'm fine." He covered her hand with his own.

She bit her lip to keep from pointing out that he wasn't fine. If he wanted to pretend he was fine, she was supposed to let him.

A*SAD*

He wasn't fine.

That was the worst dinner he'd had with his family in a while. He didn't know why. He wasn't going to blame Morgan, but he also wasn't sure if her presence had made him more sensitive. He'd gotten used to letting comments slide off his back, yet tonight, it was as though he hadn't been able to let a single one go by without saying something about it.

And he didn't know why.

Or maybe it was because Cyrus was getting married, and his parents were glowing with approval for him.

Or maybe it was because they'd been glowing with approval over Morgan because having a suitable girlfriend was the only way he could get their approval. Though he would pay good money to watch his dad's expression when he checked out Morgan's ASMR channel. Imagining Darius Khan having his brain tickled... he couldn't even imagine.

Personally, Asad didn't love having his brain tickled, he'd found. He'd checked out Morgan's channels out of curiosity and could see how many followers she had and how much love she got. A lot of them said she helped them fall asleep or that they found her relaxing or soothing. For Asad, it made him shiver in a way he didn't particularly like.

His brain was either too ticklish or not enough.

"I'm sorry about my behavior this evening," he said finally into the silence, rubbing his thumb over Morgan's fingers. He didn't want her to think she'd done anything wrong. She hadn't. She'd been trying so hard, despite her discomfort with social situations, to make the evening a success, and he was really grateful. "I know that was... not the best family dinner, and I wasn't helping."

"It's okay," she said. "I don't really understand regular family dynamics, so..." She shrugged. "I could tell you were uncomfortable and angry, but I wasn't sure what was going on."

There was that bluntness. As much as Asad wanted to say he wasn't angry, he couldn't honestly deny it. Still, he didn't like Morgan thinking she didn't understand regular family dynamics.

"My family isn't exactly regular. My brother's leukemia... well, it made everything harder." Somehow, it was easier to talk about this in the darkness when she'd already met his family, met his brother, and seen how things were. "Growing up, I was always the good older brother, watching out for him, doing what I could to make things easier for my parents. But then... he got better. I was really happy about that, don't get me wrong, but I thought they would start showing up for some of my stuff once that happened."

His stuff that he finally got to do because he'd had friends who could drive him there. During elementary and middle school, his parents hadn't been able to take him anywhere regularly enough to join any teams or group activities. Once he'd gotten to high school, though, he'd had friends with cars, and as long as he did the same things they were, they were happy to take him.

He'd understood when his parents couldn't show up to anything his freshman year. He'd even understood during his sophomore year when Cyrus was officially in remission because that was Cyrus' first year of being able to do *anything*. Of course, his parents had wanted to be there to watch Cyrus. Asad had gone to Cyrus' first baseball and basketball games, too, as a supportive big brother.

"They didn't show up?" Morgan asked tentatively, breaking the silence that filled the car.

Asad sighed.

"My junior year, they said they were going to come to a science fair I had entered. Unfortunately, one of Cyrus' baseball games fell on the same day. It was his second year playing baseball, but it was the first time they'd made the playoffs, and well..." Asad shrugged, but he still remembered the bitter hurt. The realization that he'd been pushed off the side *again*.

His mother's apology was quickly followed by, 'But it's his first playoff game, and there will be another science fair next year.'

Except there hadn't been because upon winning first prize at the fair, with no one there except his friends, while his parents and grandparents cheered Cyrus on at his first playoff game, he'd decided he was done. He'd finished his junior year, then announced he was dropping out of school.

Turned out his parents *did* care what he was doing, as long as he wasn't doing what he was 'supposed' to do, but it was already too late.

"I'm sorry," Morgan said quietly.

"It turned out for the best. I ended up getting my GED, then going to MIT a semester earlier than I would have otherwise, and I'm very happy with where my life is now. It probably wouldn't have gone that way if I'd stayed." He'd spent the fall semester of his 'senior' year couch surfing between his friends' houses and working in fast food before heading to MIT.

His parents had paid for his degree, likely guilt money on their part or maybe because they'd been afraid he wouldn't get a degree at all after he'd dropped out of high school. There had been a moment when he'd thought about rejecting their money, but he'd gotten over that pretty quickly. At that point, he figured they owed him something, and he wasn't so stupid as to start his life with a mountain of debt when he didn't have to. Pride wasn't one of his vices, at least not when it came to being financially stable.

"It's still hard." Morgan leaned over, resting her head against his shoulder while they sat at the red light.

Considering her family life, the fact she was now offering him comfort wasn't lost on him. He leaned his head against hers, before lifting it again, acknowledging her compassion and desire to soothe him. Strangely... he actually did feel soothed. Or, at least, the edges of his emotions felt less raw as she focused on him. It didn't feel like pity, coming from Morgan. She'd been through worse, so why would she pity him? But the sympathy was there, the acknowledgment that what he'd gone through had sucked, and that helped a lot.

He found he couldn't stop talking. The words spilled out of him like they'd been bubbling under the surface for far too long, and now that he'd started, he couldn't hold them back anymore.

"I still love them. I do want to fix things. But when I'm around them, it feels like I just kind of revert back to high school. I'm glad my mom and dad like you, and I'm annoyed that part of me still wants their approval. I'm even more annoyed that the approval comes from a relationship with someone else and not just... me. I don't know how to change it."

The light turned green, and Morgan lifted her head. They sat in silence for a few long moments before she finally responded.

"Maybe it's not up to you to change it," she said. "Maybe it's up to your parents."

Maybe.

But Asad still felt a little guilty. Even if it was, he wasn't exactly making it easy on them.

It didn't help his mood that now he had to go back to his hotel room and sleep in the same bed as a beautiful woman without touching her rather than losing himself in her body and fucking her until he could forget why they were there.

This week was going to suck.

8

———————

Asad's bad mood was like a black cloud following them back to the hotel. He didn't let go of her hand, though, and he seemed more relaxed after they'd talked, but the bad mood still lingered. At least, she thought it did. Since they rode the rest of the way in silence, she figured it was still there.

She knew of one sure-fire way to get any man out of a bad mood. She thought about trying to do it in the car, but she wasn't sure how he would react. She also wasn't brave enough to just reach over and undo his pants. She wasn't really his girlfriend, and even though they'd scened together before, that had been at Stronghold in the known quantity of the club.

"Well, at least that's the family dinner over with," Asad joked as they got out of the car. It seemed as if he was shaking off his bad mood, or trying to, returning to the charming joker he normally was. "Now we just have the rest of the week."

Morgan giggled because he seemed to expect it, though her heart hurt for him. She hadn't expected anything like the admissions he'd made in the car. She couldn't help picturing a little boy, desperate for his parents' attention, and so hurt when he finally thought he was going to get it only to have them prioritize his brother yet again.

Morgan hadn't had siblings, but sometimes, it had felt like she was competing with the son her father wished he'd had instead of her. At least she'd been able to hate that figment of her father's imagination. She thought it must be worse for someone who loved their brother and still had to compete.

"Let me know if there's anything you want me to do," she said, meeting him behind the car. This time he didn't take her hand, and she felt the loss. The connection.

She was feeling even antsier because, after that dinner, she felt as if more was riding on this week for Asad than she'd realized. She didn't want to mess it up for him, and she needed something to calm her nerves—like a really good spanking or even better, a flogger or whip.

"You're already doing it," he said as they headed inside to the elevators. "You were perfect tonight. Trust me, my parents loved you, and that really is a good thing, even though I'm all up in my feels about it."

This time, Morgan truly laughed when he winked at her, just because he sounded so silly using the slang.

"Okay, good."

As they got into the elevator and headed up to their floor, she could feel her nerves starting to rise. She wanted to comfort Asad, and she wanted a scene, or at least a spanking and an orgasm, but she couldn't tell if that was what he wanted. She was starting to second-guess herself based on how distant he seemed, as though he was lost in his own thoughts.

He wasn't holding her hand anymore or looking at her, even though he said she'd done a good job. It was hard to feel as though that was true. Morgan didn't know what to do or say, so she waited quietly next to him as the elevator came to a halt, then followed him to their room.

"I'm going to go get changed in the bathroom," he said once they were inside. Heading to his suitcase, he scooped out what looked like pajama pants.

"Oh... okay." Morgan's hands fluttered at her side. She wasn't sure what she was supposed to say or do. That wasn't what she'd expected him to say. Maybe he needed a minute or two of privacy after the dinner. But she hadn't expected him to get changed in there... she'd thought they'd...

Well, she was wrong.

Trying not to feel put out—this wasn't about her, it was about him—Morgan went to the dresser where she'd put her things, and took out her nightgown. It was a silky, lacy little thing with a matching robe that she'd brought but hadn't been planning on wearing. Now it felt like maybe she should put it on, so she did, tucking her dirty clothes neatly away in another drawer.

Then she looked at the closed bathroom door. Should she knock? She needed to take off her makeup and do her skincare routine, especially if she wasn't getting a spanking tonight. Her routines helped soothe her, the very act of putting makeup on and taking it off always calming her. But if Asad needed some more time and privacy, she didn't want to interrupt him.

She supposed he wasn't feeling all that amorous after the dinner with his parents, which she could understand. Maybe sex wouldn't be the same kind of relief for him it would be for her. He was a Dom, after all. Taking control might not be something he wanted right now. Maybe he wanted to relax and not have to deal with a needy sub.

Going over to the bed, Morgan pulled out her phone. She'd had it on silent, so it didn't interrupt the dinner, and there were several missed texts. She answered the one from her friend Freddy first, letting him know she was doing fine and that she hoped he had a good week. Then she checked in on her group chat.

Amy: How did dinner go?

Sam: They're probably still eating.

Noelle: I'm sure you're doing great!

Neither Carolyn nor Marissa had texted, probably because there wasn't anything new to say.

It went well. His family is nice. We just got back to the hotel.

That wasn't the total truth, but she didn't think Asad would want her sharing everything he'd told her. If it was all public knowledge, she was pretty sure she would have already heard about it. Like her with her past, he probably wanted to be able to choose who he talked to about it.

Noelle: You just got back, and you're talking to us instead of banging that hottie? Girl, get off the phone!

He's in the bathroom.

She didn't know how to say that she didn't think he was going to be up for sex after the dinner since she'd told them it had gone well. Which was too bad because she would have liked their advice about it, but she couldn't ask for it without explaining that she'd just lied.

This was why she didn't like lying, but she couldn't regret respecting Asad's privacy.

Marissa: Ew, hope he didn't eat something that disagreed with him. How's your stomach?

Carolyn: Maybe he's man-scaping for her.

Amy: Um… aren't they supposed to not be having sex?

Noelle: Wait, what? Who said that? I thought that was the point of this trip.

Amy: Zach told me they were doing this week
platonically. I think he heard it from Kincaid.

Marissa: I hadn't heard anything about that.
But no one tells me anything.

Sam: Yeah, I overheard some of the guys
giving Asad a talking-to about it. They're
worried about Morgan's emotions getting
confused.

Morgan stared at her phone in shock, then shook her head. The door to the bathroom opened, and she automatically hit the off button on the screen, pressing the phone to her lap. Feeling oddly vulnerable, she was very glad she'd put on the robe.

People were making choices about her life without her again.

Pressing her lips together, she swallowed back the emotions, putting her usual practiced smile on her lips.

"All done?" she asked as Asad emerged.

It wasn't just pajama pants. He also had on a t-shirt she hadn't seen him pick up. His gorgeous body was basically completely covered from bicep to ankle. The Persian Excursion was wearing more clothing than she was.

"It's all yours," he said, gesturing back at the bathroom. Then his hand came up to cover his mouth as he yawned, his other arm stretching out. The expression on his face was one of exhaustion.

Hm. Maybe he really was just tired. It had been a long day with the drive, then dinner with his family. An emotional day for him, though not for her. Maybe Sam had heard wrong. And just because someone had told Asad to keep his hands to himself didn't mean he would. It wasn't like they hadn't scened before.

She would give him the benefit of the doubt tonight.

Still, as she closed the bathroom door behind her and began her nightly routine, she couldn't help but check the text messages again. Her friends were discussing whether or not Morgan should sleep with Asad—as if it was their decision.

Morgan shook her head, shaking away the unhappy emotions, the resentment.

She took a deep breath.

Then another.

Then she looked at the messages again.

They were just talking, not trying to decide for her. It was gossip. And they were making some good points—like Carolyn's point that pretending to be in a relationship all week might be easier if they were having sex and that it wasn't anyone else's business what they did.

They weren't trying to decide for her.

Not like some of her other friends, who meant well but kept interfering in her life...

Morgan took another deep breath and let it out slowly, counting to ten as she did so. She didn't want to be angry. She didn't know how much of what Sam said was true. It was hearsay. Sam had overhead the guys talking to Asad. She might have misinterpreted.

But if someone was... what did Amy call it? The female version of cock-blocking. *That's right.* If someone was clam-jamming her, she was going to be pissed. No matter what their intentions were.

She took another deep breath and counted to ten.

There was no point in being mad when she didn't know for sure what had happened.

Texting her friends that she was going to bed and that she'd update them later, Morgan turned her phone to do-not-disturb so she could get a break from all of it. The whole point of coming here was to get away from everything.

She started on her nighttime routine, beginning with the soft, fuzzy headband that pushed her hair out of her face, then her makeup remover. Just the touch of the furry band pulled some of the tension from her body, and as she began rubbing the makeup off her face in rhythmic, circular motions, she could feel more of it sliding away. There was something hypnotic about skincare, at least for her.

It allowed her to think. Mistress Julie had been working with her on thinking through why people might act or react a certain way to various situations, to help her understand. This was the perfect time to apply some of those techniques.

She wasn't going to assume Asad was bowing to anyone else's edicts. That wasn't really the kind of person he was. That was part of why this trip had been so appealing. He was respectful of her, but he'd never been overly protective, and he'd treated her like any other submissive in the club, even when they scened. Some of the Doms tiptoed around her when they scened with her, as though her past meant she was going to melt down at any moment. She understood their trepidation, but it made it hard to enjoy those scenes.

That had never been a problem with Asad.

That was why it was even more ridiculous to think that someone would tell him not to scene with her or be intimate with her this week. They'd done plenty of scenes in the past. Just because they were away from everyone this week...

She was getting mad again without knowing if that was the root of the problem.

It was far more likely that any amorous intent had been squashed by the dinner with his family. She completely understood if that was the case. Everyone had been trying... but it had been a very uncomfortable dinner. And the revelations afterward had hurt her heart.

While she wanted to comfort Asad, it was very possible he just wanted to be left alone. He had certainly seemed stressed.

The feeling of rejection faded as she finished rubbing lotion into her face.

There. She felt much better now.

The whole world didn't revolve around her. Despite what Sam had said, there was every reason to think that Asad's actions were connected to his family and the dinner.

Taking off her fuzzy headband, Morgan quickly stuffed her hair in the bonnet she wore to help keep her curls under control before opening the door and peeking out. The whole room was dark, and she could hear Asad's even breathing. He'd fallen asleep. She sighed. Definitely no orgasms tonight... unless she wanted to masturbate right next to him while he was sleeping—which felt odd—or in the bathroom, which sounded uncomfortable.

Which was probably for the best since she was all ready for bed as well.

Turning out the light, she crept through the darkness, using the dim light from her phone screen to find her way to her side of the bed. Plugging the device in, she slipped between the covers. The king size bed was more than big enough to fit both of them, and it felt like Asad was very far away on the other side of it.

She was tempted to reach out and touch him just because she could, but she didn't want to wake him. Yawning, she realized her breathing was starting to match his, her eyelids getting heavy in the darkness. It didn't feel odd to be in bed with someone else. It felt rather nice to know she wasn't alone and that she *could* reach out to touch him if she chose to.

Even though she wasn't right now.

But she wanted to.

As her eyes adjusted to the darkness, she could see that he was facing away from her, and she had the oddest urge to scoot up behind him and curve her body around his, hugging his back to her front. Spooning. That's what it was called. She wanted to make him the little spoon even though he was a lot bigger than her, and men were supposed to be the big spoon.

No, not 'supposed to be.' Can be. They don't have to be. There's no gender to spoons.

Sometimes, her upbringing or her training with Master Richard came through in the oddest ways, ways she was still working on recognizing. She didn't know who to blame for that one. Master Richard had certainly never been interested in spooning, and her parents would have never talked about something like spooning.

I can be the big spoon if I want to be.

The thought was defiant. Rebellious even. She smiled and closed her eyes, yawning again before her smile fell away. The urge to cuddle Asad was still there.

He'd said he wanted a fake girlfriend to keep his mom from trying to hook him up with someone, but after tonight, Morgan thought it might be more than that. He was here for his brother's wedding, and although it was clear he loved his brother, there was also a lot of tension there, as well as a lot of tension between him and his parents.

Maybe what he'd really wanted was someone here for him.

Which meant this wasn't just about getting his mom to leave him alone but also about supporting him.

An odd feeling of warmth rushed through her. It was the same feeling she'd gotten when she'd realized Brian actually did require a roommate and that the offer hadn't been made out of pity. Asad really did need her. While she didn't think she'd be able to do anything for the relationship he had with his family, she could be here for him as his friend and help him through the week.

Whatever he needed, she'd be there for it.

It wasn't that she was happy he had a strained relationship with his family, of course, it was just... it felt nice to be needed. To be able to be there for someone instead of everyone being there for her without allowing her to reciprocate. Still smiling, Morgan hugged her pillow and dropped off to sleep.

9

———

Asad

Someone was wrapped around him, warm and clinging, and snugged up against his butt. Asad opened his eyes, frowning as he twisted to see who it was before his brain caught up to his situation and reminded him that he was sharing a room with Morgan.

Morgan of the very soft breasts pillowed against his back and the hand just above his groin, so the back of her hand was brushing against his morning erection.

Do not fuck Morgan.

Strangely, he heard it in Lexie's voice, not Patrick's. Or maybe not so strange. At first glance, Patrick was far more intimidating, but anyone who knew them also knew the real threat was Lexie—at least when it came to having an enjoyable time at Stronghold or Marquis. Patrick could kick his ass. Lexie could mobilize every single submissive in the club to make his life hell. He had no interest in being covered in glitter for the rest of his life.

Which means you need to get out of bed and away from the sexy sub you're supposed to be keeping your hands off, asshole.

Well, technically, she was the one with her hands on him. He wasn't touching her with his hands. Or his cock. He was on his side of the bed where he belonged. Morgan had cuddle-migrated over to his side of the bed and spooned him. Surely, he couldn't be held account-able for that.

No, but now that you're awake, you can be held accountable for anything else that happens from this point forward.

Sometimes, his brain made too much sense in ways he didn't want it to.

He kind of wanted to pretend he was still asleep, so he could enjoy being cuddled, which was... unexpected. Asad was not a cuddly person. It wasn't that he disliked it, but it wasn't his first instinct. Then again, most submissives expected to be cuddled, not to be the cuddler.

If he liked being the little spoon, did that mean he had to hand in his man-card? He pondered it for a moment. Nah. He was secure enough in his manhood to be able to enjoy being the little spoon.

His alarm went off, and he groaned. *Yes, thank you, world.* Time to get up and get back to Cyrus' wedding week.

"Oh! Sorry!" Morgan jerked away, the warmth that had engulfed his back disappearing as she realized where she was.

Asad rolled onto his back, which allowed him to take advantage of the warmth she'd left behind where she'd been sleeping while she scooted back to her side of the bed.

"No problem," he said, grinning at her. He didn't want her to feel bad. It wasn't her fault he woke up horny, and she was there. "I can't remember if I've ever been spooned before. It's not the worst way to wake up."

Morgan blushed, the pink color of her cheeks contrasting nicely with the shiny green thing she was wearing on her head. Her face was scrubbed clean of makeup, which he found almost surprising. He'd half expected her to sneak out of bed to put it on before he woke up. One of his college roommate's girlfriends had done that.

"I didn't realize I'd moved over in the night," she said, fussing with the sheets in front of her. The strap on her nightgown slipped down her shoulder.

It didn't matter that he'd seen her naked before. It didn't matter that they'd had sex before. Asad couldn't help but look at that little strap and think about peeling the rest of the nightgown off of her and having sex with her right *now*.

"Like I said, I didn't mind at all." Except he now had a throbbing erection and nowhere to put it. He cleared his throat. "I'm, uh, gonna hop in the shower, unless you want to go first?"

Morgan shook her head.

"I'll shower tomorrow. Today's the spa or golf day, right?" she asked, even though they'd gone over the schedule again in the car yesterday.

Smiling reassuringly at her, he scooted over to the edge of the bed and grabbed his phone. His pajama pants weren't going to hide much. As he stood, he angled his hips away from her so she couldn't see the giant bulge tenting his pants. Or he hoped she couldn't.

"Yup." He rolled his eyes. "You know, the true bonding experiences one can have. Still interested in going golfing with me?"

"As long as you understand that I'm going to be absolutely terrible." She watched him as he moved around the bed, heading for the bathroom, her green eyes alight with interest.

Could she tell that he had morning wood? Was she laughing inwardly at him? He couldn't tell.

"Me, too," he said, chuckling and pretending he didn't feel like a teenager trying to sneak his woody by an attractive girl and hope she wouldn't notice. At least in high school, he'd had books to cover his groin with. His phone wasn't nearly big enough.

Skirting around the bed, he made it to the bathroom and breathed a quiet sigh of relief as he closed the door behind him. It was only Tuesday. He still had to get through an entire week of sleeping in the same bed as Morgan and *not* fucking her.

A cold shower was in order.

He'd been so distracted getting into the bathroom, he'd forgotten to bring his clothes in. Once he was out—and his dick was thoroughly depressed—he had to wrap himself in a towel and go back out into the room. Morgan was waiting, her hair still in the green thing, dressed in plaid capris with a white blouse that had a lacy collar and puffy sleeves. She looked adorable.

"Is that your golfing outfit?" he asked, realizing how the question could sound as the words left his mouth. "It looks great."

"Thank you," she preened, reaching up to undo the bow on the top of her hair thing as she walked past him into the bathroom. "Carolyn said it would work."

"It does."

The fan turned on in the bathroom, drowning out anything else he might have said, which was probably for the best. He needed a minute or two to collect himself. He wasn't used to having sleepovers with women, and he sure as hell wasn't used to having to keep his hands off them. If he'd had his way this morning, when he'd rolled onto his back, he would have kept right on rolling until he was on top of Morgan.

He really needed to stop thinking that way, or he was going to get himself into trouble.

Golf.

He could focus on golf. There really wasn't much that was less erotic than golf. He would have honestly rather done the spa day, but Cyrus wanted to do golf, and Asad was his best man, so golf it was. Which, when it came down to it, was probably better than being naked and getting a massage next to a naked Morgan.

He wasn't sure if it was his desperate desire for a distraction or that she was now forbidden fruit, but he couldn't remember ever wanting to fuck a specific woman this badly.

Morgan

Golf was fun.

She was absolutely terrible at it, but no one seemed to mind, least of all Asad. It didn't hurt that she was in a group with him, his brother, their dad, and their cousin Mason, so she wasn't totally surrounded by strangers. Actually, what weirded her out the most was Asad and Mason looked so much alike, she'd had to pause and double-check she was holding Asad's hand when they walked up.

It quickly became clear they were very different people, but when they stood next to each other and had the same expression, they could easily be mistaken for each other. They looked more like twins than cousins. Mason's glasses were the main way to tell them apart at a glance.

"Okay, so... this club?" Morgan asked, lifting the club in question from her bag.

"That's right." Asad grinned at her. Even though he'd told her he wasn't a huge fan of golf, it turned out he was very good at it. He'd been helping her through all the rules and the techniques.

After picking her club came her favorite part. She stood beside the tee, purposefully gripping the club not quite correctly. Asad came up behind her, his big body wrapping around her as he helped her adjust her position. As soon as she'd realized that was how he'd be 'assisting,' she'd stopped trying to get it right the first time. If she could wiggle her butt against his groin a little, even better. She really liked the little growly noise he made when she did that.

There was a growing heat in his eyes that made her tingle all over.

Teasing him like this, flirting with him... it was fun. It was also good practice. She just had to remember it wasn't real. Well, the heat in his eyes was real. He was attracted to her, but he was Master Asad. He wasn't flirting with her because he wanted to be with her, but he definitely wanted to fuck her.

And that was good.

She could enjoy practicing flirting, knowing it wasn't going to lead anywhere, and he wasn't going to take her too seriously or read too much into it. Which meant she could truly relax.

"You need to cut that out," he growled under his breath as she wiggled her butt against him for the umpteenth time.

"Cut what out?" she asked innocently, as if she had no idea what he was talking about. When she peeked over her shoulder to look at him, his eyes were narrowed, as though he was trying to decide if she was sincere or not. Morgan giggled.

Asad groaned.

"Mercy, save me from a righteous brat," he muttered.

Morgan grinned. 'Bratty' was not a word that had ever been used to describe her. She'd recently actually overheard one Dom calling her relentlessly obedient—he'd made it sound like a good thing, and at one time, she would have taken it as such. Now that she knew there were other options for submission, she wanted to explore. She just hadn't known how to, especially not without disappointing a Dom who expected her to be a certain way.

Right now, she could be whoever she wanted to be with Asad because they weren't in a scene, and a girlfriend could tease her boyfriend if she wanted to.

It also helped that she knew Asad because she could tell he wasn't really upset with her. That was also important to her.

"Stop playing around with your girlfriend. We're here to golf," Mason said from where he was standing by Cyrus, his drawling tone filled with annoyance. Darius coughed into his hand, turning away to look elsewhere, as if he was uncomfortable with the observation about his son and son's girlfriend.

"You heard him." Asad's breath was warm against her ear. Unlike Mason, whose competitive nature had become clearer with every hole, he sounded amused. "We're here to golf."

As much as Morgan wanted to keep teasing Asad, she didn't want to hold everyone else up.

"Yes, Sir," she said, adjusting her grip on the club. She heard him make a low noise in reaction—she'd been teasing again with the 'Sir.' Then Asad stepped away. Taking another moment to aim, she swung the club, and it connected to the ball with a satisfying *thwack*. Everyone watched as it sailed across the green, bounced, and came to a halt even closer to the hole than Mason's had. Morgan bounced. "Yay!"

"Good job, baby," Asad said loudly, wrapping his arm around her waist and pulling her to him for a hug. Behind them, Mason muttered something about beginner's luck, causing Cyrus to laugh and tease him about being a sore loser. Shaking his head, Darius looked up to the sky, as if appealing to a higher deity for patience. And maybe he was.

Everyone was getting along. Asad was clearly having a good time, which meant she was doing a good job and was enjoying herself as well. It was a good day. The only cloud on the horizon was she couldn't quite shake what Sam had said about the other Doms telling Asad to keep his hands off of her.

As long as things kept going the way they were, she supposed she'd find out tonight.

10

Patrick: How's everything going?

Great. Morgan is having a good time.

Asad wondered if he should confirm he'd been a good boy and kept his dick out of Morgan, or if his text would be good enough to reassure Patrick that everything was going well.

Patrick: Glad to hear it. Keep up the good work.

Gritting his teeth, Asad swiped out a quick text back.

Yes, Dad.

He resented that Patrick felt the need to check up on him, yet he inwardly acknowledged the need for it. Morgan was having a really good time, and he was having a really good time with her.

And after she'd spent the majority of the day rubbing her delicious ass against him, he absolutely wanted to fuck it.

The text from Patrick had been a good reminder that it really wasn't worth it. He didn't need the whole club mad at him. And he sure as hell didn't need Patrick and Lexie mad at him. He didn't think they'd kick him out of the club if he had sex with Morgan... but he also wasn't one hundred percent sure they wouldn't. They, and everyone else, could definitely make being at Stronghold and Marquis uncomfortable enough that he might not *want* to be there.

Better not to risk it.

No matter how badly his dick ached.

And it ached a lot.

Forget the cold shower. He needed a hot one that he could get his rocks off in and give his poor blue balls some relief.

Sighing, he exited the clubhouse bathroom and headed back to the table where he'd been sitting with Morgan, Mason, and some of his other cousins. Morgan hadn't been the only woman to go golfing, but she was far outnumbered by the men—most of the women had chosen to go to the spa. Cyrus and his dad were at another table with Anna's father and two brothers. He was relieved to get a bit of a break, even if it meant putting up with Mason.

In some ways, he and Mason were more like brothers than he and Cyrus were. Mason was a little older than Asad, and they'd spent a lot of time together while Cyrus was in the hospital when Asad had been dumped on his aunt and uncle to take care of. They'd been rivals academically, although Mason had chosen to go into psychology and the army rather than taking the engineering route.

They even looked more alike than he and Cyrus did.

Which was why he wasn't surprised to come back to his seat to find Mason flirting with Morgan. He was leaning over the empty space of Asad's seat, holding Morgan's fingers in his, talking earnestly about... something. Their other cousins were arguing over their golf game, ignoring Mason and Morgan completely.

"Hey, hands off my girl," he said, reaching down to break their hands apart as he retook his seat.

"Maybe your girl likes my hands on her," Mason retorted.

Morgan frowned, opened her mouth, then closed it again, looking conflicted. She met Asad's gaze.

"I didn't dislike them, but not in a sexual manner," she said after a long moment, and Asad laughed, replacing Mason's hand with his. He squeezed her fingers to reassure her.

"Don't worry, Red, he's just giving me shit. I know you were being a good girl." Leaning over, he gave her a kiss on the temple, right next to her red hair. Morgan's eyes widened in surprise, but she seemed pleased by the new nickname. It had jumped to his lips without thinking, but he felt it suited her.

When he turned back to Mason, his cousin was watching them with narrowed eyes. Asad pointed a threatening finger.

"Don't you dare try to psychoanalyze us," he said warningly. Beside him, Morgan shifted uncomfortably, so he gave her fingers another squeeze. "Did he tell you he's a psychologist?"

"I'm not that kind of psychologist, and I'm not trying to analyze you," Mason said, shaking his head.

Asad was pretty sure that was a lie. He didn't think Mason could turn off the part of him that analyzed people. It was just in his general make-up and always had been. He'd been a quiet, competitive kid who liked to know what made other people tick.

Mason looked past Asad to Morgan. "I'm currently a profiler for a security company, Black Fox Elite."

"You didn't tell me your cousin works for Black Fox Elite!" Morgan leaned against Asad's shoulder as she focused on Mason. "You must know Drew."

"I didn't know he did," Asad answered before Mason could respond, frowning at his cousin. "I thought you were offered the job and turned it down."

"I did, then I reconsidered after my last job didn't work out." Mason shrugged. "If you kept in better touch, you would know that."

"Phone works two ways, asshole. We're supposed to call each other for important life events."

"Important life events like getting a serious girlfriend?" Mason raised his eyebrow, his focus narrowing on Asad as if he'd just caught him in a trap. Which he kind of had. The fucker had a point.

"Oh, we're not that serious. I mean, we're not not-serious, but we're not like—" Morgan stumbled over her words.

Asad turned his head to catch her lips with a kiss to shut her up. She was adorable when she was stammering. Part of him wanted to know how she planned on digging herself out of that verbal hole, but he didn't want to give Mason any clues that things weren't as they appeared.

His cousin could probably be trusted, but one never knew. Especially since Mason's mom would definitely tell Asad's mom if she found out the relationship was fake. Mason could lie to everyone except his mom, who always saw through him. It was better to keep everyone in the dark for now. He'd confess to Mason after the wedding was over.

"It's okay, baby, he's just trying to figure out how serious we are. And you don't need to worry about hurting my feelings." He grinned at her, and she relaxed, relief clear in her eyes. Turning back to Mason he gave his cousin a look. "We're serious enough that I figured I'd bring her to the wedding and get mom off my back, but neither of us are interested in marriage or anything like that, so you can stop the fishing expedition. Tell your mom we're nowhere near getting engaged."

Mason chuckled. "Well, it was worth a try. I was curious, too. It's not like you've ever brought a girl home before." Mason didn't look entirely convinced, but he'd leave it alone for now.

"My little brother doesn't get married every day. I notice you don't have a date."

"No, no dates for me. Drew is the only one on my team with a wife. Our jobs don't lend themselves well to relationships. And I didn't want to give my mom any ideas by bringing a casual date." Mason frowned. "Don't be surprised if your mom takes Morgan's presence as an indication of something a lot more serious than you anticipated."

"I know." He turned to look at Morgan. "Ready to head back and relax before tomorrow?" Tomorrow was the Jahāz Barān, where he and his cousins would take the gifts from the bridal shower from Anna's parents' house over to Cyrus' house, a combination of traditions that Asad thought went together beautifully. Everyone was happy with it.

"Ready." She pushed her seat away from the table, getting to her feet.

"Have a good night, you two," Mason smirked. Asad grinned, as if he was actually going back to the hotel to get laid. Fuck, he wished it were so. The smile faded from his lips as he turned away.

They said goodbye to Cyrus and his dad and headed out the door to the car. A small weight lifted from his shoulders. Another day's activities done without any drama or issues. In fact, today had gone better than expected. Maybe because they'd had something to do other than sit and talk.

Activities to keep them busy were good. And more buffers. As obnoxious as Mason could be, hanging out with him or the other cousins was easier than with Asad's immediate family. The rest of this week should go even more smoothly since Monday had been the only time his immediate family was gathering on their own.

His shoulders relaxed even more at the realization.

"I think today went really well," Morgan said brightly as Asad opened the car door for her. She was beaming, her wide smile going practically from ear to ear, obviously very proud of herself.

"It did. Thank you for coming with me instead of going to the spa." He didn't think today would have gone nearly as well if it had been just him, Mason, his brother, and his father in their group. Way too much opportunity for the small talk to veer into dangerous territory with Mason as the only buffer.

Being able to concentrate on helping Morgan learn how to golf had kept them all focused on something outside of themselves. Definitely not a bad thing when it came to his family.

"You're welcome." Morgan's eyes sparkled. She sighed happily as she sat down in the car. The fact that she was clearly pleased made him feel even better. "Golf is fun."

He laughed as he closed the door. Yes, she'd had fun today, the little tease. And despite having blue balls all day, he'd enjoyed watching her have fun. He'd also really appreciated her being there and taking some of the heat off his back.

"I'm glad you had fun," he said, getting in the car. "Golf is not my favorite activity. Too much walking, not enough doing."

"You're good at it, though." She sounded like she didn't quite understand. Asad shrugged as he started the car and pulled out of the parking space.

"I learned." It was one of the things he, his brother, and his dad had done together once Cyrus was in remission. It hadn't lasted long, but he'd been a bit of a natural. It had all come flooding back today when he'd gotten on the green. He'd done it because he'd wanted to spend time with his family, not because he'd enjoyed it. Just like today. Except today it had been more of an obligation than a choice. "You did a good job with it today, too."

Morgan preened at the compliment, making him smile again.

"So... I was a good girl today?" she asked coquettishly.

Asad chuckled.

"You were a very good girl."

"Does that mean I get a reward?"

The tone of her voice was still very flirtatious, and Asad paused, glancing over at her. She was looking at him with expectation clear in her expression, her eyes practically glowing. His brain scrambled to keep up with what was happening.

"Uh..."

"Because I think I deserve a reward." Not just flirtation. Determination. Morgan wanted something, and she was determined to get it.

Asad's palms suddenly felt a little slick against the steering wheel. She did deserve a reward. If she had been anyone else, he would have been planning out the reward she was going to get all day in his head. And not just because she'd been rubbing her ass against his dick for hours.

"Do you want to go for ice cream?" It was the first thing that he could think of, and the words popped out of his mouth before he could assess whether it was a *good* response.

When he glanced at Morgan again, her eyes weren't just hot, they were furious.

"I'd rather have an orgasm," she replied tartly, confirming the supposition his brain had been trying to tell him. The obvious conclusion that he'd rejected—of *course,* if he'd been told to keep his hands off of Morgan, someone would have also passed the same message along to Morgan.

But nope.

It appeared no one had told Morgan the Persian Excursion was closed for the week.

Well, fuck.

11

———————

Sam had been right.

Someone had beaver-dammed her with Master Asad.

They mean well.

But they're wrong!

"Woah, hey, don't cry... don't cry, let's talk about this... I didn't mean to upset you." Master Asad was gripping the steering wheel so tightly, she almost expected it to creak.

Reaching up, Morgan dashed the tears away from her eyes. She hadn't realized she'd teared up. Crying was not something she did outside of a scene, but she was so... so...

"I'm not upset, I'm pissed!" She was so angry, it was leaking out her eyeballs, which was unexpected.

Mistress Julie would call it an overwhelming response to new emotions. Morgan hadn't been allowed to be angry for basically her entire life, but she could be angry now.

It didn't feel good. She didn't like it.

She felt like hitting something. Hurting someone.

Or, really, she wanted someone to hurt her until she could _really_ cry, but apparently, that wasn't an option right now. Her breath hitched. She was losing the battle to get herself under control, and she didn't know how to handle it. She'd never lost that battle.

When you feel safe, you'll also feel safe to express yourself, Mistress Julie's voice whispered through her mind. She did feel safe. She also felt out of control, and she knew that's why she was sinking back into the more familiar mindset of Asad being Master Asad. Because if he was Master Asad, it didn't matter what she wanted. She could cede the control to him, let him decide how the rest of the evening was going to go.

"I take it no one told you that this week was supposed to be platonic?" His tone was dry, but she could hear the frustration laced through it, which was reassuring. At least she wasn't the only one who was frustrated.

Arms crossed over her chest, as if she could hold in her emotions by sheer physical force, Morgan shook her head, pressing her lips together. Blinking quickly, she swallowed hard.

No, no one had told her that this week was platonic. Her decisions had not only been made for her, she'd also been kept out of the loop. No one had even thought to tell *her* what they'd decided about her life.

Master Asad sighed and reached over to put his hand on her thigh.

"I'm sorry, Morgan. I didn't realize no one had told you... They mean well. It's just that spending a week together can be very intimate and adding sex to that..." He shrugged. "Apparently, there's a lot of worry about magic penises and vaginas."

"What?" Bewilderment cut through her anger and hurt.

By the time he was done explaining what he meant, they'd reached the hotel, and Morgan was actually laughing. Her anger wasn't gone, but it no longer felt as though she was going to explode. It had decreased to a low simmer, bubbling under her other emotions but not boiling over.

"You've never heard of magic penises and vaginas, huh?" Master Asad asked, breaking the silence between them. Morgan was staring up at the hotel in front of them. Some of the windows were lit from within, some were not. The setting sun was on the other side of the building, casting them in shadow.

"I don't read a lot of romance."

"Why not? It feels like most of the subs at the club do."

"I don't think I'm a romance person." She looked down at her chest. Her fake breasts. "They're not really written for me."

"What are you talking about? They're for women. Usually. Some of the guys are even reading them now, I hear."

"Have you ever read one?" She wasn't surprised when he shook his head. "Well, magic penises and vaginas might be a big part of them, but so are women with fake breasts, and big hair, who wear lots of makeup and dress in sexy clothes. They're always the villain. If a woman is described that way, you immediately know she's going to be trouble for the heroine. It got depressing, so I stopped trying to read them." She'd just started liking herself and the books had made her feel like she wasn't supposed to like herself the way she was, so it hadn't been a hard decision.

"Well, if there's any question, I like your breasts, and hair, and how you dress, and I think you do an amazing job with your makeup."

"Thank you." She smiled at him, her spirits lifting a little before they sank again. She sighed. If she'd ever wanted proof that she wasn't cut out for romance, the fact that her friends didn't think she could even go away for a week without setting a bunch of rules around it was a telling sign. "So... where does this leave us? I thought I was going to truly get away this week, get to make my own decisions, and... I wanted to scene. I thought I was going to get to scene with you."

"Trust me, it's not from lack of desire on my part." His fingers toyed with hers. "I don't want anyone pissed at me, though. Patrick and Lexie especially."

"How would they know?" The line from the popular app sound fell from her lips, and Morgan sat up. "No, wait, seriously, how would they know?" She turned to look at him. The shadows made it a little harder to read his expression, but he looked like he was listening.

"We just won't tell anyone. No one at the wedding knows anyone back home, right?"

"Well, there's a line from Mason to Drew to Patrick…"

"So, we won't tell Mason. He's not going to know what we do in our hotel room, alone." Excitement fizzed through her, along with the defiance she'd felt yesterday. The rebellion.

Everyone thought they could tell her what to do, how to act, what she could and couldn't do. Not just her parents and Master Jason and Master Richard, but all her friends now. They might have good intentions, but they were boxing her in while telling her it was for her own good.

It was different.

She knew it was different.

But right now, it didn't feel that different. The biggest difference was that she felt like she could do what she wanted to do, anyway. Was part of her afraid that if people found out, they'd be angry at her? That they'd feel like she wasn't worth helping if she went against what they wanted? Absolutely. Yes.

It wouldn't happen if they didn't find out.

No one needs to know.

Everything hinged on how Master Asad reacted, and right now, he was sitting silently, thinking about what she was saying. He wasn't convinced yet.

"What was the point of being rescued if I still don't get to make my own decisions?" she asked a little desperately. He winced. "What was the point of getting away from everyone for a week if they're still controlling everything I do? I was supposed to be able to think for myself this week."

"You're right." He said it so quickly, and it was so unexpected, for a moment, she wasn't sure she'd heard him correctly.

"What?" Those were definitely not words she was used to hearing. She stared at him, at his lips, like maybe she'd be able to read them to see if she'd misheard him.

"You're right." He nodded his head, obviously having come to some kind of decision. "No one needs to know. And you should be allowed to make your own decisions. If you want a scene, if you want sex, then you should be able to choose that."

Relief flooded her, along with an odd sense of joy. She was right. She was *right*. And he was going to let her choose. Really choose. Not just a small choice, like what she was going to eat for a meal or what movie she wanted to watch, but a big choice like having sex, even though they weren't supposed to.

Those small choices had been scary in the beginning, but she was past that now. She wanted to be able to make big choices, like who she had sex with and when. Even if she wasn't planning on telling anyone about it, she would know.

"Thank you."

Master Asad shook his head.

"Don't thank me. That's a choice you should always have, and I'm sorry I was a part of taking that away from you." He tilted his head back, looking up at the ceiling of the car for a moment, thinking, before bringing his gaze back to meet hers. "We do need to go over a couple of ground rules, though."

"Like what?" Did he mean like a contract?

"Like, we obviously both agree we're not going to tell anyone. Even if you want to tell them that you can make your own decisions, which you can and should, you need to leave out that you made some of your own decisions this week. No matter how mad they make you."

That was fair. Morgan nodded.

"And we both agree, this is just for this week. Fake relationship, real sex, and it's all over when we get back to Maryland. And if you start feeling any emotions for me that go beyond friendship, you will tell me, and we'll cut this off immediately."

She wasn't sure exactly how she would tell what her emotions were, but she nodded. They'd had sex in the past and scened together multiple times, so she didn't see why this should be any different just because it was a week instead of a night. Less than a week now. Five nights.

She'd never been in love before, though she thought she had been with Master Jason. They weren't in danger of love at first sight, and she didn't think five nights was long enough to suddenly go from friendship to a romantic relationship. At least, not from what she'd observed. Of course, she'd seen it in movies, but everyone kept pointing out to her that those weren't real life. They were on a two-hour time crunch to get the characters together, so the timelines were accelerated.

Therefore, she and Master Asad should be fine, especially with established ground rules.

"I'm not worried about that," she reassured him. "I'm not ready for a relationship. But I was looking forward to practicing this week."

He flashed a grin at her, looking more like himself than he had since they'd arrived.

"Then let's go practice, baby."

Asad

No one had told Morgan. He couldn't help but be pissed on her behalf. Maybe everyone had assumed she wouldn't want to have sex while she was away. Or that someone else had talked to her about the rules for the week.

He didn't know, but it was a glaring oversight, and it made him furious on her behalf.

If anyone found out, this might be a colossal mistake, but he'd never been much of a rule follower. Morgan was. Since she was looking to rebel a little, he was going to go ahead and enable her. He would have even if it hadn't involved getting something he wanted, too. The fact her rebellion included his cock was just the cherry on top of the sundae.

Of course, since he was supposed to be keeping his hands off of her, he didn't have his play bag or any of his toys here with him. Which meant he was going to have to get creative.

At least happy Morgan was back. Her entire demeanor had changed between the car and their room, and she was back to the flirty, happy woman she'd been on the golf course. Which meant she was teasing him again.

"Get in there," he growled, slapping his hand against her butt to get her moving. The hotel hallway was empty, and he was pretty sure no one he knew was on their floor anyway, but he did get a little thrill out of spanking her in a semi-public place. Yeah, he definitely didn't like following rules. They'd been chafing him, even though he hadn't realized it until now.

Would there be consequences if they were found out? Yes. But as Morgan had said, how would anyone know?

He'd keep his hands to himself in front of Mason, and he wasn't going to tell anyone. It didn't sound like Morgan would, either. They'd spend an enjoyable week together, she'd get to 'practice,' he'd get to reward her the way he truly wanted to, then they'd go home, and no one would be the wiser.

Morgan pranced past him, shooting him a little look over her shoulder. Yup, finding out she could get a scene had changed her entire mood, and he couldn't regret that. While he might not want to be a long-term Dom, the first rule of being a Dom was that the submissive's needs came first.

She both wanted and needed this. It was his responsibility to give it to her.

Yes, and I'm sure Patrick would buy that line.

Patrick would never know.

"You have been a very naughty girl today," Asad said with mock severity, stepping through the doorway and closing the door behind him with a satisfying thud.

Morgan's eyes widened.

"Me, Sir?" Sincere innocence shone from her face and eyes. She was a little too good at that.

"Oh, yes. You've been a little cock tease all day, and now, you're going to pay for it." He advanced on her, reaching for his belt as he did so.

12

———————

Sliding the belt through the loops of his pants, Asad doubled it over in one hand.

Morgan's gaze followed the path of his belt, her little pink tongue flicking out over her lower lip in anticipation before she blinked and looked up to meet his eyes. The air around them felt different, as though they were standing in their own little bubble, the rest of the world outside the room separate from them.

He felt lighter, freer than he had in days.

"Oh, no." Morgan pressed her hands against her chest, but a little smile curled the edges of her lips. "I didn't mean to tease you, Sir. I'm so sorry."

"It's too late for that, baby." He tapped the folded-over belt against his leg. The scenes he'd done with Morgan had never involved role play before. To be honest, he hadn't really intended for it to happen this time. He'd been completely sincere when he'd said she'd been teasing him all day. He certainly wasn't going to object to it, though. "Naughty girls get the belt. And you're not going to make a sound while I do it."

A shiver went through her, but it was one of excitement, not fear.

Asad could tell. For Morgan, an implement like the belt was more of a reward than a punishment. Would it hurt? Yes. But she was a masochist, so she wanted it to hurt.

And Asad was a sadist, so he enjoyed making her hurt.

Normally, he would want to hear all the delightful sounds she made while he hurt her, but they were in a hotel. There was a club nearby... but the owner happened to be the father of another Dom whom both Asad and Morgan knew, so going there was probably not the best idea. This room was their best place for privacy, even though it would mean they needed to be quiet.

"Please, I'll be good," she whispered, backing up toward the bed, her hands clasped in front of her, upper arms pushing her breast together enticingly.

Little tease.

He barely managed to hold back his smile. That would ruin his 'stern disciplinarian' role.

"Then show me. Be a good girl and pull down your shorts and bend over the bed." As soon as he gave the order, he could see the warring desire in her eyes. Part of her wanted to say 'no' and turn it into a force scene while part of her realized that was probably not the best idea when they were trying to be quiet in a hotel room.

Discretion won out, but Asad made a mental note. They would be able to scene again when they returned to Stronghold. If Morgan wanted a consenting non-con scene in the future, he would be happy to oblige. He doubted anyone else would, considering her background, but it made sense to him—he didn't think she'd ever been *allowed* to say 'no' and still get what she wanted. Of course, it was a fantasy for her.

Turning around, Morgan made a show of reluctance as she tugged her shorts down and bent over, revealing a very cute pair of lacy undies. The white lace hugged her curves, the gusset damp from her arousal. Asad's cock, already thickening, immediately hardened to fully erect.

Was there a part of him still worried this would all blow up in his face?

Sure.

But it wasn't going to stop him.

Morgan had the right to decide what she wanted. As a good Dom, it was his duty to provide it to her.

Could he give her an orgasm without sex? Absolutely. But that wasn't what she'd asked for. More than anything else, she wanted to make her own choices. She needed to. For this week, she'd chosen him and sex.

And, most importantly, no one will know.

Bracing her forearms on the bed, Morgan peeked over her shoulder at him, fluttering her eyelashes.

"Please, Sir, I'm sorry I teased you all day. I'll suck your cock to make it better." There was a hint of laughter in her voice, though she managed to suppress any actual giggles.

Asad shook his head, shaking away his own desire to laugh as well as denying her. Which was exactly what she wanted.

"No, baby, first you're going to pay the price for teasing me. Then, maybe, if you take the belt like a good girl, I'll let you suck my dick." Yeah, he was definitely going to have her suck his dick before he fucked her. Morgan gave fantastic head. But he liked the idea of making her 'earn it,' and from the way her eyes lit up, so did she.

"I'll be good, Sir, I promise. Please, just don't spank me too hard."

Asad nearly snorted. She'd be disappointed if he didn't spank her hard enough, but he appreciated the effort.

"Don't worry, baby, I'll go easy on you since this is your first offense this week. Don't expect me to be so gentle after this."

He almost ruined his line and snickered as her expression fell. As a sadist, he definitely wasn't past a little mental torment to go with the physical. Fucking with her head and pretending he was going to go light on her was almost as fun as actually spanking her.

Stepping to her side, so he was in position to wield the belt, he didn't lift it immediately. Instead, he hooked his fingers into her panties and began to slowly drag them down over her ass to join her shorts around her knees. Morgan wriggled a little, maybe to help and maybe because she was aroused.

Lowering her own shorts was its own kind of submissive humiliation; having her underwear slowly stripped away was another. Were the gossamer thin panties going to do much to protect her bottom? Absolutely not. Her shorts wouldn't have done much, either, but removing her own shorts at his order emphasized submission to his command, then stripping her of the last line of her defenses—negligible though it was—would have a mental effect.

"There we go," he said with satisfaction, running his hand back up her thigh and over her upturned bottom. "Now it's time for your punishment."

***

<u>MORGAN</u>

Excitement thrilled through Morgan. This was why she liked scening with Master Asad. He was willing to do the kind of scenes with her that no one else was. Any other Dom at Stronghold would have worried that a domestic discipline scene was too close to her past for her to enjoy. They'd have tiptoed around every possible trigger rather than trusting her to use her safewords.

Master Asad just dove right in.

Although she was a little worried he wasn't going to spank her hard enough.

The first slap of his belt against her upturned bottom seemed to confirm that fear. It hurt, the way a belt would always hurt when it snapped against flesh, but he'd been very gentle, and the light sting didn't nearly satisfy her.

It was... a tease. The way she'd teased him today.

Oh, that mean, sadistic Dom.

Morgan groaned, dropping her head down as she realized what he was doing—making the punishment fit the crime.

"Oh, was that too rough, baby?" Master Asad said with false sympathy. "Maybe I should just use my hand."

"No!" Not that he couldn't spank her hard with his hand, but she'd been anticipating the leather from his belt—wanting it.

Switching to his hand would be another form of torment for her, and not the fun, painful kind she really wanted. That she craved. "I mean, please, Sir, I won't feel fully absolved of my transgressions without a proper punishment."

He coughed, and she was pretty sure he was covering up a laugh, which made her smile. Thankfully, he couldn't see it because that would have ruined the little game they were playing. She canted her hips upward, offering her ass for more punishment.

Belts were something she'd been unfamiliar with as an implement before coming to Stronghold. She'd known paddles, floggers, canes, and whips in their many variations, but belts... not so much. And she did like the leather. It could be stingy but gentle, the way he'd just done, or it could bite into her flesh deep enough that she'd feel it the next day—which was her favorite.

"Very well, baby. I'll make sure you get your deserved punishment."

This time, the belt came down much harder. Morgan moaned, her toes curling at the stinging, throbbing sensation that flared through her. The top surface of her skin flamed, but where she really felt it was an inch or two into the soft flesh of her ass. It ached underneath where the belt had hit and made her pussy ache in return.

She dropped her head as the belt came down again, leaving a welt just under the previous one. Master Asad's hand brushed over both marks, so she could feel the way her bottom was already swelling.

She was going to feel this tomorrow.

Good.

That was exactly what she wanted. It would help keep her calm and centered since tomorrow, she was going to be on her own a little more since Asad would be helping his brother. She was going to watch the event, then in the afternoon she had an appointment with Mistress Julie, during which they were definitely going to talk about this whole 'no sex' edict that no one told her about.

She had a feeling Mistress Julie didn't know, either. Her therapist would have never approved. And it meant a lot to her that she could trust that.

Knowing she was finally getting what she wanted—needed—allowed her to relax into the strokes of the belt as Master Asad laid them down horizontally across her ass. They hurt. Burned. And stoked the fires of her arousal, making her squirm and moan. When he reached the sensitive spot where the curve of her bottom met her thighs, she pressed her face against the mattress to cry out, suddenly acutely aware of the rooms on either side of them.

She'd never had to worry about being quiet before. There was something rather exciting about it, about muffling the sounds she was making because someone might overhear them. Being watched, being listened to, those things were so normal that trying to hide was as arousing as the burning lick of leather against her skin.

"Good girl." Master Asad brought the belt down on a diagonal, crossing all the previous welts he'd left before.

She cried out against the mattress again, panting for breath as the delicious pain coiled through her and turned to searing pleasure. It came down again, making another diagonal, so there would be an X across her ass. The fire licked her skin, stoking the heat in her core, and her pussy clenched emptily. Master Asad ran his fingers over the ridges of the welts, stimulating her sensitive skin, making her writhe against the bed.

Everything was so focused on her ass, the myriad of sensations so localized, the rest of her was aching for attention.

"I was going to do your thighs, but I think your skirts might not go low enough," Master Asad murmured.

Morgan squeezed her thighs together. She wanted the belt against them, but she worried he was right. She had several dresses for the week, and none of them was super short, but the skirts were flowy, and she didn't want them lifting up to reveal anything.

"Turn over onto your back and roll onto the bed."

A little unsure of how he wanted her positioned, Morgan did her best, and he helped move her where he wanted her. She ended up perpendicular to him, her hands stretched toward the headboard of the bed, arms resting on the pillow, while he reached down to strip her shorts and underwear completely off. Still wearing her shirt, she was now naked from the waist down, and somehow, it made her feel more vulnerable than being fully naked—just like when he'd pulled down her panties to expose her bottom.

There was something about being partially clothed that made the parts of her that didn't have clothes feel even more laid bare.

Her breasts stood up on her chest, nipples pointed toward the ceiling. The lack of sag when she was on her back was one of the indicators of her implants. Morgan couldn't help but glance up to see Master Asad's reaction, the way she always did when a Dom focused on her breasts. Some liked them, some were indifferent, and some... well, they judged. She'd never seen anything but appreciation in Master Asad's eyes, and this time was no different, which allowed her to relax even further.

Reaching down, he pulled up her shirt above her breasts and tugged down her bra, exposing them completely but framing them with her clothing. Morgan wriggled, making them jiggle a little, and Master Asad couldn't hide the flash of his smile.

"Very pretty," he commented, reaching down to palm one with his warm hand, giving it a caress before pinching her nipple hard enough to make her moan. When her lips parted, he shoved her balled-up underwear between them.

As gags went, she doubted it would be very effective, but her arousal shot up even higher. She could taste the faintest hint of her cream on the cloth, and the dry lace in her mouth would help her remember to be quiet, even if it didn't actually muffle much of her sounds. Her tongue rubbed against the fabric, unable to leave it alone.

It had been a while since she'd tasted herself, and she wasn't sure how she felt about the memory. Not bad, but not good either. It was just there, unable to hurt her, though it didn't arouse her.

"Don't move your hands," he ordered before bringing his hand down on her breast. Morgan moaned, arching her back up as he began to spank her breasts, making them jiggle with every hard slap. He didn't start off overly gentle, as he had with her ass, but each sharp smack seemed to be growing in intensity, turning the skin of her breasts from creamy white to bright pink. Nothing that would linger long enough to show in the morning but certainly enough to make her squirm and writhe.

Then, rather than stopping there, he lifted the belt and brought it down across both breasts at the same time.

Morgan's jaw clenched against her high-pitched cry, her back arching as her nipples exploded under the lash. It hurt—it hurt so bad—as the stinging, throbbing sensation shot straight through to her core, making her pulse as her ears rang.

Fuck.

No one had ever used a belt on her breasts before. When she looked down at her stretched out body, panting for breath through her nose, she could see the pink welt across both mounds. Her nipples were darker red than usual and standing even more erect, swollen from the abuse.

"Good girl. One more."

Yes, please.

This time more prepared for the sensation, she didn't cry out, though she did suck in air through her nose as tears sparked in her eyes. The belt went directly over her nipples again, horizontally, hitting her most sensitive spots while simultaneously ensuring that nothing she wore would show the marks. Fuck that hurt so good. Her nipples felt like they were about to burst. She wished he had clamps to pinch them more tightly and confine them, flatten them out.

"Now, spread your legs." His voice was deep, dark as he gave the command.

Her legs parted automatically as she floated on a sea of erotic pain. More. She wanted more. Needed it. She was so close to the precipice, and he was going to push her over it.

Yes, yes, yes, yes.

Her thighs spread apart wide, opening for him, and when the belt came down between her legs, the shocking exquisite agony of leather against her swollen lips and clit sent her soaring. Hot bliss exploded within her, and she felt his hand cover her mouth, muffling her cries of ecstasy the panties had barely muted.

13

Watching Morgan writhe in painful orgasm from having a belt applied to her spread pussy, Asad's cock pushed against the front of his pants, straining to reach the gorgeous redhead. Fuck, she was gorgeous. And she loved the belt. He pressed his hand down hard enough on her mouth to keep her in place and muffle her cries, making sure she was still able to breathe through her nose without any problems.

She was staring up at the ceiling with wide, glazed eyes, filled with sparkling tears that slid from the corners of her eyes down into her hair, all while shuddering in abject ecstasy. Fucking perfection.

Then she blinked, awareness returning to her gaze through the erotic haze. Asad smiled as she slumped, panting. He lifted his hand from her mouth, enjoying the bit of lace peeking between her pouting lips. It was the little things in life.

However, he wasn't going to enjoy it very long because he wanted in her mouth.

Dropping the belt onto the bed for the moment, he grasped her shoulders to spin her, pulling her to the side until her head was hanging off the bed. Tugging the panties from her lips, he freed his erection with his other hand. Morgan moaned as he reached out to fondle one of her sore breasts, his fingers rubbing over the welts the belt had left behind.

Her nipples were tightly budded on the tips of her breasts, a much darker pink than they had been before. She moaned again as he pinched one while placing the tip of his dick at her lips. The moan was cut off as he thrust in, sliding his dick between her lips as her tongue danced over the top of it.

This wasn't a position he'd want to keep her in for too long, but the good news was, he wasn't going to last very long. If that could be considered good news, which it probably was for Morgan's airway.

The hot suction of her mouth around his dick while he played with her breasts was pure fucking heaven. She wrapped her hands around his body to stabilize herself in the precarious position, holding on to him just enough to help keep her more comfortable. If she needed to safeword, she'd give him a double tap where she was touching him.

Though, since it was Morgan, he was extra aware of what he was doing. There was always the worry she wouldn't safeword, even when she needed to, though it hadn't yet been an actual problem.

So, he enjoyed himself, using her mouth, playing with her breasts, enjoying her body for several long minutes while his need mounted higher and higher. Slick heat surrounded his dick, her low moans creating a humming vibration as he pushed into her throat, the muscles convulsing around the tip of his cock, her body spread out before him... his to play with, to torment, to use. Her fingers dug into his ass, nails scraping his skin.

"Fuck, Red..." He thrust, shuddering as his balls tightened in reaction. "I'm going to cum."

A low hum answered him, her suckling intensifying in encouragement. He groaned, thrusting hard, careful not to bang her head against the bed but using her mouth with vigor. His hands closed around her breasts, fingers tightly pinching her nipples as his pleasure surged.

"Fuck!" He slid in deep until her lips were against the root of his cock, the full length buried in her mouth and throat as the hot bliss gripped him. Pulse after pulse of sweet release went straight down Morgan's throat while he shuddered with pure pleasure.

It was everything he'd been wanting, craving, since the moment they'd gotten into the car.

But he wasn't done yet.

As his dick softened between her lips, he bent forward, leaning over her body to slide his tongue into her pussy. A classic sixty-nine position. He felt her gasp around his half-hard cock, felt the shudder of her body beneath his as he tongued her clit. The little nub was still swollen from the lash of the leather, extra sensitive from her orgasm, and she writhed as he sucked it into his mouth.

He could feel her gasps around his dick, making it twitch as another ripple of pleasure swept through him like an aftershock. It didn't matter that he'd just cum; feeling her reaction was like an aphrodisiac. He fucking loved it.

He loved being able to do this. To give her what she needed. What she craved.

He hadn't realized how constrained he'd felt about scening with her at the clubs until now. He'd always enjoyed the scenes they'd done together, but he hadn't truly felt able to do whatever he wanted with her. Hadn't felt like he could push any of her limits.

Because someone was always watching.

Usually several someones.

Watching and waiting to step in when *they* deemed someone had gone too far.

The realization made him even more determined to give Morgan what she needed this week. If he'd been holding back with her, just a little, he could only imagine it had been a lot worse with the other Doms who cared what other people thought. Not that Asad didn't care... he just didn't care as much as most people.

Feeling her shudder and relax beneath him as her orgasm subsided, Asad straightened, pulling his cock free of her mouth. Morgan didn't move. He didn't panic because her chest was rising and falling with slow, steady breaths, but he didn't want to leave her head hanging at that angle if she'd fallen asleep.

"Up you go, Red," he murmured, curling his arm under her head and the other around her knees to move her around on the bed.

"Mmm." She snuggled in against his shoulder.

Which felt... nice.

Aftercare was not his forte, but he did know what to do. He just didn't usually enjoy it. It usually felt like a trap. As though intimate aftercare was where submissives started to get confused about what the relationship was. Asad veered toward doing the bare minimum, then jetting out of there as soon as his sub's needs were taken care of.

But there was nowhere for him to go.

Then again, it was Morgan. It wasn't as if he needed to worry she was going to suddenly start thinking or wishing they were in a relationship just because of a little cuddling. Hell, they were sleeping in the same bed all week. And she knew the score.

<u>Morgan</u>

That had been...

Morgan shivered, even though she could hardly be cold when she was curled up next to Master Asad. He was hot, and not just on an attractiveness scale. He physically ran warmer than she did. With the air conditioning running high, the room was cold, but next to him, she barely felt it.

No, her shiver had everything to do with the sensations still tingling over her skin. Everything hurt in the most delicious way possible. Her ass. Her breasts. Between her legs. Her throat felt raw, her lips bruised. She was tingling and smarting all over.

He hadn't held back at all.

"How are you feeling, Red?" Master Asad asked, running his fingers through her hair and pushing it out of her face.

"Good, Sir." So, so good. Satisfied in a way she hadn't been in so long.

It wasn't that she wanted to go back to Master Richard, but some of the things he'd done with her had been things she liked. Craved. And she hadn't been getting all of those things since her rescue. She'd been getting some of them, but not as much as she wanted. It felt as if she'd been snacking for months and now she'd finally eaten a full meal.

"No need to call me 'Sir' anymore, Morgan, scene's over." His tone was teasing but firm.

Right.

Asad.

Not *Master* Asad. Scene was over. She gave her head a little shake.

"I'm good." She yawned. "Tired. I need to take off my makeup."

"Okay."

He moved his hand away from her hair, and she rolled off the shoulder she'd been using as a pillow. Everything felt dreamy. Nice. She glanced back at him. He was frowning, looking down at the bed in front of him around where his feet were under the covers.

Her stomach dropped.

The urge to drop to the floor in supplication and beg for forgiveness for whatever she'd done wrong slammed into her, leaving her breathless. It took physical effort to resist the compulsion.

Asad glanced up at her.

"Everything okay, Red?" He reached out to touch one of her long curls, twisting the end of it around his finger.

Suddenly, she could breathe again. He wasn't mad at her. She hadn't done anything wrong. She didn't need to placate him.

"I was about to ask you that," she replied, doing her best to sound playful rather than panicked.

"Yeah... just, normally I'm the one slipping out of bed and running away. Feels odd to be on the other side." He winked at her.

Morgan laughed, the last knots of her tension sliding away. Everything was okay. He wasn't upset with her, not really.

"I'll come back," she said, though the end of it lilted upward in a question. Asad raised his eyebrows at her. She firmed her tone. "I'll come back." Because she was going to be sleeping in the bed with him, again.

The thought was more disquieting than before, and as she walked to the bathroom, she pondered the issue. Why did the idea of sleeping beside him feel strange now? Just because they'd had sex?

Yes, just because they'd just had sex.

Because she didn't get to sleep in a bed with someone she'd just had sex with.

Ouch.

It hadn't been revealed as an issue yet because she hadn't gone home with anyone she'd had sex with. She certainly hadn't been to anyone's home to have sex with them, and no one had been to hers. Her sex life had been carefully confined to either Stronghold or Marquis, and never to the hotel rooms within the latter.

Morgan made a mental note to bring up her discomfort during her appointment with Mistress Julie tomorrow. She had a feeling the therapist would want to unpack that instinct. It was a good thing she was discovering these things with Asad. She would feel awful if he was her real boyfriend, but since he was just her fake boyfriend and secret lover, it didn't feel like as big a deal that she clearly still had some things to work through.

Doing her nightly routine helped get her into a better frame of mind—the mind of someone who didn't think it was weird to sleep in the bed with their lover. This was good practice, and that was exactly what Asad was supposed to be. Her fake practice boyfriend.

Squaring her shoulders, Morgan looked at herself in the mirror. She hadn't put any clothes on—it seemed pointless, and she was always most comfortable in her own skin, anyway. Well, she was wearing her bonnet, but that was it. Looking at the welts across her breasts and turning to see the lines across her ass made her feel a little better.

She couldn't say why it comforted her to see those marks; she just knew that it did. Maybe one day she and Mistress Julie could work through why, but so far, there had been a lot of other important topics to focus on during their sessions.

Lifting her chin, she headed back out the door into the hotel room—where she was going to sleep in the bed with Asad. Although she hoped she didn't end up wrapped around him again in the middle of the night. She didn't want him to get the wrong idea, especially since they were having sex now.

Especially since everyone else seemed to think *she* would get the wrong idea if she had sex with him this week. If he thought she was getting attached or emotionally involved, he would probably cut off the orgasms. So, no extra cuddling. Just a practice relationship and real orgasms.

Asad was laying in the bed on his back, his hands behind his head, propping it up along with his pillow. He opened one eye as she walked back into the room, then the other, his gaze traveling over her body with admiration.

"I have to admit, I like that look," he said, grinning. "There's something about the silky head thing and no clothes that is very appealing."

Giggling, Morgan got into the bed. It did feel weird, but she pushed those feelings away. That was half the point of this fake relationship—getting to practice so when she had a real relationship, she knew what to do and was used to things like this. Settling onto her side of the bed, she tried to push away the uncomfortable feelings and just relax.

Turning onto his side, Asad stroked her bonnet after she'd pulled the sheets up over herself. There really was an intimacy to being in bed together, doing nothing. No wonder Master Richard hadn't wanted it.

"So, why do you wear this?" he asked.

"It's called a bonnet. Naomi introduced me to them." She reached up to touch it. "It helps keep my curls from getting frizzy or wild while I'm sleeping." Curly hair was a pain in the butt, and Naomi's hair was far curlier than hers. She'd never known about bonnets until Naomi, and they had made her life and morning routine a lot easier.

"Huh. Well, it's cute." Asad looked at her. She looked at him.

Awkward.

She didn't know what to do. It didn't seem like he really did, either. Maybe because he didn't normally do sleepovers with his lovers. That actually seemed very likely and made her feel better. She wasn't the only one out of her depth. Sure, Asad's reasons for not sleeping with the people he had sex with were different from hers, but it was something they had in common.

Yawning, she stretched and smiled up at him.

"It was a nice day, thank you," she said. "Good night."

The expression on his face made her giggle, then his lips quirked into a smile. He shook his head at her.

"Good night."

Pulling away, he turned over to turn off the light. Snuggling down into the sheets, Morgan was very aware of the large, hot body on the other side of the bed. She wondered if he was naked as well or if he'd put something on while she was in the bathroom. She couldn't exactly reach over to find out.

Yawning again, she closed her eyes. The soreness of her body, the cool sheets against the warm welts, and the satisfaction of having her needs satisfied lulled her off to sleep in record time. In her dreams, she moved across a great expanse to snuggle up against a hot man who curled his arms around her and held her tight.

14

———————

Morgan

"I keep cuddling Asad in my sleep. I don't mean to. It just keeps happening. He called it 'cuddle migrating' this morning." Morgan stared glumly at the computer screen where Mistress Julie stared back at her.

"Did he seem upset?"

"No, but..." Morgan couldn't quite put her finger on what bothered her about it. It had been a good morning. She'd woken up wrapped around Asad again. He'd chuckled and patted her hand, which she'd quickly removed from his body before he got up.

He'd been fine.

She'd been disturbed.

Mostly because she couldn't figure out why she kept doing it and why she didn't wake up once she did.

"Are you upset?"

"I don't think upset is the right word. I don't like that I'm doing something without knowing I'm doing it." Yes. That felt right. "I also don't want him to think that I'm clinging to him or getting emotionally involved."

Mistress Julie's eyebrows raised. Morgan hadn't gotten to the whole 'people told Master Asad no sex this week, but no one told me' thing yet. She was working her way up to it. From the expression on Mistress Julie's face, this might be a good time to bring it up.

"Sam told me that she overheard the guys telling Master Asad no sex this week. They think I'll get confused if we have sex this week, even though we've had sex before. And it wasn't just his friends. I confirmed with him. Master Patrick and Lexie even talked to him about it." She did her best to sit still, even though she was getting upset, pressing her hands down against her thighs to hold them in place.

Of course, that made her lean forward a little, and she found herself rocking a little. Which... helped. Since Mistress Julie didn't say anything, she didn't stop.

"How does that make you feel?"

Morgan had known the question was coming, so she had her answer prepared.

"Sad. Mad. Like they don't trust me." Because they didn't. "Like I'm not getting to choose what I want."

"Do you want to have sex with Asad?" Mistress Julie's tone was carefully contained, and Morgan couldn't tell what the Domme thought about it at all. At least she didn't seem as though she was judgmental. If she thought it was a bad idea, it wasn't showing on her face or in her voice.

"Yes." Morgan tilted her chin up defiantly. Then her shoulders slumped. "But I don't want anyone upset with me. Or him. I don't see why it can't be our business what we do."

Which was why she couldn't yet admit to her therapist that they'd already had sex. Wonderful, hot, painful sex she was still thinking about this morning. She did want to talk through all of it with Mistress Julie, and everything they talked about was supposed to be confidential, but...

There was also a part of her that wanted to keep it to herself. Not because she thought Mistress Julie would tell anyone, but because right now, it was something about her that no one knew. A thing that was hers and only hers. No one could judge her on it, no one could tell her she was doing the wrong thing, no one could change how she felt about it because they didn't know.

"It should be. Do you understand why people are concerned?" Mistress Julie asked gently. Morgan pressed her lips together, moving her hands under her thighs so she was sitting on them, the pressure helping keep her focused.

"I do. I'm glad they care. But no one else has people meddling in their business."

"Well..." Mistress Julie coughed, a small smile appearing on her lips. She wasn't known for smiling in the club, but she did it fairly often when talking to Morgan. "That's not strictly true. Our whole club runs on gossip and meddling. I think half the club's couples would have never gotten together if it wasn't for meddling from their friends."

"Like who?" She couldn't help her curiosity, which gave her a little taste of being on the other side of things.

Morgan had never meddled in someone else's relationship. If she was going to meddle with anyone, it would be Amy. But she stayed out of it because it wasn't her business. Right? Or was that the wrong thing to do?

"Well, for instance, when Sam and Q were assigned to each other for Q's submission class, Master Patrick and Lexie had me and Master Law talk to them to make sure they were okay with being paired up. We were all worried they'd end up at each other's throats."

Huh. She hadn't known that. It wasn't quite the same thing, but... there were similarities.

"And believe me, Master Andrew had plenty to say about Master Law and Iris at first." Mistress Julie's dark eyes sparkled. "Actually, Master Patrick meddled a lot when it came to keeping Iris at the club, in part because she's Andrew's sister but mostly because he could see she was a submissive in need." She tilted her head, giving Morgan a *look* that was effective, even over the computer.

"I still think I should be able to choose who I have sex with and when I want to have sex with them," Morgan grumbled, then clenched her jaw because part of her couldn't believe she'd just contradicted Mistress Julie. Her pulse started to race a little faster, and a fine tremor went through her muscles.

"Good girl," Mistress Julie said, as though she knew Morgan needed to hear those words. She relaxed. "You think that because you're right. And I'm glad to hear you speaking up for what you want."

Morgan frowned as a thought suddenly occurred to her. She knew Mistress Julie was right, that she should be allowed to speak up for what she wanted, and it was something they'd been working on.

"Is this a test? To see if I'll rebel and have sex with Master Asad, even though I'm not supposed to?" She didn't know how she felt about that.

From the way Mistress Julie's eyes widened, her jaw dropping, Morgan thought if it was a test, no one had told her therapist. It only took the other woman a moment to think about it before responding.

"No." She shook her head. "Patrick would have mentioned it to me if it was. But I'll be honest, Morgan, he didn't say anything to me about it. I don't know why he talked to Asad but not you. Maybe he thought Lexie would. Maybe there was a miscommunication in there somewhere. I honestly don't know. But they wouldn't have set this up as a test. My best guess... they have your best interests at heart and didn't realize how it would make you feel."

That did make her feel a little better. She didn't like the idea that it was a test.

"But Morgan, choosing your own path through life is not rebellion. If someone doesn't like what you're doing, that's for them to deal with. Now, actions have consequences. If you do something someone doesn't like, they might not want to spend time with you, but that doesn't necessarily mean you shouldn't do it. Especially when what they want is something that affects you and not them." Mistress Julie paused, waiting for Morgan to nod her head before continuing. "If you decide to have sex with Asad this week, that *is* something that will be your decision... and should have been in the first place. I'll have a talk with Master Patrick."

"No, don't. Please." She didn't want to get Asad in trouble, and he might be if Mistress Julie was the one to talk to Master Patrick. If Master Patrick or Lexie was upset that Asad told her, she wanted to know and also to defend him, whereas Mistress Julie would be more focused on protecting Morgan. "I want to talk to him and Lexie. When I get back, I should be the one to do it."

There was another long pause, then Mistress Julie nodded her head in agreement.

"If you feel up to it, I think that would be good for you and for them as well. The more they see you taking ownership of your deci-sions and your life, the better. You should be prepared for some push-back, though, as you take these steps. Not because people don't want to see you grow but because there's always some pain associated with change. It's probably going to be frustrating at times, for everyone, as they adjust to the new standard, but that's normal, and it will work out in the end." A little smile haunted her lips. "This is what we refer to as growing pains."

"I think I've been holding myself back because I didn't want to disappoint anyone or have to go against anyone who has been helping me." Also, going with what other people wanted felt more natural to her. It was what had been trained into her—starting with her parents, then Master Jason and Master Richard. She saw that now, though she hadn't at the time.

This week was the first time she'd really felt comfortable going against what others wanted of her, and that might be because they weren't actually there to see her do it. They would only know if she told them about it, and she currently wasn't planning to, and neither was Asad. Which might contradict the whole point of making her own decisions, but the important thing was that *she* knew.

Maybe it would help give her the courage to make a stand on making her own choices once she got back to D.C.

Choices she would actually tell people about.

In the meantime, doing it without telling anyone was good practice.

She squared her shoulders.

"I'll talk to Master Patrick and Lexie about being able to make my own choices when I get back," she said firmly.

"Good for you." Mistress Julie nodded encouragingly. They chatted for a few more minutes, then it was time to go. Morgan signed off and leaned back in the chair. Asad had let her have the room, going down to the hotel bar to meet up with Mason, Cyrus, and Anna. He'd told her she could join them if she wanted to when she was done.

She wasn't sure whether or not she wanted to.

The morning had been a lot of fun, watching Asad participate in the Jahāz Barān. He'd explained it was a ceremony to bring presents from Anna's family to Cyrus' house, preparing the new couple for their life together. He and the other groomsmen had dressed up in some festive traditional outfits and carried the gifts on their heads from the car into the house Cyrus and Anna shared. The gifts had all come from Anna's bridal shower.

Morgan had thought it was a beautiful way to combine the traditions of the different families, and she could tell it had meant a lot to Asad to be able to participate. After that, everyone had stayed at Cyrus and Anna's for a catered lunch provided by Anna's family, then they'd broken up to do whatever they needed to for the afternoon.

For Morgan, that had meant her appointment with Mistress Julie, which she'd been grateful for. She really hadn't meant to end up wrapped up around Asad again. But Mistress Julie was right, he hadn't seemed to mind, and he hadn't recoiled or acted any differently toward her today.

If anything, he'd been even more affectionate, though she knew he was playing that up for the benefit of his family. His mom had been busy explaining things to some of Anna's family, but she kept beaming at Morgan whenever they looked at each other. It was simultaneously gratifying and uncomfortable.

She wasn't sure she was ready to step back into the arena, so instead of texting Asad that she was going to join them, she checked on her social medias, making sure her scheduled posts and things were loading the way they should. She texted her friends to let them know that Sam had been right about interfering Doms, but she didn't tell them that she and Asad had had sex.

She still wanted to keep that to herself.

15

Asad

Hanging out with his brother was a lot easier when their parents weren't around. He didn't know what his mom and dad were up to this afternoon, probably some kind of preparations for the weekend, but he was glad to get the breather. Especially since he didn't have Morgan by his side to play buffer.

Everyone was more relaxed without his parents there, including Cyrus and Anna. They were cuddled up to each other in the booth, practically cooing with little hearts floating around their heads. It was sickening but also really cute. Should he be doing that with Morgan to really sell their act?

Could be fun.

With any other woman, the idea would have sent him running, but since it was fake with Morgan, it felt like a possibility.

Not because he wanted to coo and have hearts in his eyes for a woman so much as after watching Cyrus and Anna together, he was curious what it would be like. Granted, some of his friends acted very similarly with their girlfriends, and he'd never had that reaction before, but he'd never had a fake girlfriend he could try it out on before.

"If you two want to go get a room somewhere, I'm sure Asad and I can entertain ourselves." Mason's tone was dry and tinged with amusement as Cyrus and Anna played kissy-face again. Rather than taking insult, Cyrus grinned as he turned back to their cousin.

"Maybe we like an audience," he teased, then grunted as Anna elbowed him in the side.

"Oh my God, don't say things like that!" Anna covered her face with her hands. "They're *family*. You want them to think you want your family watching us?"

The phrasing of her response was throwing him off. Asad couldn't tell whether or not they were actually exhibitionists—was it just that they were family that she objected to or was she just worried they would take Cyrus seriously when he said he liked an audience?

He'd heard that kink had a genetic component, which was something he really didn't want to think about, especially when it came to his parents. One of the other Doms at Stronghold had recently found out the hard way that his parents were kinky—his dad owned the BDSM club up here in Pittsburgh, called the Outlands. Poor Mitch hadn't known until his dad came down to visit Stronghold to talk business with Master Patrick.

How likely was it that his brother and Anna were kinky just because he was?

Next to him, Mason shook his head.

"I could write up an entire psych profile on you two."

"You say that about everyone." Cyrus rolled his eyes, then turned his attention to Asad. "Though if you were going to write one up about anyone, I think it should be Asad."

"What? Why me? I'm not interesting." Out of all of them, he was the most normal. Sure, his parents had been way more focused on Cyrus than him during their childhood, but it hadn't been all bad. He hadn't had to overcome a deadly illness when he was just a kid, and he hadn't gone into the army and seen the kind of shit Mason had. Plus, Mason was way too interested in killers and what made them tick.

Asad was just a normal guy who'd gotten his GED, gone to

college, gotten a job, and was now living the bachelor life. Well, and brought a fake girlfriend home to meet his family, but that was the most interesting thing about him, and they didn't know she was a *fake* girlfriend.

"Because I want to know why you're here with a woman who isn't actually your girlfriend."

"Excuse me?" The words popped out of his mouth as he sat up straight in his seat, his arms automatically crossing over his chest as he leaned back. *Fuck.* His brother knew. And had said so in front of Mason. He was so fucked.

"Oh, come on, Asad." Cyrus' eyes were full of something that looked a lot like pity, and it made every part of him bristle. He didn't like his little brother looking at him like that. "You show up to my wedding with a woman we've never heard of, and you expect us to believe you're in a serious relationship with her? I mean, you're doing all the right things with her, and I can tell you're friends, but I don't remember PDA particularly bothering you, and while you hold her hand a lot, you barely touch her otherwise."

"Have you considered that it might bother *her?*" Asad snapped back. His phone buzzed, but he ignored it. Why he was digging his heels in instead of admitting that he'd been caught out? Yeah, he didn't want it accidentally getting back to his parents, and no he didn't entirely trust Mason to be able to keep it a secret from his mother, but that wasn't all of it. Something about the way Cyrus had said it was putting his hackles up.

It didn't matter that Cyrus was right.

Or maybe it made it worse that he was.

Cyrus blinked at Asad's vehement response, as if no, he hadn't considered that before. Next to Asad, Mason remained silent, watching both of them carefully. It was hard not to be hyperaware of his far-too-observant cousin whose focus was now on him, but Asad ignored him as best he could.

"It didn't occur to you that maybe Morgan doesn't want me all over her in front of my family, who she *just met*, especially my parents?" Granted, he had no idea how Morgan would actually feel about that, though he was pretty sure she would have gone along with whatever he suggested. That wasn't the point.

"Told you so," Anna muttered under her breath, elbowing Cyrus again. His side had to be hurting by now, even though he didn't say anything. He did reach under his arm to catch her elbow and pin it to his side, so she didn't have so much leverage, but his focus remained on Asad. He was frowning thoughtfully, but he clearly wasn't convinced yet.

While Cyrus was thinking, Asad picked up his phone to check it. Morgan had texted to let him know she was on her way down from their room.

"She's on her way down from the room," he said, turning the phone back off and looking at Mason. His cousin immediately began to move out of the way to let Asad out of the booth. "If you could refrain from casting aspersions on our relationship in front of her, that would be great."

Getting to his feet, he ignored his brother as Anna whispered something furiously to him. Cyrus looked like he was pouting a little. Good. He didn't know why Cyrus being correct had gotten under his skin the way it had, but he was still full of completely unjustified indignation. And Mason was still watching him.

He hadn't taken more than a couple steps away from the booth when Morgan walked into the bar. As always, she looked stunning. She was dressed the same way she had been that morning, in a flirty blue dress with tiny sleeves that flared out around her knees. It had a wide neckline but wasn't low cut enough to show more than a hint of cleavage. Against her auburn hair and creamy skin, the pale blue looked incredible.

Striding up to her, he pulled her against him. Her eyes widened in surprise as she tipped her head back to see his expression.

"Just go with it," he whispered as he lowered his lips to hers for a searing kiss.

No need to fake anything. Morgan's hands pressed against his chest, then slid up around his neck as she kissed him back. The urge to reach down and cup her ass was there, but he ignored it. First of all because he really wasn't sure how she felt about full-on PDA in public—in the club was entirely different—and also because he'd just finished telling his brother that she wasn't completely comfortable with PDA.

"Hello," she said, eyes sparkling when he lifted his head. She kept her arms around his neck, but her gaze flickered to the side, cluing him in to the fact that someone was coming up behind him. "Miss me?"

"Of course. Poor Anna and I had to put up with Mason and Cyrus without you. Now that you're here, we'll outnumber them."

Morgan laughed as he stepped back, letting go of her hold on his neck. He slid his hand around to twine her fingers through his, turning to see Cyrus coming up behind him. No longer pouting, he looked more anxious than anything else.

"Hey, Morgan," he said, his gaze flickering back and forth between them.

"Hi." Her reply was cheerful but didn't invite further conversation.

Asad almost snickered. His brother didn't know exactly how to respond to her guileless greeting.

"Sorry, but uh,"—he cleared his throat—"do you mind if I steal Asad away for a moment? Mason and Anna are right over there." He turned slightly to point back at the booth they'd both come from.

Morgan looked up at Asad for direction.

"Go on, baby. We'll be there in a minute." He gave her hand a squeeze. Cyrus wanted to talk to him alone, so he'd give him that. "I'll go get you a drink. White wine?"

"Yes, please." Her smile was dazzling. She leaned over, going up on her tiptoes to give him a kiss on the cheek before letting go of his hand and sauntering away. Her ass looked great in that dress.

Cyrus muttered something under his breath.

"What was that?" Asad arched an eyebrow at his little brother before turning to head to the bar, so Cyrus had to follow after him. He could hear Cyrus' sigh as he had to hurry to catch up.

"I was just wishing I hadn't said anything," Cyrus admitted as he fell in to step beside Asad. Raking his hand through his hair, he gave Asad a nervous side glance. "I just... I don't know. Anna thinks I'm upset because you showing up with a girlfriend I didn't know about makes me feel like I don't know what's going on in your life at all."

That was fair. Though, truthfully, there was a lot Cyrus and their parents didn't know about Asad's life, and he preferred it that way. But he hadn't meant to hurt his brother's feelings. At least, he didn't think he meant to, but hearing Cyrus admit to it gave him a little feeling of satisfaction he didn't want to examine too closely.

"I don't really talk about my relationships because I don't want mom getting ideas in her head." And also because he didn't actually have relationships. He doubted his family wanted to know the details on his most recent fuck.

"But you brought your girlfriend to a family wedding? Mom is definitely getting ideas." They reached the bar, and Asad raised his hand to catch the bartender's attention. "She's not even mad that this was the first she'd heard about Morgan."

Asad shrugged because he didn't really have a good answer for that. Thankfully, putting in the order for a glass of Sauvignon Blanc and paying for it meant he didn't have to answer his brother right away. Cyrus was still watching him when he had his card back and the wine glass in his head.

"I figured it was better to introduce Morgan than to have mom trying to hook me up with someone when I already have a girl-friend." That was close enough to the truth to feel realistic. "I don't think Morgan would have taken that well."

"Huh." Cyrus cleared his throat as they headed back to the table. "Well. Anyway. I just wanted to say I'm sorry, and you don't have to worry about me saying anything rude to Morgan. I like her. She seems good for you."

Asad didn't quite know what to say to that, so he didn't. He also wasn't amused to get back to the table and find that Mason had scooted into the booth, so Morgan could sit next to him, and he was holding her hand... completely platonically, he was admiring her nails—as if the bastard cared anything about nail polish.

"Hey," Asad said, setting the wine down on the table and sliding into the booth next to Morgan. He reached his arm around her, pulling her against him, which had the happy side effect of pulling her hand from Mason's. "If you want a woman, get your own. Stop touching mine."

He was joking, but a hint of irritability had come out in his voice, enough that Mason raised his eyebrows and his hands in surrender. Out of the corner of his eye, he could see Anna and Cyrus exchanging glances over his display of jealousy. It wasn't entirely an act. He'd always been competitive with Mason. That was all. Mason didn't know that his relationship was fake, so he shouldn't be flirting with Asad's girlfriend.

"I was just admiring her nails. They're very pretty."

"Uh huh." Asad gave his cousin the dirty eyeball over the top of Morgan's head while she snuggled into him and reached for her wine. "Planning on getting yours done sometime soon?"

"I get a manicure every other week, thank you. It's why my hands are so soft."

"They are very soft," Morgan chimed in, because of course she did.

Asad shook his head and sighed.

"Are you saying I need a manicure?" he teased, settling comfortably into the seat. It felt strangely right to be sitting there with her, Cyrus and Anna across from him. He'd thought he was relaxed before, but he was even more so now. Having her as a buffer really did make a huge difference for how comfortable he was.

"Oh no, I like your hands rough. I mean..." Her cheeks turned very, very pink as everyone laughed. Anna elbowed his brother again as if to say '*see?*' At least his soon-to-be sister-in-law was on his side. He was going to make sure she never found out he was lying to them. He liked Anna and didn't want to hurt her feelings.

"Let's talk about something else before we embarrass Morgan too badly," Anna said, smiling kindly. "What's everyone up to tomorrow before the rehearsal dinner? I know there's a couple options to choose from unless you're going out on your own."

"Yeah, what's with all the activities?" Mason asked. "I figured I'd have some more downtime, but every time I turn around, something's been added to the schedule."

Anna and Cyrus both grimaced.

"It's the parents," Cyrus explained. "It's like a competition to see who's the best host, except they're not being cutthroat about it."

"It's like the nicest game of one-upmanship ever." Anna rolled her eyes, then shrugged. "But it makes them happy. It'll all be over after this weekend, then we can escape to our cruise and shut out the rest of the world for a week."

Yeah, that sounded just like his parents. It was also a good ice breaker.

Relaxing in the booth, his arm around Morgan, Asad sat back and enjoyed and afternoon with his family. Later, he'd reward her for being such a great fake girlfriend. An orgasm or two should do it.

16

Tied down to the bed with her hands bound above her head with one of Master Asad's ties and her ankles spread and secured with two of her scarves, Morgan moaned as Master Asad pinched and twisted her nipples. Only the faintest traces of her welts remained, but the little buds were still extra sensitive from the lash of the belt the night before. His pinching and pulling was sending little shots of pain and pleasure straight to her spread, neglected pussy.

Straddling her waist, Master Asad appeared to be entirely focused on tormenting her breasts and nipples. He'd started off with little slaps and fondling, taking the time to suckle the tender buds before moving on to pinching and pulling, ignoring the bottom half of her body completely. It was driving her wild.

He scooted down slightly, so he could bend over and take a pert nipple between his lips again, causing Morgan to moan even louder and arch her back to try to thrust it deeper into his mouth. Between her thighs, her pussy ached with need, craving whatever kind of sensation he wanted to give her.

He was playing with her nipples—why not her clit?

"Yes, Red?" he asked, lifting his hand. His other hand fondled her opposite breast, brushing his thumb over the sensitive bud while he palmed the mound of flesh. "Something you need?"

"Whatever pleases you, Sir," she said automatically.

"And if it pleases me to fuck these beautiful breasts and leave your pussy completely unattended?" Saying the words, he pushed her breasts together, plumping them next to each other and creating a deep valley he could thrust his cock into if he wanted.

Morgan squirmed underneath him. Part of her understood he was trying to get her to say what she wanted from him while another part of her was insisting it didn't matter what she wanted. It only mattered what he wanted. She'd never been good at lying when Master Richard had played this mind game with her, even though she'd known the desired response.

"Please, Sir, let me cum." She couldn't outright deny him what he wanted, but she could talk around it.

"Did you bring any toys with you, Red? A vibrator? Anything?"

She shook her head.

Though she had some toys at home, for some reason, it hadn't occurred to her to pack any of them. Maybe because she preferred sex to masturbation.

"Hmm. I need to find a way to sneak out so we can get some more things to play with." Master Asad was thoughtful as he mused aloud, though he didn't stop playing with her breasts while he was distracted. Her swollen nipples throbbed in the tight grip of his fingers as he pinched and released, making her pant as the pleasure-pain combination thrummed through her.

"We could go to the Outlands, Sir," she said hopefully.

Master Asad raised his eyebrows at her.

"Mitch's dad owns it. It might be hard to stay a secret."

"I've never met Master Gavin." She smiled up at her sadistic lover. "He won't know who I am, even if he knows about me."

"I thought you said Naomi told you about the Outlands."

"She did." Morgan gasped, her back arching as he crushed her nipples, pulling on them at the same time. The sweet, hot need spilled through her, and her legs jerked, trying to press her thighs together to find some relief for her aching clit. "But I've never been. I met Naomi before they moved here."

"And if Naomi and Drew are there?"

"They won't be. I already asked Naomi if she was in town this week because I thought I might be able to see her." She'd been disappointed when Naomi had said they'd be away, but now it seemed like everything was working out in a good way. Though she probably would have been able to convince Master Asad to go to the Outlands, anyway, she wanted to play there, too. "They have private rooms."

"You've thought this through, haven't you?" Master Asad asked, chuckling. He released her nipples and began to move down her body, so he was no longer straddling her waist. As he moved, he reached over to grab a condom from the nightstand. They didn't need to worry about STDs, thanks to being regularly tested, but Master Asad was well known for wanting extra protection when it came to pregnancy prevention. "No glove, no love" was the way he'd explained it to her the first time they'd had intercourse during a scene. Morgan didn't mind either way. Considering she'd never gotten pregnant while on her birth control before now, she felt safe on it, but she didn't think extra precaution was a bad thing.

"I really wanted to go to the Outlands this week." She batted her eyes up at him, knowing he would see right through the blatant manipulation attempt, but also that he would enjoy it enough, he was likely to indulge her. If he wasn't considering it, he would have shut her down already.

"Okay, Red. I'll see if I can get us into the Outlands and into a private room." Master Asad grinned at her. "I can't promise anything, though, since things are a little busy this week."

The fact he was willing to try just because she wanted to, despite the packed schedule, sent a rush of warmth through her.

"Thank you, Sir." There were a lot of people willing to help her get what she wanted as long as they thought it was a good thing for her to have. But here was Master Asad, agreeing to try to get them some time at the Outlands, even though it would make his week a little more difficult and possibly run a bit of a risk to their cover.

She didn't think they would run into anyone they knew there. No one else from the Stronghold or Marquis clubs was supposed to be in Pittsburgh this week—or she or Master Asad would have heard about it—but there was still a risk. He was going to do it, anyway.

It made her want to suck his cock all over again... unfortunately, she was a little tied up at the moment and completely at the mercy of what he wanted to do, so it was hard to show proper appreciation.

"Trust me, Red, I'm going to enjoy it just as much as you if I can get us in." With that, he lined his cock up with her pussy and sank in. Morgan moaned, lifting her hips as much as she could in her bound position, shuddering as her pussy finally got the stimulation she'd been aching for.

His thick cock stretched her open. She was so aroused, she didn't need much time to adjust. It felt good to be filled, to feel him moving inside her, and she gasped as he sank in hilt deep with one long thrust. His lips moved over her neck, the scruff on his jawline scraping against her sensitive skin, and the curly hair on his chest rasped against her overly sensitive and tormented nipples.

It wasn't nearly as painful as the freshly applied belt had been, but the lingering soreness was enough to fulfill her masochistic desires, while being bound and unable to move added to her enjoyment. There was nothing she could do but lie back and take his cock as he moved with exquisite slowness, teasing her senses with long, slow thrusts while his lips moved over the sensitive skin around her neck and collarbone.

Morgan writhed against the scarves and tie, tugging on them as her body demanded she move, wanting to wrap her arms and legs around him. She wanted to dig her heels into him and urge him onward, but his weight pressing her down and the ties around her limbs kept her from being able to do anything but squirm as he took his time. Every thrust teased her senses, his big body moving over hers, taking her, using her in the most delicious way possible.

Her pleasure swelled as his groin bumped against her clit, over and over. Closing her eyes, she canted her hips upward, rubbing herself against him as best she could every time he thrust home.

Whether or not they made it to the Outlands, Master Asad was going to make sure it was a pleasurable week.

As his pace picked up, her ecstasy began to spiral upward, outward, and her body tightened to an almost unbearable degree with every stroke of his cock. She clamped down around him, pulling helplessly against the restraints, as hot bliss exploded inside her. He fucked her harder, faster through her climax until he buried himself inside her, panting for breath as he shuddered with his own release.

When she woke up the next morning, she was wrapped around him again, but this time she didn't mind so much.

A_{SAD}

National Aviary, rehearsal dinner, Outlands. The rehearsal dinner was happening tonight and from what Anna had said, it was basically going to be a pre-reception for the wedding. It was on a Thursday night because on Friday she was doing the Hana Bandān with his mom and the bridal party. Morgan had been invited as well and had already said she would go, so tonight it had to be.

Thankfully, it hadn't been difficult to get guest passes for him and Morgan since they were already members at Stronghold and Marquis. He *hadn't* been able to get them a private room, but that was probably for the best. If Master Patrick happened to ask Master Gavin if he and Morgan had visited the Outlands at all, Asad would be able to say they'd just gone to look around because Morgan wanted to see another club. A private room would have been a lot harder to explain.

He was feeling a little nervous about going to the club, but hey, sometimes it was fun to live dangerously. And, if nothing else, he could pick up some toys there for them to use back in the hotel room. Although last night had been fun, and Morgan hadn't had any complaints, there were more things he wanted to do with her while they were here...

If she was going to secretly rebel with him this week, he wanted to make it worth it for her.

"Does this look good for the aviary?" Morgan asked nervously, coming out of the bathroom and twirling around so he could see her full outfit of shorts and tank top. Her hair was pulled back in a ponytail that cascaded down her back, and he had a brief image of wrapping it around his hand while she knelt in front of him flash through his mind.

"It looks fantastic. *You* look fantastic." He glanced at the clock. No, they did not have time for him to order her onto her knees for a little morning enjoyment. Damn being the best man, anyway. Any other wedding and he'd be perfectly happy to fuck off from his responsibilities.

Yesterday had been really good with him and Cyrus, and he didn't want to fuck that up. Plus, his parents were going to be at the aviary today, and he didn't want his mom complaining that he'd been a no-show. Or late. Especially since they would be leaving the rehearsal dinner when dinner was over and not joining in whatever after-dinner activity he was sure would be suggested. There was no way tonight was ending with dinner.

"Okay, good. I've never been to an aviary before." Morgan twisted her hands nervously in front of her. Getting to his feet, Asad smiled reassuringly at her, but didn't hold out his hand. Sometimes, she wanted to hold on to him, like an anchor in a storm, but sometimes— like right now—her nervous energy gave off the impression that she needed space.

"I haven't, either. I guess we'll find out what it's like together." He put his hand on her back to escort her out of the room and felt her slowly relax as they headed to the car, talking about what they both wanted to see there. Unsurprisingly, the penguins were at the top of both lists.

Even though there was a large group of wedding guests coming to visit the aviary together, they naturally ended up splitting apart as people lingered at one exhibit, hurried on to the next, or chose to go in a different direction. Asad was rather surprised to find his parents tagging along with him and Morgan—and even more surprised when they all enjoyed themselves.

Anna and Cyrus had disappeared to who knew where, and his mom and dad spent the time mostly chatting about the various exhibits and talking to Morgan. His mother even shared a few embarrassing stories about when Asad had been little, like the time he'd decided to interrupt a dinner party that had gone on after his bedtime. Even as a kid, he'd liked to sleep naked.

It was surprisingly relaxing, and it wasn't until they were at the rehearsal dinner that he had the disturbing thought that he seemed to be able to get along with his parents when Cyrus wasn't there and Cyrus when his parents weren't there but not when everyone was all together, which was disheartening.

"This was lovely," his mom said when they reached the exit, beaming at him. He couldn't help but wonder if she'd made the same observation or if she was just relieved to have reached the end of the exhibit without some kind of argument. "I know it's been a very busy week, but I'm glad we got a chance to spend some time together, especially with you, Morgan. I'm sorry we haven't been able to do more."

"It's fine, Mom. We knew you were going to be busy this week," Asad said, shrugging off the apology. Beside him, Morgan twisted slightly, putting her free hand over top their conjoined ones, so both of hers were holding his.

"I'm glad we were able to spend some time together, too," Morgan replied brightly. "I appreciate you taking time out of a very busy week to do so. I'm looking forward to the Hana Bandān tomorrow."

His mother brightened even more.

"I as well, dear." Stepping forward, she went up on her tiptoes to give Asad a kiss on the cheek and wrapped her arms around him for a hug. Startled, he released Morgan's hand to give his mom a full hug back, shocked and a little worried at the sudden display of affection.

"You okay, Mom?" he asked as she pulled away, sniffling a little, her eyes bright. Behind her, his dad only appeared a little concerned, so whatever was making her emotional, it wasn't something serious enough for his dad to know about.

"Yes, dear. Just realizing how fast time flies." She looked up at him almost mournfully, the expression on her face tugging at his heart. Her gaze moved over his face as if she was trying to memorize and capture this moment in time.

To be honest, she was starting to freak him out a little.

"We've still got a few more days this week, Mom."

"Of course." She smiled at him tearfully.

"Come on, Lena. We'll see the boy in a couple hours." His dad gave him a sympathetic look as he came up to capture his mom's arm. She stepped back, sniffing again, but pulling herself together. "You'll be at the rehearsal?"

"Yup. See you there." Something in his chest clenched again as he gave his dad a quick hug while his mom said goodbye to Morgan. He'd almost rather be fighting than have his mom look at him like that again. There had been something disturbingly vulnerable about that moment. He didn't like it.

17

The Outlands was wildly different from either Stronghold or Marquis, yet familiar in a way that meant Asad relaxed the moment he walked in. The smell of leather, the cries of pain and pleasure, all felt like his comfort zone. After an evening of avoiding his parents at the rehearsal dinner as much as possible, he *needed* this.

A place away from all the family stuff, a place where he felt comfortable, and a place where he could get fun toys to torment Morgan with. There was an entire array available at the front desk for anyone who needed something.

"Do you want to get some toys or look around first?" he asked as they looked around the main floor, which boasted a bar and a dance floor, but most of the space was taken up by a huge opening that allowed people to look down onto the kinky scenes happening below. That's where the real Dungeon was. There were some doors along the back wall he assumed were the private rooms or at least some of them.

"Look around?" Morgan answered, though her voice lilted up to make it a question, and she looked at him anxiously as if she wasn't sure she'd made the right choice.

Asad smiled easily, moving his hand from her lower back up to the back of her neck to give it a reassuring squeeze, and she relaxed.

"Let's look around. That's smart, then we can see what's available, and that will help me choose what we're going to do."

The place was busy for a Wednesday night. It also wasn't as large as Stronghold, which might explain why the private rooms were all full. That or maybe there were just more exhibitionists at Stronghold. Who knew?

The dance floor was pretty sparse, but there were plenty of people hanging out around the bar, mingling and talking, which reminded him the most of Stronghold. The local kink hangout, where people could just come and be themselves while wearing fetwear. No wonder he felt at home.

Walking along the circular edge of the balcony, they looked down on the scenes below. This was something cool neither Stronghold nor Marquis had, and Asad appreciated the view from the top. It was a completely different angle and made for a fun voyeur experience as they could see a spanking, a whipping, wax play, a threesome...

"Master..." Morgan leaned against him, alarm in her voice. Asad turned his head to see what she was looking at and saw... himself.

No.

Shit.

That was Mason. Down on the lower floor of the Outlands, flogging a woman bound to a St. Andrew's cross.

Well, fuck.

It looked like he had a lot more in common with his cousin than he'd known.

"Sorry, Red, I don't think we're going to be able to play here tonight." He stroked his thumb down the side of her neck in apology and felt her sigh through the tips of her fingers.

"Do you think he'd really tell someone if we asked him not to?" Morgan pouted. "He's here too."

"And he works with Drew, and who knows what his other connections to Stronghold are. But if you want to stay, we will. This would definitely convince him that we're a real couple if he saw us here." They looked over the balcony again. His cousin had a good form with the flogger. Pausing, Mason stepped forward to check in with his sub, rubbing his hand over her back and ass before moving away again and changing out the light flogger he was using for a heavier one.

Even though there was nothing wrong with watching, Asad felt strange about it. He'd had no idea his cousin was kinky. He was pretty sure Mason had no idea Asad was kinky. It would be fun to fuck with him, but Asad wasn't sure how much he wanted to watch, especially when Mason didn't know he was there.

So, they either needed to go downstairs and let Mason see them so he could feel comfortable again, or they needed to go.

Morgan cast a longing glance down at the lower floor again, then shook her head.

"No, Master Asad, I think we should go. I don't want to get you in trouble, and I think it would cause me more stress to worry that Mason might let something slip that would get back home than it would pleasure to be here."

She had a point. Otherwise, Asad might have decided to override her decision because protecting him shouldn't be their only reason for leaving. However, he didn't want to cause her anxiety.

"We'll get some toys on our way out," he murmured. "Trust me. We're still going to have a fun night."

"Yes, Sir." She grinned at him, apparently eager, regardless of whether they were at the club or the hotel.

Asad felt a little reluctant to be leaving the club so quickly, but he did enjoy picking out a few things for him and Morgan to play with back at the hotel. A gag, of course, to help her stay quiet and not disturb the other guests, which meant he felt no qualms about also picking up a rattan cane and a Delran cane. Lube and plug were a must—he chose a heavy glass one covered in ridges from the tip to the thick bulb. Morgan's eyes widened with interest when she saw it. He also grabbed a knotted leather flogger and a tiny rubber pussy whip that would be nice and stingy on all her most sensitive parts. The last toys were a finger vibrator and a pair of clover clamps for some extra fun. And, of course, some toy cleaner and arnica cream to help with any possible bruising.

Was it more than he needed? Probably. But he liked the options for flexibility.

Picking them out and buying them also turned out to be more fun than expected because he kept looking over his shoulder to make sure Mason hadn't come upstairs. He felt reasonably safe, yet the idea that they might get caught purchasing naughty toys added a little level of excitement that wouldn't have been there otherwise. Morgan seemed to feel it, too, glancing around nervously, then giggling.

The woman manning the register watched them with amusement. She probably thought they were tourists, which didn't bother Asad. Likely, he was never going to see her again. Though she did raise her eyebrows when they brought everything to the front.

"Um... have you used one of these before?"

"Frequently. I prefer it for stingy pain." He gave her his best 'I'm a knowledgeable sadist, not a tourist with no experience' smile.

"So do I," Morgan chirped brightly. "Oh, should we get a paddle? Then I can have the thuddy and the stingy."

"The rattan cane is for the thuddy. Or I can use my belt again if you want." Paddles weren't his favorite. He didn't know why; he just preferred the lighter instruments of torment. Maybe because his arm didn't tire out quite so quickly.

Bemused, the woman bagged up their purchases and wished them a good evening. Morgan happily told her that she planned on having a great one. Taking another quick look around to make sure Mason wasn't upstairs, they went back out the front door. Asad couldn't help but feel a bit of gleeful pleasure at knowing a secret about his cousin.

Of course, he could hardly reveal that secret without revealing that he had the same secret... but he could certainly have some fun with Mason without tipping his hand during the rest of the weekend.

Right now, though, he was going to concentrate on getting back to the hotel room with Morgan and salvaging their evening. She deserved a fun night, and so did he.

<u>MORGAN</u>

Leaving the club wasn't as disappointing as Morgan had thought it would be. Really, she'd mostly been curious about it and had liked the idea of scening in a place where no one knew her, but going back to the hotel to scene with Master Asad felt really good, too. She didn't feel like she was missing out on anything by leaving, other than an audience, which she didn't need.

As soon as they were back in the car, Master Asad put his hand on her thigh, his fingers stroking the soft inner skin as he navigated them back onto the road. Already aroused from looking around the club and picking out the toys, Morgan squirmed in her seat. She could feel that her panties were wet, and having his hand so close to her pussy, his palm warm on her thigh, was making her squirm even more.

"Lean back and spread your legs, Red," he ordered, though his eyes were on the road, almost as though he was ignoring her.

Biting back a whimper, she leaned back in the seat, scooting her butt forward as much as she could with the seat belt on, and spread her legs wide.

The loose skirt she was wearing slid across her skin, leaving her thighs almost completely bare and exposing her underwear. Master Asad's finger stroked over the wet fabric, tracing her labia, and Morgan shuddered.

"Play with your nipples. You can do it over the top of your dress, or pull them out if you're comfortable."

From his tone of voice she couldn't tell if he had a preference. She wasn't sure what she should do, but she reached up to brush her hands over her breasts. The top wasn't low cut enough for her to pull down comfortably, so that made her decision for her...

Still, she couldn't help but think about what it might be like to pull the top of her dress down. It was dark outside and the likelihood of anyone being able to see in the car to see her topless was small, despite the streetlights. The area they were driving through didn't have a bustling nightlife.

Even though she was used to exhibitionism at the club, a small thrill went through her at knowing she was playing with her breasts and nipples in an area where they *wouldn't* want to be seen by anyone. It would be even more profound if she did pull her top down.

"Good girl," Master Asad murmured, his finger slipping under her panties to stroke her pussy.

Morgan whimpered again, closing her eyes and tipping her head back as she cupped her breasts, pinching her nipples hard through the fabric. It wasn't hard enough. It was a tease, not a fully satisfying sensation.

She wanted more, and she was going to get it...

She just had to be a good girl and wait till they got to the hotel.

Somehow, fifteen minutes stretched to feel like an hour as she kept playing with her breasts, trying to get a satisfactory pinch on her nipples as Master Asad's fingers slipped through the slippery folds of her pussy. The puffy lips became more sensitive with every stroke, her inner muscles clenching emptily as he teased her clit, then slid away.

By the time they reached the hotel, she was a hot, wet mess of arousal and need, but she kept her legs spread far apart, just liked he'd ordered her to.

"Good girl," Master Asad said, sliding his fingers out from beneath her panties.

Morgan turned her head to look at them as he brought them to his mouth and sucked them clean. Even in the shadows cast by the lights, she could see the gleam in his dark eyes.

"You taste delicious." Reaching back down, he tugged her skirt over her thighs. "Let's go."

Yes, please.

Thankfully, the bags the Outlands had provided were big and were completely opaque, so no one could see what they were bringing in. The tips of the canes stuck out, but only someone familiar with exactly what they were would be able to guess from what they could see.

They walked right through the lobby without anyone giving them weird looks. She felt as if she was ready to jump out of her skin, everything was tingling and buzzing, yet no one knew. The elevator was empty, so Morgan couldn't help leaning against Master Asad, brushing her hand over the front of his pants. She twisted her hand around and the thick bulge of his erection pulsed against her palm.

"You are looking for trouble, Red," he growled into her ear, a slight hitch in his breath as she wrapped her fingers around him through his pants.

"Yes, Sir," she agreed, lifting her chin to meet his hot gaze. He looked as though he wanted to strip her down and devour her right there in the elevator, and her heart thudded in her chest.

She'd never gotten to be playful like this with anyone before. It was exciting. Unnerving. Wildly arousing. Completely different from the scenes she did at the club, where everything was carefully negotiated ahead of time. Even if no one was watching, which someone always was, her scenes never included this kind of flirting beforehand.

She was starting to understand why romance books had felt so strange to her—it wasn't just that she felt more like a villain than a heroine, it was because she'd never gotten to flirt. To play. To tease. She hadn't understood how it could feel. In comparison, the scenes she did at the club felt more controlled, more sterile, even though they were enjoyable. The very spontaneity of leaving the club, starting the scene in the car, and now teasing him in the elevator was a whole new world for her.

The doors to the elevator opened.

"Move," Master Asad growled, his hand smacking against her ass. Morgan jumped forward, giggling, the spot on her butt where he'd spanked her stinging deliciously.

More, more, more.

She could feel her swollen pussy between her legs, slippery and sensitive, pulsing with every step she took. It didn't matter that he hadn't really hurt her yet, she was more turned on than she'd ever been in her life. She still wanted the pain, but if he bent her over the bed the moment they got in the room, she wouldn't have been disappointed.

What she really wanted was him inside her.

Master Asad fumbled with the door key, making her giggle again, and he gave her a dark glare. Covering her mouth with her hands, she blinked innocently at him and saw the side of his lips quirk up in amusement before he scowled again.

"You're in so much trouble, Red. Now, get inside."

Scampering through the door ahead of him, Morgan's heart fluttered in her chest as she came to a stop in the middle of the room, unsure what to do next. The sound of the door shutting behind her had a finality to it that made her pussy clench. She couldn't wait to find out what he was going to do next.

18

Asad

Well, he had her in the room. Now what?

He should have been formulating a plan on the way back to the hotel, but all of his attention had been taken up by concentrating on driving while playing with her pussy—and *not* allowing himself to be distracted watching her play with her breasts.

Doing things on the fly was not his norm, although apparently, it was for this week. Which was more enjoyable than he would have thought. Having a fake girlfriend came with some serious perks. Things he couldn't do at the club because they were at the club. Since he never took his interactions outside the club, playing in the car or getting his cock fondled in an elevator was completely out of the question.

A week ago, he would have said none of that mattered to him. He liked his life the way it was—he liked his scenes the way they were, he didn't need anything more—but he was really enjoying getting a taste of it. It was something to savor because next week it was going to be gone, which was fine.

Asad was all about seizing the moment. He would enjoy it while it lasted. And he'd use it in the club the next time he scened with

Morgan there. After this week, he was going to be much more comfortable doing so with her than he would be with any of the other submissives.

Standing with her hands clasped in front of her, she stared at him with wide eyes, waiting to see what he wanted her to do. Her nipples were little pebbles pushing against her dress, her lips were slightly parted, and from the way she was standing, he could see that she was squeezing her thighs tightly together to put pressure on her pussy.

His dick was aching to be inside her, but since they'd just bought a bunch of toys, he didn't want to disappoint her. What was the point of the purchase if he wasn't going to use them? The fact he was more interested in fucking her than in scening with her was a little concerning.

Then again, going to the Outlands, then the drive home had been one massive tease. If he counted all of that as foreplay, he didn't feel quite so disturbed by his impatience.

"Okay, naughty girl. Get undressed while I get these bags unpacked. Strip. Slowly." That would get them started.

Sitting down in the chair, his gaze locked on Morgan, Asad pulled the bags onto his lap and started to unpack them one by one, pulling them out of their packaging and removing tags. Looking a little uncertain, Morgan reached behind her to unzip her dress. She was flexible enough to handle it on her own and doing so thrust her breasts forward in an enticing way.

Reaching up, she pulled one shoulder off, then the other, holding the fabric over her breasts until both her arms were free of the sleeves, then she let it drop. The bra she was wearing was a lacy forest green that made her skin glow in contrast, and when she shimmied the skirt over her hips, he could see that the underwear matched.

His dick throbbed in response.

"Very nice, baby. Now the bra." He cracked open the packaging for the nipple clamps. Not because he was going to apply them immediately; the timing was just fortuitous.

Slipping off the straps first, she reached behind her to undo the clasp, and the bra dropped away, revealing her pert nipples.

"Touch yourself."

He couldn't remember ever requesting a strip tease of a sub, but on the other hand, he'd never had his hands full like this at the beginning of a scene. There was something intimate about it, but he tried not to let it bother him. This whole week with Morgan was different, more intimate than what he usually did, which was fine.

They both knew the score.

So, he might as well enjoy it while he could.

Morgan let out a happy sigh as she ran her hands over her breasts, cupping and fondling them, then moaned when she pinched her nipples. The little buds were crushed between her fingers. Asad suspected she hadn't been able to get the stimulation she'd wanted when she was playing with them in the car. But he didn't want her enjoying herself too much while he was still getting the toys out. That didn't seem fair.

"Now, the panties," he ordered. Morgan pouted at him, and for a moment, he thought she might actually disobey, but then her hands moved, gliding over her stomach. She hooked her fingers through the waistband and pulled them down.

The little tease bent forward at the waist. If anyone had been sitting on the bed, they would have gotten a fantastic view of her pussy. All Asad got to see was the top of her head. Something she'd done purposefully, he realized, when she straightened back up, and he saw the mischievous expression on her face—she glanced at him nervously, but he wasn't upset. He enjoyed 'bratty' Morgan. It was more like 'playful' Morgan, but he had a feeling she was trying to be bratty. Testing the boundaries, as it were.

The packages were all open now, all the toys at his disposal. He wanted to clean the vibe and plug before he used them on her, but that still left him with plenty of options.

"Very pretty, Red, but I think your nipples could use some decoration. Come here." Her eyes lit up at his words, and she came forward eagerly. She'd seen the clamps he'd chosen.

Clover clamps could be nasty little things. They tightened when they were tugged on, and they were Morgan's favorite. Asad liked them a lot, too, though they meant keeping an eye out to make sure they didn't stay on *too* long. He wanted them to hurt, not harm.

Still sitting in the chair, he reached up to cup her breast. With the way she'd been pinching and tugging on her nipple, there was no need to stimulate the little bud to further hardness. He applied the clamp, enjoying the way she went up on her toes for a moment, closing her eyes as the tight grip of the clamp bit into her sensitive flesh. A thin chain hung between the clamps, dangling against her stomach as he fastened the second.

Eyes still closed, lips parted, Morgan panted for breath as her body adjusted to the crushing pinch of the clamps. When her eyes opened and she looked down at him, they were practically glowing with her need. Asad smiled.

Morgan

The clamps gave her poor nipples all the pressure they'd been aching for and then some. It hurt, it always hurt, but it felt so good, too, the pain going straight to her pussy which was already dripping. If she could just rub her thighs together, her clit was so swollen and slippery, she'd probably be able to get herself off with just that...

As if he could hear her thoughts, Master Asad's gaze sharpened.

"Spread your legs, baby. I want to see that pretty pussy." Not like he didn't have a good view already since he was sitting in front of her. Her pussy was basically at eye level. She obeyed, spreading her legs, since she knew seeing it wasn't the point. When he ran his hand up her inner thigh, her hips canted forward, and her hands fluttered in the air as she tried to keep her balance. "Hold on to my shoulders, Red. You don't need to tip over."

Relieved, Morgan rested her hands on his shoulders, shuddering and moaning as his fingers found her pussy again. This angle was much easier for him to toy with her body, and his finger slid inside her, pumping and twisting and setting her nerve endings ablaze with hot need.

"Oh!" She rocked on her feet, able to do so since he was letting her hold on to him. His thumb rubbed against her clit, and she felt her knees buckle. "Oh... please..."

The unsteady position made her feel like she might fall over if it wasn't for his fingers in her pussy, and she shuddered, her muscles clamping down around him. She was already so aroused, she was on the cusp of climax.

"Come for me, Red. Come all over my fingers."

That command was all she needed to push her over the edge. She cried out, her muscles clenching around him, fingers digging into his shoulders, as waves of pleasure crashed over her. Her head tipped back, and she cried out, shuddering, her knees buckling. A strong arm wrapped around her, helping her stay on her feet as the hot ecstasy filled her and retreated, leaving her floaty and quivering.

"Good girl."

Morgan moaned again. She felt Master Asad getting to his feet, his clothing sliding against her bare body, his fingers slipping away from her pussy. Her hands slid from his shoulders down to his chest, resting against the muscles, and she could feel his heart beating fast beneath her palms. The scent of feminine arousal filled her nose as his fingers pressed against her lips, and she opened them obediently. Licking and sucking, she cleaned his fingers, raising her gaze to his as she did so.

With his arm still around her, helping to keep her upright, he held her close, watching as she licked her cream from his digits. She leaned into him, pressing her breasts against him, as she twisted her head to get every last drop. The sweet-salt flavor was faintly citrusy and not unpleasant. Her confined nipples throbbed as they were caught between her body and his, adding to both her pain and plea-sure. In the wake of her orgasm, the sensation was almost too much, yet she loved it.

As soon as his fingers were clean, Master Asad dropped his hand and claimed her lips for a kiss, tasting her on her lips. His tongue delved into her mouth, dancing with hers, and she moaned, opening for him and letting him take over. The kiss deepened, as though he was trying to lick the taste of her from her mouth. Morgan shuddered as his hands ran over her body. She was hyper-sensitive post orgasm, and now that her arousal had been satisfied, the sensations were much starker.

Lifting his head, Master Asad smiled down at her, a cruel glint in his eye that stirred her belly.

"Now, it's time for your punishment, Red."

Morgan blinked. She'd forgotten that he'd promised a punishment. She'd been too preoccupied with what he was doing to her in the moment to spare a thought for the future. Now that she'd had her orgasm, her senses were no longer dulled by her desire... and it was going to hurt so much more.

Devious sadist.

Releasing her, Master Asad placed his hands on her hips to maneuver her, stepping around her and turning her at the same time. Now he had a lot more room to move around her, and she was trapped between him and the chair he'd been sitting in. Not that she minded. The feeling of being confined by him was comforting.

"These look very nice," he said, reaching up to tug on the chain between her clamps.

Morgan yelped as the tug on her sore nipples flashed through her, the clamps tightening from the pull. That was the best and worst part about clover clamps—every time her nipples got used to the pressure, it could be increased, and she'd feel it all over again with a sharper and sharper bite.

Master Asad grinned wickedly. "Very nice."

"Thank you, Sir." Compliments were always appreciated.

He lifted the chain upward, lifting her nipples and breasts at the same time. She could feel cool air on her skin where her breasts normally rested against her body. The urge to go up on her toes was nearly impossible to resist, but he wasn't pulling upward to make her—he was just lifting her breasts.

"Hold this here."

Use the chain to hold her own breasts, pulling on her nipples in a way that stretched them out, even as they were crushed by the clamps? *Owie.* But he'd ordered her to do so, and it was hardly as painful or humiliating as many of the orders she'd followed in the past. Morgan reached up to take the chain, holding it up with both of her hands, using her thumbs.

Master Asad stepped away, looking her up and down as though he was enjoying the view. Her nipples throbbed, making her insides ache. It hurt so much. Her arousal was starting to curl in her belly again, but not enough to entirely offset the pain. At the moment, the pain-pleasure balance was off and entirely in pain's favor. Eventually, she'd catch up again, but right now, she breathed through her nose, her jaw clenched against the burning ache in her breasts, trying to breathe through it and fighting the impulse to rip the clamps from her tortured nipples.

"Good girl. Now, keep holding it there."

Moving around behind her, he picked up something. Morgan whimpered when he came to the side of her, and she could see the rattan cane loosely gripped in his hand. A sense of dread started to fill her as she had an idea of what he was going to do. He was eying her breasts as she held them upwards, her nipples straining. The undersides of her breasts were far more sensitive than the top or sides.

Confirming her thoughts, he lifted the cane, gently tapping it against the underside of her breast as he gauged the distance and angle. Morgan bit her lip against another whimper.

This is going to hurt.

Her pussy pulsed in excited response—that was how she was wired.

The impact wasn't very hard.

It didn't need to be.

"Oh!" Morgan went up on her toes, her nipples protesting as her hands automatically jerked, tugging on the clamps and tightening them around her poor, tortured buds. The angle was somewhat awkward, and he hadn't used nearly the force he could have, but it didn't matter. The sensitive undersides of her breasts screamed with the sting, especially in conjunction with her tormented nipples.

His sadistic chuckle rolled through the room.

"Hurts, does it?" The mock sympathy in his voice grated over her nerves, and she turned her head to glare at him before she realized what she was doing and dropped her gaze. The tip of the cane moved to beneath her chin, lifting her head so he could see her expression. "No, no, Red, I don't want you to hide your responses from me. I want every glare, every whimper, every reaction. I want to be able to savor them."

The sincerity in his eyes was impossible to deny. He wanted it all from her because it wasn't just about what he was doing to her; it was about how she reacted to it. Something her previous Masters had never cared about, or they'd only wanted specific reactions from her rather than the truth.

Master Asad wanted *her*, uncensored. Her pussy fluttered along with the pain still throbbing through her breasts.

"Yes, Sir," she whispered.

19

———

Asad

Morgan's reactions were so fucking perfect.

He'd chosen the underside of her breasts because he hadn't been able to get the idea of caning her breasts out of his head once it had gotten in there, but he also wanted to get maximum pain with minimum impact. Morgan loved breast play. And though she'd reassured the Doms that she wasn't worried about the implants and impact play, especially considering how her previous master had treated her breasts, he still felt a little nervous. So caning the underside, causing her to pull on her nipples with the clamps, was the perfect compromise in his mind.

The little glare she'd given him before she'd tried to hide it had made him grin. He didn't like that she hid her reactions, though he understood why, but he wanted to see them.

"Now, normally I would want every scream, too, but since we're in a hotel room..." Stepping to the side, he bent down to pick up the gag. "I'll settle for hearing every muffled scream."

Putting the cane down, he walked over and lifted the gag up to her lips. She automatically opened, anxious arousal filling her gaze as he pushed the red ball between her lips. Unlike the underwear he'd used to gag her before, the ball gag would absolutely keep even her loudest screams muffled enough that no one outside the hotel room should be able to hear them.

"I'm not going to be restraining you, so if you need to use your safe word, use the tap out signal."

Morgan rolled her eyes. Asad pressed his lips together. Well, he'd said he wanted her to be honest with her reactions. Yes, he knew that she'd never used her safeword before, but it was there for a reason.

"Drop the chain, Red."

Her eyes widened, but she did as he said, dropping the chain. Her breasts fell, bouncing, and she cried out behind the gag, going up on her tiptoes as the jiggling caused the chain to pull some more. Asad knew it was well within the bounds of what she could handle, just like the cane was, but a little reminder that this *could* be painful certainly didn't hurt, especially when she was rolling her eyes at him.

Granted, he didn't expect her to need her safeword, and he didn't plan to go anywhere near her limits. She did have several edge play items on her hard limits, including permanent markings and being kept in a cage, but none of that interested him, anyway. Something permanent on a sub? No thank you. And he wasn't interested in humiliation play, pet play, or confinement. He wanted to be hands-on.

"Good girl. Now, put your hands up behind your head. I'm going to take these off." He waited till she'd positioned herself the way he wanted, her back slightly arched and pushing her breasts out at him, before he hefted one in his hand and removed the clamp. Lowering his mouth to her nipple, he sucked on the little bud, smiling around it as she screamed behind the gag, knowing that sensation was flooding back into the nub as blood flow returned and plumped it back to its natural proportions.

He laved his tongue over it, sucking hard to make it swell and expand even faster, knowing it would add to both her pain and pleasure. His cock throbbed in time with her muffled cries and panting breath as he moved to her other breast and repeated the process.

The need that was driving him made him want to rush, to move faster, but he didn't want to deny her the fun of the cane.

When he pulled away from her breasts, her nipples were shiny and rosy red from their abuse, and when she opened her eyes, he could see they were glazed from arousal. Perfect.

"To the bed," he ordered gruffly. It only took moments to get her positioned exactly how he wanted—bent over so her ass was high in the air, propped up on her elbows. The position would cause her overly sensitized nipples to brush against the sheets below her every time she moved—and he planned on making her move a lot.

He ran his hand over the pristine curve of her ass. Nothing was left from the belting she'd taken the other day, leaving him with a delightfully blank canvas. He started with his hand to warm up the skin, enjoying the way she wriggled and squirmed under the spanking, knowing it was also brushing her nipples against the bed at the same time. His hand came down harder and harder, turning the pale cream of her ass to a hot pink that was ready for the cane.

"Good girl," he murmured. "Now five with the rattan cane and five with the Delran for being such a naughty girl and teasing me."

Morgan moaned behind her gag, dropping her head and lifting her ass up as if begging for more. Between her thighs he could see that she was already highly aroused again, her pussy swollen and slick with her cream. The reddened cheeks above them made quite a pretty picture.

He brought the cane down across both cheeks, right in the middle, and she squealed as the thuddy rattan smacked against her skin, leaving a thin red line across the pink mounds. Asad smoothed his hand over her heated skin, his own desire pulsing as he touched her, feeling the warmth emanating from her.

"Good girl. Four more."

The cane came down again, horizontally across her bottom. The second blow fell an inch above the first, the third an inch below the first, the fourth an inch above the second, and the last an inch below the third, leaving a pretty row of lines evenly spread across her bottom. He'd made sure to leave room between them for the Delran, which was much stingier and would bite into her skin between the other lines.

Panting, Morgan dropped her head down, wriggling a little and going up and down on her toes as Asad switched out the canes. As soon as he was done with them, he was going to be sinking balls deep into that pretty pink pussy, which was now dripping wet and waiting for him.

***

Morgan

Agony and ecstasy, two sides of the same coin—at least, according to her senses. Her nipples were burning. Her ass was burning. And her pussy was burning with hot need. She could feel each individual line across her ass as they slowly faded into a meld of painful throbbing.

Master Asad's hand smoothed over her skin again, making her want to squirm and buck beneath him. It was almost a soothing touch, except that when he reached the exact center of one cheek, he squeezed, digging his fingers into her skin. Her choked cry was barely audible beyond the gag, but she felt the sensation pulsing through her. Then he did it again to her other cheek, and she felt her elbows buckle as she did her best to writhe in place and not move too far away.

Her brain told her to move away from the pain.

Her pussy told her to lean in.

Then his hand moved away, and she braced herself for the next slice of the cane.

"Relax," Master Asad murmured, tapping the whippy cane against her bottom gently. Taking a deep breath, Morgan made her muscles relax, even though it went against every instinct she had. She knew he was right.

The sound of the cane moving through the air barely reached her before the slice of burning fire across her bottom exploded. Morgan screamed into the gag, comfortable in the knowledge that no one but Master Asad would be able to hear her—and that he wanted to.

The Delran's sting didn't go as deep into her flesh as the rattan, but the initial burst hurt so much more. Her insides clenched as she panted through the pain, her teeth biting into the gag, drool beginning to drip from the sides of her mouth. Master Richard had never gagged her. He'd demanded she stay silent without any assistance from a gag.

There was freedom in being gagged, just like there was freedom in bondage. It didn't matter what noises she made, didn't matter how indelicate they sounded—she literally couldn't help it. Master Asad wanted her genuine responses, so she gave them to him and didn't worry about what she sounded or looked like.

With each stroke of the cane, she jerked forward, her sore nipples rubbing against the bedsheets, stimulating them further. That part didn't hurt, though it was almost too much sensation on her abused nubs. Yet she didn't try to lift herself up or pull away because deep down she wanted it.

She wanted more.

The final count of the Delran cane landed against her sit spot. Morgan screamed, rocking forward and dragging her nipples across the bed. Her whole bottom felt as if it was on fire, especially on that delicate area where her ass met her thighs. She would likely be able to feel that one all day tomorrow... which she loved thinking about. She'd enjoyed it with the belt and didn't doubt this weal would last even longer.

Shuddering and panting through the pain, she breathed through her nose, her insides quivering with need.

Rough hands gripped her thighs, Master Asad's fingers digging in as he pinned her in place. The tip of his cock pressed against her pussy, then thrust in, hard and fast. It didn't matter that she was aroused or that the condom he was wearing was lubed. The rough entrance meant she felt every inch of him as he impaled her with one thrust. Her toes curled as her senses came alive.

The hard planes of his body slammed into her bottom, smacking against the sensitive stripes he'd just left, and the pain blossomed all over again. He pulled back and slammed into her again, holding her down, fucking her roughly as if he didn't care whether she came... and all of it added to the delicious sensations coursing through her.

Her pussy was already extra sensitive from her previous orgasm, and having his cock pistoning back and forth made her writhe—or she would have if his weight wasn't leaning on her, keeping her in place. The lack of mobility, the gag in her mouth, and the way her bottom burned as he fucked her roughly, jiggling her cheeks with every stroke, was sending her higher and higher.

Morgan sobbed against the gag as the tumult of sensations overwhelmed her, crashing into her from every side and pulling her under the chaotic waves of dueling pain and pleasure. Behind her, Master Asad kept moving, thrusting as her body clamped around him in a vain effort to control the hot bliss that was shattering her apart.

If she could have begged, she would have. All she could do was grip the sheets and let him have his way with her, letting him ravage her from the inside out as every nerve ending in her body went on overdrive until she broke into a million pieces.

Then he thrust in hard, pressing his body against her, grinding and rubbing against the swollen, seared flesh of her ass, and Morgan screamed again. Her pussy gripped him, convulsing around his thick cock, and she could feel him pulsing against her shuddering walls. Rocking his hips, he groaned her name as he filled the condom while her pussy milked him.

"Fuck," he said hoarsely before collapsing on top of her. His heavy weight was strangely comfortable atop her, making her feel surrounded and secure as her body shuddered in the aftershocks of pleasure. She was still throbbing from the assault of erotic agony, the overwhelming climax.

Even if he wasn't on top of her, she was pretty sure she wouldn't have been able to stand. Her legs felt like rubber. So did her arms. So did everything else. Lying underneath him was about the limit of what she could realistically handle.

Closing her eyes, she savored the moment of feeling him surrounding her, inside her... as if they belonged together. She knew it couldn't last, but just pretending felt nice.

20

Asad

Organizing a bachelor party long-distance hadn't been easy. Asad had mostly left it up to the other groomsmen to help him out. Mason had taken the lead, not surprisingly, and he'd done a good job.

They'd rented out a huge private room and set up a projector to put some movies on one side of it with several couches and armchairs—not that most people were paying attention. Some of them were talking and drinking at the tables in the center of the room, which were set up to eat. There was a massive buffet, complete with meat stations to grab food from, and an open bar. Most of the guests were at the tables set up for playing cards on the other side of the room. There were tables for poker and blackjack—and very cute young women in very skimpy outfits were dealing.

Cyrus had specifically said no strippers, and Mason could honestly say they weren't strippers. They were getting plenty of attention from Cyrus' single friends, though. His brother, on the other hand, was sitting on the couch, drink in hand, watching the movie and looking contemplative.

As much as Asad would have liked to join the party, though none of the women were as attractive to him as Morgan, he felt like it was his duty to keep his brother entertained. That's what the best man was there for. Did it go against the grain to put aside what he wanted? Absolutely. At the same time, it was like slipping on an old worn-out shoe he'd just found again. It was a little too comfortable, yet painful.

"No cards for you?" he asked as he took the seat next to Cyrus. Unsurprisingly, Mason followed only a moment later, sitting on Cyrus' opposite side on the couch.

"Nah." Cyrus stared at the movie screen, but it didn't seem like he was really seeing it. His finger tapped against the side of the glass he was holding. Frowning, Asad leaned back to glance over Cyrus' shoulder at Mason to see what he was thinking—and Mason was looking back at him in the exact same manner.

His brother loved Anna. Asad had seen it. Was he having second thoughts?

"Everything okay?" Mason asked. "Is this where you get cold feet, and we have to talk you into showing up at the ceremony tomorrow? Because I'm pretty sure Anna will castrate you if you do a no-show."

Cyrus snorted, and the tension inside Asad relaxed.

"Trust me, I'm marrying that girl tomorrow, come hell or high water." A real smile appeared on Cyrus' face, and he finally turned his head, glancing back and forth between Mason and Asad. "What is this, an intervention?"

"Nah, just wanted to check on you since it's your bachelor party, and you're staring off into space." Asad raised his eyebrow at his little brother, inviting him to explain. Cyrus shrugged one shoulder. "So, if it's not Anna, what is it?"

"It's you."

On the other side of Cyrus, Mason sat back, a look of satisfaction on his face. Asad narrowed his eyes at his cousin but addressed Cyrus.

"What about me? What did I do?" He tried to keep his tone light rather than defensive, but he could hear it creeping in. He knew damn well he hadn't done anything. As always, he'd put aside all his own issues to be there for Cyrus when his brother needed him.

"I was hoping this week would be more of a bonding experience,"

Cyrus said, refocusing his attention on his glass, as if looking at Asad while confessing his feelings was too difficult. "I thought maybe we'd... I don't know. It's not that you haven't been around, it just hasn't been what I thought it would be."

Confusion filled Asad. He had no idea what his brother was talking about.

"Well, I'm here, right? What do you want to do to bond?"

"I don't know." Cyrus sounded mournful. "I just thought... I mean, I know things got messed up when we were kids. First the cancer, then you leaving, and I guess I just thought this week we'd be able to change all that. Sometimes, it feels like things will never really change." He turned to look up at Asad again, his dark eyes filled with emotion. "But I am really glad you're here."

He suddenly leaned forward, grabbing onto Asad and wrapping him in a hug. Asad blinked, looking at Mason and mouthed the words 'how much has he had to drink?' Mason held up his hands in confusion, but he didn't seem surprised by Cyrus' confession or his emotional outburst.

"Maybe you and Asad could talk about when and where you're going to see each other after this," Mason suggested gently, patting Cyrus on the back.

"Yes." Cyrus sat up straight, staring at Asad like he could burn a hole through him. Even though he was sitting up, he still gripped Asad's shirt tightly, keeping him in place. "We're going to get together after this. I want you in my life, Asad."

"I am in your life," Asad protested, but even as he said the words, he knew that Cyrus had a point. He hadn't been in his brother's life the way he could have been. He'd been avoiding Cyrus as much as he had their parents.

"I want you in my life more."

"Okay," he said soothingly, patting Cyrus's hands. "I can do that. We'll make it a point to see each other more. Okay?"

"Okay." Nodding, Cyrus loosened his grip on Asad's shirt. "I know Mom and Dad didn't really treat you fairly, especially when it came to showing up for you. I just don't want you to resent me."

"I don't." At least, he didn't mean to. It wasn't Cyrus' fault he'd been sick or that their parents had focused on him above all else. It was a relief to hear his brother say their parents favored him, confirmation that it hadn't all been in his head. Cyrus saw it, too. "Okay maybe that's not entirely true, but I know it's not your fault."

He didn't really know whose fault it was. His parents had been in a shit position. Sure, they eventually were making the choice to continue prioritizing Cyrus, even after he was better, but at the same time... Asad got it. They hadn't known he would have a future. Seeing Cyrus have one had been miraculous. Asad just wished there had been room for him as well.

That wasn't Cyrus' fault—it really wasn't—and hearing him address the elephant in the room made Asad feel a lot better than he would have thought.

He did want to be in Cyrus' life more. He wanted them to be brothers in every sense of the word. His brother was now a fully-fledged adult, getting married, and in a lot of ways, Asad didn't even know him.

Well, they could fix that now.

"So," he drawled. "Let's bond. What should we talk about?" Truthfully, he didn't really know. He and his guy friends tended to talk about kink and the people they knew. That's what they bonded over. They all liked the same kind of movies and doing nerdy shit like the Renaissance Fair, but his brother had always been more of a sports guy.

He wasn't actually sure what they had in common. Which backed up Cyrus' point. But it was okay.

They could start now.

Morgan

Friday evening... the second to last evening of her week being Asad's fake girlfriend, and she wasn't even getting to spend it with him. Which shouldn't matter because he *was* her fake boyfriend, not her real one, yet...

Her phone buzzed, and she glanced at it. A text from Master Patrick.

> Master Patrick: Just wanted to check in and see how the week is going. We're looking forward to having you back in the club next week. You've been missed.

A strange tightness smacked her right in the chest. She hadn't texted him to check in because she'd been mad about hearing that her activities for the week had been curtailed. Truthfully, she'd expected the text from him earlier in the week, then she'd been so distracted by all the activities, she'd forgotten to look for them. Besides, her friends had been checking in regularly, and she'd been lying to them about having sex with Asad, so she'd figured it was probably trickling back through the Stronghold and Marquis grapevine.

> Doing great. I miss the club, too. It's nice to be away for a while and do something different, though.

She wanted to confront him about the 'no sex' edict and the lack of communication with her, but that was better done in person than over the phone, especially over text message. Besides, it would be rude, considering she was being included in one of the more intimate events of the week. She wasn't entirely sure why she'd been invited to this other than her dubious position as "Asad's girlfriend." Everyone else was one of Anna's bridesmaids or family.

Anna, Anna's sister, Anna's mom, Asad's mother, grandmother, and some of his aunts... she was the odd one out. She didn't want to be disrespectful, so she sat quietly in her chair, sipped her drink, nibbled on the refreshments, and watched henna being carefully applied to Anna's hands.

Asad had explained the evening would be based on a very old tradition called Hana Bandān. Cyrus hadn't been interested, and he'd wanted Asad to be able to be there for his bachelor party, but Anna had wanted to indulge her almost mother-in-law—not to mention the grandmothers—so she'd had her bachelorette party the weekend before. Tonight, the night before the wedding, she was doing the henna. It was beautiful, the swirls and dots creating stunning, lacy patterns as it was applied.

"Can I get you something more to drink?" Asad's mom asked, coming to stand next to Morgan.

"Oh, no, thank you." She was already too full because she didn't know what to do with herself other than eat and drink. "I'm enjoying watching."

Rather than moving away, Lena sat down beside her, folding her hands on her lap. Morgan eyed her nervously. At the beginning of the week, knowing she would be attending a 'ladies only' event hadn't felt daunting, but she hadn't realized it would be just family and bridal party when Asad had told her.

She wasn't sure he actually knew how intimate it was, to be perfectly honest, or if leaving her in ignorance was an oversight. The only thing she was certain of was that he wouldn't have thinkingly put her in an awkward situation. He had been very distracted, though, so he might have just forgotten to tell her.

"I'm so glad you were able to come up this week," Lena said. Her greying black hair was swept back from her face in a complicated-looking updo, giving Morgan a clear view of her profile as Lena watched Anna laughing at something one of the grandmothers said.

"Thank you. It's been nice to meet everyone."

"I'm so glad to hear that. We're hoping to see Asad more often. We've missed him." Lena turned to look at Morgan. There was something in her eyes, some emotion Morgan didn't recognize. "We'd love it if you joined him, too."

There were undercurrents to the conversation. This was one of those times where there were hidden meanings beneath the words being said. Morgan had learned to recognize when it happened because Carolyn and Marissa both did it a lot. Unfortunately, she wasn't as good at figuring out what wasn't being said. Usually, she had Amy explain it to her.

"Um," was the only response that popped to her mind.

She didn't think Asad would want to continue their fake relationship beyond this week. That was the deal, after all, which made her feel a little sad. She was enjoying this week. She was enjoying having a fake boyfriend. Even beyond the sex, she liked spending time with him and being his 'girlfriend.' She wouldn't mind doing it again, but she had a feeling he would.

The plan was for them to 'break up' before he visited his family again, and there wasn't much point in changing that.

"You don't have to commit to anything, of course." Lena smiled, but it was strained. "I just wanted you to know that you're welcome. We'd love to get to know you better. This week has been such a whirl-wind, I feel like I've barely been able to talk to you."

That was true, but it had also been an upside to the week. Not because she didn't like Lena, who seemed perfectly nice, but because Morgan was pretty sure Asad didn't want her getting close to his family. That was for a real girlfriend, not a fake one. She also felt uncomfortable with the idea. It was one thing to lie to a stranger... Right now, the lie didn't feel good at all.

"We were able to talk on Monday... and now," she pointed out. "Although if you need to spend time with your family, I understand. That's what this week is about."

"Yes." Lena paused and then took a deep breath. "That's why I want to spend more time with you, dear. You're clearly important to Asad, and... well, my relationship with him isn't what I would wish. I was hoping maybe this week we could change things, but..." Her expression didn't change, but Morgan got the sense Lena was feeling sad.

"I know he enjoyed yesterday at the aviary," Morgan said. "Maybe if you spent more time paying more attention to him instead of Cyrus. Or as much attention to him as you do to Cyrus."

There was another long moment of stunned silence while Lena blinked as she processed Morgan's statement. The expression she had was one Morgan was all-too familiar with—it meant she'd said some-thing wrong.

"I'm sorry, I um... I probably shouldn't have said that." Pressing her hands flat against her thighs, Morgan leaned her weight back and forth, rocking slightly, so she could put new pressure on some of the marks the cane had left behind. They didn't hurt nearly as much, but it was enough to help distract her as her pulse began to race so she didn't go straight into panic.

"No, no you're right. And you're very direct, which isn't a bad thing. My husband and I have made many mistakes with Asad, and most of them we didn't realize until it was far too late." Lena's lips pursed. "Sometimes, it's hard to break out of habits."

"It is." Morgan knew that better than anyone. "I think it would make him very happy to know how you feel, regardless." Sometimes, knowing someone's intentions helped.

Lena nodded slowly. "That's good to know. Thank you, Morgan."

Oh, good. She'd said the right thing.

"So… tell me more about you and Asad. I know he said it's casual, but we can all clearly see you two make a perfect couple. Do you think you'll become more serious soon?"

Oh, crap.

21

Asad

The room was dark when Asad stumbled in. He'd had a few more than he'd meant to, spurred on by the 'bonding' with his brother, which had gotten even easier when lubricated with alcohol. He blinked, carefully closing the door behind him with exaggerated slowness so as not to wake Morgan. Slowly, his eyes adjusted to the darkness, which wasn't actually total thanks to the alarm clock and the streetlights that were barely filtering in through small gaps in the curtains.

It was quiet, other than the faint sound of Morgan's slow, even breaths.

Knowing she was there spread warmth across his chest, far warmer than any shot he'd taken. The feeling of satisfaction, knowing she was there, was new and odd. Why would he be satisfied knowing she was there?

Maybe he'd just gotten used to having her around in this room. They'd been together in it all week, after all. Her being in the room felt right. Good. Like coming home at the end of a long day.

Stop thinking like that.

He was drunk, and his brain didn't have the defenses against unprovoked thoughts the way it normally did. The thoughts kept coming as he padded across the room, stripping his clothes as he went, and slid into the bed.

I wonder if she's naked.

I wonder if she would mind if I woke her up.

She probably needs her sleep.

I can just cuddle her.

Since when do I want to cuddle someone? She's not a fucking teddy bear.

But I do like cuddling her.

I like it when she cuddles me, too.

Maybe she'll cuddle migrate her way— Oh, hello. Perfect timing.

Morgan snuggled into him with a happy little sigh, nestling her head in the crook of his arm. His hand curved around her shoulder. Now he really did feel like everything was right, just like it was supposed to be.

Warm. Safe. Wanted.

His brain registered all of these things, and he yawned, tilting his head to rub his cheek against the silky cap on her hair.

"Your mom wants to spend more time with you," she murmured.

If he wasn't so drunk, he would have jumped out of his skin.

"I didn't know you were awake."

"I'm not." She yawned. "But I wanted you to know."

Asad chuckled. She did sound like she was half-asleep. The warmth in his chest felt like it was spreading.

His brother wanted to bond.

His mom wanted more time with him. And if his mom was saying it, that meant his dad felt the same way. They operated as a pair, always.

This week wasn't anything like what he'd expected it to be. Part of that was Morgan.

"I'm glad you're here with me." He whispered the words into the darkness, not knowing if she'd heard them or not. Somehow, that made it easier to say them.

"Mmm." The little noise she made in reply didn't give him any clues about how she took the words. It seemed she'd fallen right back asleep. Which meant it didn't matter that he cuddled up around her, hugging her like a teddy bear, wrapping himself around her the way he really wanted to, rather than holding back the way he felt he had to.

His eyes were growing heavy.

It felt like he blinked, and all of the sudden, the sun was shining in through the window, and Morgan was stirring in his arms. She yawned, stretching in his arms, and he released her so she could roll away. This time, he hadn't been little spoon. Neither of them had been the spoon.

They'd slept facing each other, her head on his arm, his other arm wrapped around her, and his leg trapping her against him. He'd tucked her head under his chin. It was the exact kind of sleeping arrangement that should have horrified him, yet as she rolled onto her back, all he felt was a sense of loss.

Bad, Asad.

He covered up his unexpected emotions by rolling away as well.

"What time is it?" he asked.

"Oh shoot, it's nine!" Morgan jumped up out of bed.

"What's wrong?"

"I've got to get started. I need to shower and do my hair and makeup and be ready to leave by three." She was already headed to the bathroom, not giving him a second glance. It was silly to feel abandoned. It really was. Yet...

"You need that long to get ready?" As soon as the words were out of his mouth, his brain started screaming at him—*Mistake! Mistake!* It didn't matter that he'd never had a serious girlfriend, he knew better than to ask questions like that.

Morgan glanced at him, pausing before she went in. She didn't seem offended.

"Yes. The shower will take me at least half an hour because I need to wash and condition my hair, plus shave everything. Then it will take me about another half hour to an hour to dry it, another hour or possibly two to get it into the hairstyle I want. My skincare and makeup take me at least an hour, but it might be a little more since I want to do a glam look for the wedding. And I need to factor in time for food and travel." All of this was said in a matter-of-fact tone that laid out how she was going to be spending her day.

"Right." He nodded his head, relieved she wasn't upset with him for questioning how long it would take her. Coffee. He needed coffee. "Do you want some coffee?"

"That would be great, thank you," she called out as the door to the bathroom closed.

Coffee and breakfast. He could get those things for her since it was going to take him a lot less time to get ready than it would her. He did need to shave and style his own hair but that would take him half an hour combined.

Morgan would have had more time if he wasn't a groomsman, which made him feel a little guilty. She had to be there early because he had to be there early for pictures, unless she was going to arrive separately, which she didn't want to do. So, the very least he could do was get her coffee and feed her while she got ready.

Then the whirlwind would begin.

<u>*Morgan*</u>

"It was a lovely ceremony." That was the first thing she said to Asad when he was finally able to rejoin her after the cocktail hour, and it was the same refrain she'd been repeating since the ceremony ended. It popped out of her mouth automatically.

It was also true. The ceremony had been lovely. She didn't have anything to compare it to other than movies, and she'd never seen a movie with a Persian wedding. The blend of traditions from Cyrus' and Anna's families had been beautiful, made even more so by the love shining from the two of them. Morgan had gotten a little teary when they were saying their vows to each other. Asad had been beaming with pride for his little brother.

"Yes, it was." Asad winked at her, wrapping his arm around her.

"Now I'm starving, and Anna and Cyrus are going to be at least another half hour. What's good?" He looked at the stations set up for the cocktail hour and the servers walking around with trays.

"Everything," Morgan said honestly. All the food had been incredible.

Asad chuckled. "Sounds about right."

With him at her side, the cocktail hour didn't feel so awkward. There had been plenty of friendly people asking how she knew the bride and groom, but small talk was not her forte, and everyone she'd gotten to know during the week had been taking pictures. Asad's mom had tried to get Morgan to go with them, but she had begged off.

She wasn't Asad's real girlfriend. She didn't belong in the wedding pictures. Lena wanted their relationship to be more than it was, even after Morgan's explanation last night that they weren't making plans to get serious. Considering Asad had brought her to the wedding, when he'd never introduced a girlfriend to his family, made her task more difficult, but she'd tried.

The cocktail hour was much more enjoyable with Asad at her side, chatting easily with acquaintances, introducing her, finding topics of conversation that everyone could be involved in, and making everyone laugh. She could relax and let him take the lead, not just in the sexual Dom way, but in a way that allowed her to be herself.

By the time she went into the reception, she was feeling much better, even though she had to walk in on her own. Asad and his family were being announced before Cyrus and Anna came in.

Finding her table, she was a little nervous about sitting down by herself, then was relieved when Anna's sister's husband, Kirk, joined her. They hadn't talked much, but at least she knew him. The rest of the table would be filled once the wedding party came in—it was her and Asad, his parents, the grandmothers, and Anna's parents and sister.

"This is beautiful," Kirk said as he took his seat, looking around at the tables and flower arrangements. The location itself was practically a work of art, with a vaulted ceiling, columns going up the entire length of the walls, and greenery lit with twinkling lights decorating the balcony that looked down on where the tables were arranged.

The table linens were bright white, set off with gold chargers underneath white plates. Gold and white vases were in the center of each table, tall enough that they didn't block much of the view of the rest of the table, but huge enough at the top to have giant arrangements of white flowers that spilled over the edges. She felt like she'd stepped into a fairy tale.

"It really is," Morgan agreed, looking around with appreciation. She'd discovered that when in doubt, for wedding small talk, just comment on how lovely everything had been.

Thankfully, they'd barely spoken before the music started, and the DJ asked everyone to be seated so he could introduce the wedding party. Morgan smiled and clapped along with everyone as first the grandmothers were introduced, then the parents, the wedding party, and finally Cyrus and Anna. Asad dropped a kiss on top of her head before sitting in his seat, making her smile.

She knew he was just posturing for his family, but she was realizing how much she liked those little gestures of affection. That was a good thing to know for when she got a real boyfriend.

On the other side of Asad, Darius sat down and Lena next to him. Morgan was next to the grandmothers, who both cooed over her and told her how beautiful she looked. She couldn't help but preen at their compliments and returning them. Despite the very different styles of their dresses, they both looked incredible.

"Well, what a day," Lena said brightly, reaching for her glass.

"What a week," Kirk commented with a chuckle, making everyone laugh.

At another table, someone started tapping their glass, the sharp sound cutting through conversation, especially as it was quickly joined by many glasses being tapped with silverware. Everyone turned to look at Cyrus and Anna, who shook their heads but obligingly leaned in for a kiss. Cheers erupted through the room, then everyone went back to what they were doing as servers began to move through the tables, carrying salads.

"So, son, how has work been?" Darius asked Asad. There was a moment of awkward silence as Asad blinked, looking as if he wasn't sure he was hearing correctly. On the other side of Darius, Lena smiled at her husband approvingly. Apparently, she was implementing some of what she and Morgan had discussed the night before.

Morgan smiled and elbowed Asad.

"Good, uh, I mean, it's been good. I just finished up a big project." As Asad spoke and Darius and his mom listened with their full attention on him, Morgan grinned. It felt nice to do something good for someone else.

Asad

His parents had been replaced by pod people. It was the only explanation.

Here they were at Cyrus' wedding, and all they wanted to talk about was... him. Not in a bad way, either. His dad didn't make one remark about how he could have come to work for the family or how well Cyrus was doing at the accounting firm.

The whole conversation was completely focused on him.

At Cyrus' wedding.

He felt as if he'd stepped into an alternate reality.

Once the music started, he dragged Morgan out onto the dance floor with him. Granted, he loved to dance, but mostly, he just needed to escape his parents' attention. It had been one thing at the aviary, especially since conversation had revolved around the exhibits; it was another thing at the wedding reception.

Wrapping his arms around Morgan, he swayed with her to the romantic slow song, knowing the ideas he was putting in his mom's head but deciding it was the lesser of two evils.

"You said something about my mom wanting to spend more time with me?" he murmured as they moved together.

"Yes. She worries that she and your dad made you feel like you don't matter as much to them as Cyrus does. They want to fix things with you, but they don't know how."

Bless Morgan and her bluntness. Sometimes, that's what it took to get things through. She would say the things he and his parents would have talked around for ages without actually saying it out loud. Not that he knew what to do with that information.

He glanced over to where his parents were now talking to Anna's. They were smiling and enjoying themselves. They were trying. The first steps had been made. And sometimes, taking that first step was the most important thing.

They sure as hell weren't going to fix everything in a day or even a week, but they could make a start.

The song came to an end, transitioning to a more upbeat number. Cyrus had told him that the playlist was supposed to start with music every generation would enjoy and as the night went on, it would move to more modern tunes. Right now, it was playing a song he remembered his parents dancing to when he was a kid.

"I'm going to go ask my mom to dance," he said. Morgan beamed up at him, which made him feel like a hero, as silly as that seemed.

"I think she'd love that."

Morgan was correct. His mom was as thrilled to dance with him as she was during the Mother-Son dance with Cyrus. Something he'd never expected, and it made him feel on top of the world.

22

———————

After a night of dancing, Asad's feet hurt, yet he wasn't ready for the night to be over. It had suddenly hit him that the week was over. This was his last night with Morgan. Tomorrow, they were going back to Maryland, back to Stronghold and Marquis, back to their own homes where they were just friendly acquaintances who sometimes scened and fucked.

He should have been happy about that. He didn't *want* anything more involved than an occasional scene and sex.

Yet there was a part of him that wasn't thrilled thinking about the difference between how things were now and how they would be back home. There was no stopping it, though. Soon, they'd be back at the clubs where they wouldn't be fake girlfriend and boyfriend anymore, which meant no more hand holding, no more casual touches or kisses, no more just hanging out with Morgan or holding her or sleeping next to her.

None of which should be a problem. Those were all good things. That was how it was supposed to be.

He was *not* going to give any credence to the idea that the reason he was struggling with some feelings was because he and Morgan had been having sex all week. There was no such thing as a fucking magic vagina. They'd had sex in the past, both together and with other people. Hell, he'd seen her having sex with other men and had been just fine with it.

It meant nothing that the thought of her having sex with someone else now made his jaw clench.

Truth be told, this was the closest he'd ever let a woman get to him in years, but it was more of a friendship thing. Friends with benefits. He just wasn't used to being close friends with a woman, especially a woman he was attracted to, so things were confused. That was all.

This meant they could have one last epic round of sex tonight, end things with a bang, so to speak. Then tomorrow, he'd drop her off at home, and they'd part ways. A few nights alone in his own bed, and he'd have his head back on straight. He might as well enjoy not being alone in a bed while he could.

"Weddings are exhausting," Morgan said, yawning as Asad closed the door behind them.

"Too exhausting for one more activity?" he asked, striding up to her and pulling her against him so she could feel his erection pressing against her.

Morgan's eyes widened with delight as she gave a little wriggle, her hands coming up to rest on his chest.

"No, I'm not too exhausted for one more activity." Her tongue flicked out, wetting her lips. Anticipation lit her eyes. Had she thought maybe he'd be done with her now that the wedding was over?

"Oh, good. I would hate for those toys we bought to go unused." They hadn't touched the plug or the pussy flogger yet.

"Me, too. What do you want me to do, Sir?" Morgan squirmed against him, rubbing her breasts against his chest just under where her hands rested.

"Let's play 'night before the wedding,' and you're the virgin bride, but I'm not the groom." Asad grinned wickedly as her lips opened in surprise.

She blinked, thinking it through for a long moment. If she wanted to do a straight scene, that was fine, but he rather thought she'd enjoy a little role play.

Hopefully, pretending to be different people would help him get out of his head.

"Okay... are you seducing me, or am I protesting?"

Raising his hand to her hair, he twirled his finger around a lock of it.

"Let's go with seducing since we're in a hotel room." It was the second time she'd brought up doing a consenting non-con scene. He was definitely going to arrange something for her when they were back home. Somewhere it wouldn't matter when she screamed, and he wouldn't have to muffle the sound with a gag. "Though if you want to put up a 'token protest,' that could be fun."

Her eyes lit up as if she'd just gotten an idea. She pushed her hands against his chest, though she wasn't *really* trying to push away.

"Oh no, Asad, we can't..."

"Shhh, you don't want your fiancé to hear us." Tightening his grip on her, enjoying her wriggling against him, he claimed her lips with a kiss, hushing her protests. She melted into it, kissing him back enthusiastically before trying to pull away again.

Why he'd hit on this role play idea, he didn't know. Maybe it was because he couldn't see himself getting married, but he had weddings on the brain. Role play was often about playing with taboos, like seducing a bride the night before her wedding. It wasn't something he would ever do in real life because he would never want to hurt anyone like that or cause a breakup, but that didn't mean he'd never thought about it. There was a challenge to it that was appealing, if it wasn't for all the real-life repercussions.

Which made it the exact kind of situation role play was meant for.

"Asad!" She tore her lips away, pushing a little harder this time. The way she tilted herself made her lower body rub against his groin. Little tease. "I'm a virgin... my fiancé will know!"

"Don't worry, sweetheart, I have a way around that." Which had been part of why he'd suggested she be a virgin in this particular scenario. He wanted to use that butt plug, then fuck her sweet ass before this week was over. Running his hands down her back, he cupped her bottom to press her pussy more firmly against him. "Tomorrow, you'll be his, but tonight, you're mine."

The words hit a little harder than he'd meant them to. Maybe that was why his brain had come up with this scenario. Tonight was the last night she was truly *his*.

She wouldn't be completely untouchable when they got home, but it would be wildly different.

If the words affected her the same way they did him, it didn't show in her face. She looked up at him with wide eyes, totally in character.

"I'll still be a virgin?" she asked plaintively. "How?"

"Let me show you." Pushing away all of his emotions to be dealt with later, he lowered his mouth to hers again and maneuvered them toward the bed, stripping off their clothes as they went. He moved her next to the nightstand where he'd stored all their toys before releasing her from the kiss and kneeling in front of her to pull off her underwear.

Leaning forward, he pressed his mouth to the front of her pussy, where the lips parted, and slid his tongue into the cleft. Morgan gave a little shriek, falling back against the bed. Her thighs fell open a little farther, and Asad took full advantage. She wasn't fully lying down. She was leaning against the bed, her legs parted, while he pushed his head between them.

"Oh, Asad!" She grabbed onto his head, her fingers tightening in his hair, probably partly to keep herself balanced and partly because he was tonguing her clit. His cock throbbed in response as she tugged on his hair, and he reached down to rub the thick shaft through his boxers.

It occurred to him that she was calling him by his name rather than 'Sir' or 'Master Asad' since they were role playing... and he liked it. For some reason, it made a difference he wouldn't have expected.

Delving his tongue between the cleft one last time, he teased the sensitive nubbin there before pulling away and looking up at her.

"Don't worry, sweetheart, I'm not going to take your virginity. I just needed to taste it. Now, turn around so I can prepare you." Getting to his feet, his hands on her hips, he helped her turn, so she was no longer facing him. He pushed her upper body down, bending her over the bed, her pert ass high in the air. "Stay there."

Opening the nightstand drawer, he pulled out the lube and plug and grabbed the pussy whip for good measure. He could punish that 'virgin' pussy for not being accessible to him before he claimed her ass. Then he bent down and pulled out the Delran cane from under the bed. He wanted to send her home with a few welts to remember him by.

Why it felt important to leave his mark on her, he didn't know, but he liked the idea. A little something to remember the week by, for a few days at least.

First things first, though. He needed to get her ass prepped. Putting the cane and rubber whip on the bed beside her, he opened the lube and spread it over his finger, placing it at her anus. Morgan whimpered, wriggling a little as he began to push his finger into the tight grip of her ass. Next to that tiny hole, the ribbed plug he was holding looked massive... but it was as thick as his cock, although not quite as long.

"Do you see now how I'll leave your virginity for your fiancé but still have you for myself?" he asked, moving his finger inside her, pumping it back and forth like a small cock as he stretched her open.

Morgan

Why was this so arousing?

It wasn't just that she liked anal sex. She did. Was it the role play? Or was it because her partner was Asad? Was it being able to say his name? She felt wicked every time she did so, even though she knew he would tell her not to if he didn't like it. During role play, names were used unless a new rule had been established.

Hearing him say he was claiming her, pretending she had a fiancé waiting to take her virginity the next day, was far hotter than she would have expected. In her head, she didn't love her fiancé. It was an arranged marriage, something she didn't want but felt honor bound to respect... but she wasn't married yet.

Tonight, she could have a final night with the man she truly loved and give him something she would never let her husband have.

Even though it was pure fiction, the wicked scenario was having an effect on her. She didn't understand it, but she felt it.

"Yes, Asad. I'll never let my fiancé have me there, I promise. It will be all yours."

He groaned behind her and pushed a second finger into her bottom. Since she'd been all week without any kind of anal play, she could feel the stretch of her ring as it was pushed open, the burning friction sending waves of pleasure through her core. She pushed back, taking him deeper, lifting her bottom higher for him to do with as he pleased.

"Naughty girl," he muttered, twisting his fingers as he thrust them in again, lighting up all her sensitive nerve endings. Then they were gone, and a moment later, something much harder, heavier, and colder was pushing inside her tight opening.

Morgan moaned, dropping her head and panting as a cramp rippled through her stomach. The cold glass plug was thicker than his fingers. The ridges rubbed over her sensitive ring as it was pushed inside her, then he pulled it out a little before pushing in again, using it the same way he had his fingers. The difference with the plug was it broadened toward the base, stretching her more with every centimeter that was inserted.

It moved inside her, sending ripples of pleasure through her, and she whined, lifting her ass higher to take more and more of it. When Asad pushed the broadest part past her aching ring, she cried out as a tremor fluttered through her. She was so full now, but her pussy clenched emptily.

"Very good girl," he said approvingly, twisting the base back and forth, teasing her with the sensations.

Morgan moaned, her muscles tightening around the heavy plug.

Glass warmed quickly with the body, but it was heavy inside her, making her feel extra full and as if she had to clench her muscles to keep it in position. She shuddered, and her nipples rubbed against the sheets beneath her, adding to the stimulation. She wanted them pinched and pulled and twisted. Her whole body was one big ache, needing more of his touch... more punishment.

"Please," she begged, though she couldn't quite find the words to ask for what she wanted.

"Not yet, naughty girl. First, you have to be punished for cheating on your fiancé this way." His hand caressed her ass before he lifted it and brought it down with a hard smack. Morgan moaned, dropping her head against the bed as he began to spank her. He wasn't holding back, and each hard smack was a fiery burst of pain against her skin, making her clench around the plug every time.

She whined as the heat bloomed through her cheeks, panting as he blistered her bottom with sharp, efficient slaps of his palm.

More, more, more.

"Hold still, naughty girl. I'm going to give you something to remember me by." He moved, and she realized he was picking up the cane lying beside her. She'd almost forgotten about it. What she did remember was that she had a role to play.

"Wait! You can't, my fiancé will see the marks!"

"Then you'll have to think of a good excuse for him, won't you? Or maybe you can confess everything, and he'll take a turn punishing you for your unfaithfulness." Asad chuckled, sounding for all the world like a cruel lover who didn't care what she did once she was with her fiancé. "Now, don't make a sound. We don't want anyone to hear you."

The cane thwacked against her warmed bottom, and Morgan clenched her jaw against her cry of pain. It did hurt, and the woman she was pretending to be would have felt it far more keenly and painfully than Morgan actually did.

"Oh, please, mercy," she said, allowing herself a little sob to add authenticity to the moment. Did she hear him chuckle? "I can't take another."

"Two more, naughty girl, then I'm going to whip your naughty pussy."

"My pussy isn't naughty!" she protested. The protest might also delay the next fall of the cane, which heightened her anticipation.

"Of course, it is. You're about to let a man other than your fiancé claim your ass, and your naughty pussy is soaked." He stroked a finger through the slick folds, and Morgan wriggled, letting out a happy sigh as he rubbed her swollen clit. The little bud ached, her toes curling from the delightful sensation. "Not only that, but you've denied me your pussy, which means it's earned extra punishment."

None of that made logical sense, but it didn't matter—Morgan was keen to feel the rubber strands against her sensitive lips.

"No, please, Asad, you know I can't let you take my virginity!" she protested, trying not to giggle.

"Which is why you'll be punished, naughty girl. Now, hold still for your caning."

The cane lifted again and came down across her pinked buttocks with a painful explosion of force that nearly made her squeal. She leaned on her elbows, covering her mouth with her hands to keep from making a sound. The next blow landed on her sit spot, hard enough that she had to press her hands even harder against her mouth as she panted through the pain.

It hurt so good. Her ass clenched around the large toy. She wanted him inside her so badly, but she knew he wasn't done yet.

23

Asad

The dark pink lines crossing Morgan's bright pink bottom were so darn pretty, Asad almost regretted that he wasn't laying down more of them, but he wanted most of her focus to be on his cock in her ass once they got to that point. He didn't want her distracted by too many throbbing welts from the cane.

Although they looked damn good, and he liked seeing them there, knowing they'd last for a few days beyond tonight and tomorrow. He'd heard her muffled cries and known she'd felt them harshly—which meant her pussy was even juicier than before. That was a turn-on for Morgan, though it didn't quite satisfy his inner sadist.

That's what the pussy whip was for.

He took another long moment to enjoy the view of her bottom, the plug base peeking out between her cute cheeks, before he gave her a little pat.

"On your back, sweetheart. It's time to punish that naughty pussy."

Morgan rolled over and assumed the position with her knees bent, gripping her ankles, which spread her thighs wide apart and displayed her puffy pussy lips for his punishment, even as she whined about it. Below the creamy crevice, her tight ring was squeezing the plug, giving him easy access to both holes.

"Please, Asad, don't whip my pussy! I have to be a virgin on my wedding night. You shouldn't punish me for that. I'm giving you my bottom instead." Even through her whispered pleas, he could hear the hint of laughter and enjoyment threaded through her voice. She was having fun with the pretense of being a reluctant virgin who didn't want to be punished.

"Okay, sweetheart, I won't whip your pussy right away. Let me know when you're ready for me to."

Her eyes widened as he lifted the short rubber whip and brought it down on her breast instead of her pussy. The tiny multitude of strands would sting, though even with using full force, they wouldn't be more than a tease for a masochist like Morgan, especially on her breasts and nipples rather than her pussy.

The little mewling sound she made went straight to his cock. He lifted the whip again, bringing it down on her other breast. It took several slaps of the strands against her breasts before the skin began to blush pink, and she was squirming in place, holding onto her ankles in a vain effort to help keep herself still.

He grinned, enjoying the torment he was inflicting on her—not a painful one, but a teasing one that was making her wild with arousal and need because it wasn't nearly enough. Especially after the caning, this would be a downgrade, and it was deliciously torturous.

"Too rough, sweetheart?" he asked mockingly. "Let me know when your tits have had enough. I'll be happy to punish your naughty pussy instead."

Morgan bit her lip, as though she was trying to keep from screaming, even though he knew the sting of the whip wasn't hurting her enough for that reaction. More likely, she was trying to keep from begging that he whip her pussy, which would give her more of the pain she craved since it was so much more sensitive.

He aimed the rubber whip at her breasts again, focusing on the nipples, knowing the tease would drive her wild. Closing her eyes, she moaned, arching her back and thrusting her breasts up, begging for more. Fisting his cock in one hand, he eased some of his own ache while increasing hers.

Until she couldn't take it anymore.

"Please, Asad, I'm ready. Whip my pussy!" she begged, her voice full of desperation. Not because her breasts couldn't take anymore—they were barely pink, though her nipples were fully erect and standing at attention—but because she needed more stimulation.

He didn't need to be asked twice.

Immediately, he switched his aim, stepping back so he could hit the sensitive open folds of her pussy square on. The way she was positioned on the bed gave him a widespread target, and the tiny strands rained down on her sensitive flesh. Morgan squealed behind a clenched jaw, keeping herself from becoming too loud as the rubber snapped against her spread lips and swollen clit.

The wetness of her pussy would also increase the stinging sensation, and the way she tightened her grip on her ankles and writhed in place made it clear she was struggling to stay put. The shock of the new sensation wouldn't last long, and she would get used to it after a moment, but he enjoyed seeing her struggle at first before her body adjusted and submitted to the whip... to him.

"Good girl," he purred. "I'm going to punish this naughty pussy for denying me, then I'm going to claim that sweet ass."

Morgan moaned in response, moving her hips upward to meet the stinging whip, shuddering as it landed. She was fucking perfection.

He was going to miss this.

Morgan

The delicate folds of her pussy burned as Asad applied the whip, the tiny strands biting into her flesh every time they landed. It hurt, and at the same time, it increased her arousal, her clit throbbing from the bee sting stimulation without being able to get enough to send her over the edge into orgasm.

As teasing as the whip to her breasts and nipples had been, this was worse. Her empty pussy was clenching, her hips rocking as she held position, her whole body yearning to feel Asad's weight on top of her, his cock inside of her. Even the feeling of fullness in her ass didn't replace that desire.

"Please, Asad... I want you... I need you..." The punishment wasn't the stinging pain. All that did was drive her arousal higher. The punishment was the tease. Having him standing right there, fisting his cock, rather than putting it inside her. Whipping her pussy with a tiny rubber whip that tormented but not hard enough.

"Beg me again. Where do you want me?" The whip came down, stinging her swollen lips and biting her clit, yet leaving her unsatisfied.

"In my ass. I want you to fuck my ass." Her muscles clenched around the plug, which had warmed inside her but still couldn't replace the feeling of a cock. Her pussy spasmed in sympathy.

"As you wish."

He dropped the whip next to her on the bed and reached for the base of the plug. Morgan moaned as the ridges passed through her tight ring, setting all the nerve endings afire with pleasure. The emptiness gaped. Glass tapped against wood as Asad set the plug aside on the nightstand before moving back to his position in front of her, slicking lube over the length of his cock before lining it up with her eager hole.

His eyes met hers as he pressed the thick head to her sphincter and pushed in. Thanks to the plug, gaining entrance was easy enough, and both of them moaned as he filled her ass with his cock. Morgan shuddered, fingers tightening around her heels, holding herself open for him as his dick kept going and going, deeper inside her.

While the plug had a thick, rounded bulb, the actual stem between the base and the bulb was rather thin compared to Asad's cock. There was no relief as her tight ring wasn't able to close around something smaller. Instead, his thick length kept it stretched open—if anything, he was bigger at the base of his cock than where his shaft connected to the head, meaning she was stretched even wider as he sank into her.

"Oh... yes..." She canted her hips upward, shuddering as he bottomed out inside her, his body rubbing against hers, his hard stomach flush against her pussy and swollen clit.

"That's it, sweetheart. Take my cock up your pretty little ass. I own this ass now." He leaned forward, gripping her hips as he pulled out halfway and thrust back in hard. Morgan moaned again, clenching around him, her pussy spasming in need at the dragging sensation as he retreated, then the feeling of fullness returning.

He was big and hard and hot inside her, moving easily, thanks to the lube. He began to fuck her ass in long, hard strokes that sent all of her senses blazing. Though her muscles tried to clamp down around him, the lube meant she couldn't really get a grip. He just kept thrusting, fucking her harder and deeper, while she shuddered and writhed on his cock.

Looming over her, his fingers dug into her hips, his gaze boring into her as he moved. Morgan gasped and squirmed, holding herself open for him, reveling in the sensation of him moving inside her and using her for his pleasure, even as her own grew.

It drifted through her mind that maybe she could save her ass for him from now on. Something just for the two of them, even after this trip was over.

Then Asad leaned in, his jaw clenching, as he fucked her harder. Every thrust rubbed his body against her pussy, the friction giving her clit exactly what she needed, what she'd been craving since the moment he began undressing her. Morgan cried out, closing her eyes as the waves of pleasure peaked and crashed over her, her body spasming with the release.

She could hear Asad's low groan as her muscles tightened around him, gripping him as best they could while he continued to plunge in and out of her tight ass.

"Fuck... Morgan..." He buried himself inside her, and she cried out again as she felt him pulse within her, each spurt of cum forcing its way past her gripping entrance to be expelled deep in her bowels.

Leaning in, he claimed her lips with his, breaking her hold on her ankles as he filled her with his cum. Morgan wrapped her legs around his waist and her arms around his neck, clinging to him through the last shudders of her climax, returning his kiss as best she could through her gasps of ecstasy.

He rocked against her as her clenching spasms milked him of the last of his cum, the hard thickness of his erection beginning to dwindle inside her. Morgan sighed in satisfaction against his kiss, feeling even more sleepy than before but also completely satiated.

The only cloud on the horizon was knowing this was their last night.

But it had been a really good one.

"Good girl," Asad murmured when he broke the kiss. He shifted, and Morgan smiled up at him as his big hands cradled her face.

"That was fun." He'd made it fun.

Asad chuckled, and she felt the rumble of the vibrations against her.

"It was fun." He ran his thumb across her cheek. "Do you want me to help you get cleaned up?"

She considered it for a moment. Though she didn't need help with her normal makeup removal and skincare routine, she wouldn't mind taking a shower with him, extending this moment a little longer, but she couldn't tell what he wanted. Was he offering because he truly wanted to or because he felt like he was supposed to?

He wasn't exactly known for intensive aftercare. Not that he'd been like that this week since they'd been forced to sleep together post-sex, but now, he was offering more.

Morgan decided to take him at his word.

"Yes, that would be nice, thank you."

Later, when she was curled up in bed with Asad curled around her, a heavy arm across her midsection, she wished the week didn't have to end, but tomorrow, she was going back to her own bed. So, she snuggled in against him. Felt his arm tighten around her. He was probably already asleep, but it was still a nice feeling.

Morgan liked this. She wanted more of it.

Next time, she was going to get a real boyfriend, not a fake one, so it didn't have to end.

24

Asad

"Asad, before you go, can we speak with you for a moment? Anna will keep Morgan company." His mom made it sound like a question, but it wasn't really, and Asad knew that. Otherwise, she wouldn't have brought Anna over for Morgan.

"Sure," he said. Strangely, he wasn't as bothered by the request as he would have been a couple of days ago. He didn't immediately tense up or assume his parents wanted to chide him about something to do with Cyrus, who was across the room talking to his mother-in-law. Something in their dynamic had truly shifted between the family dinner on Monday and last night at the wedding, and he was curious but not wary of the request. Although he probably shouldn't answer for both himself and Morgan. He tilted his head at her. "Do you mind?"

"Of course not." She smiled and turned to Anna. "How are you doing this morning?" They walked off as Anna answered, headed toward where the tables were set up with food. He doubted Morgan would get anything. So far, he'd never seen her get seconds of any meal, but maybe Anna wanted to grab something.

Asad turned back to his parents. They were looking at him earnestly and perhaps a little uncomfortably.

"So, what can I do for you?" he asked since neither of them jumped on the silence that was gathering between them. His parents glanced at each other, one of those little glances couples are able to do after being together for a long period of time where not a word is said, but everything is shared.

His mom cleared her throat.

"We wanted to say how nice it was to spend time with you this week. We're hoping you'll come back home more often... or maybe we could come visit you?" She looked at him hopefully.

He almost took a step back out of surprise. His parents had never come down to visit him. He'd never been sure why, whether it was because they hadn't wanted to or hadn't been sure of their welcome, but that his mom was bringing it up at all made something in his chest fill with warmth. There had always been some part of him, deep down, that believed they didn't try to visit him because they didn't care to.

"That would be great," he said, though he wasn't sure how logistics would work since he didn't have a guest bedroom, and he doubted they'd be down for sharing his couch—which was not a pullout. Definitely his apartment wouldn't be up to their standards.

On the other hand, they could definitely afford a hotel room nearby. Whatever. They could figure that out later.

His mom smiled brightly, and even his dad's lips curved into a small smile. Then her smile faded, and she glanced at his dad again. There was more. Lifting her chin, she met Asad's gaze squarely.

"We also... we need to apologize," she said before faltering.

To Asad's surprise, his dad picked up the verbal baton rather than letting the moment linger, his voice gruff but sincere.

"We weren't fair to you when you were a kid. Our only defense is that we didn't realize at the time what we were doing. We never meant to make you feel like... like you didn't mean as much to us as Cyrus. Eventually, we realized what we'd done, what we'd been doing, but it was too late to change it."

"By eventually, he means recently." His mom chimed in, and his parents shared a guilty-looking glance.

Asad was floored. This went far beyond anything he'd expected from them, even though they'd been clear about wanting to make amends.

"A friend of mine brought up 'glass children' and 'the well child,' and once I learned more about it, I realized that's what we'd done to you." She met Asad's eyes, chewing on her lower lip. "We're so sorry. We have some habits we're working on undoing, but we wanted you to know that we do want to fix things—"

Unable to listen to anymore but also unable to speak, Asad stepped forward and wrapped his mom in a huge hug. She made a little sobbing noise against his chest as she wrapped her arms around him, gripping him tightly enough to make him grunt. Then his father's arms were around him as well, holding on to both of them, and it was Asad's turn to suppress the sudden urge to cry. He clenched his teeth against it, blinking rapidly.

Then he let out a small 'oof' sound as something hit him from behind.

"Family hug!" Cyrus said loudly in his ear.

Laughter bubbled up out of Asad, breaking the tension and the threat of tears. He could hear his mom's laugh as well and his dad's chuckle. Twisting, he opened his arms to include his brother in the hug.

For the first time in a very, very long time, it felt as though they were truly a family.

He knew it didn't mean everything would be perfect immediately, but it was as he'd thought last night—these were the first steps. And they were far bigger first steps than he'd thought they would be. He hadn't expected anything more than he'd already gotten... but it felt really good to get it.

Lifting his head, he could see quite a few people looking over at them, but his parents didn't seem to care that they were making a scene. From across the room, both Anna and Morgan were watching and smiling. Anna was actually beaming. He couldn't help but wonder if she might have been the person to bring up 'glass children,' whatever that was, to his mom. He had some research to do when he got home, but right now, everything was almost perfect.

Morgan's gaze met his, and she smiled sweetly at him, making his chest tighten for reasons other than his mom's crushing grip. He could see her happiness for him, and it made him feel... odd.

MORGAN

Her home had been invaded.

All she really wanted to do was sit quietly by herself, but the group chat had blown up as soon as she'd let her friends know she was home, then all of the sudden, everyone was coming over. She didn't really know how it happened, so she hadn't been able to stop it. She also worried if she'd tried, her friends might have decided they wanted nothing to do with her.

But she was so tired.

Especially because it was nonstop questions about the week, about Asad, about the wedding, though most of the questions were easy to answer. No one asked if they'd had sex. They just assumed she and Asad had followed the 'rules,' so she didn't have to lie.

At least her friends were also feeding her, so she didn't have to worry about that. They'd ordered pizza for themselves and a salad and mozzarella sticks for her and Amy. Pizza gave her heartburn, but the mozzarella sticks seemed to be okay as long as she didn't eat too many and didn't use the dipping sauce.

"So, what happened while I was away?" she asked, trying to shift the attention from her.

"I got my bloodwork done, and I'm seeing the doctor next week to go over the results," Amy offered up. Unlike Morgan, Amy's mozzarella sticks were still sitting on her plate. She pushed some of the lettuce around on her plate, looking pretty glum, even though her voice was chipper. "Which is good. Because it doesn't seem to matter what I do, I just keep gaining weight."

"Well, I like your curves," Sam said, glancing around and almost daring anyone to say otherwise. As a curvy woman herself, Sam rocked her curves with confidence.

"Honestly... I think I'd like them too if the wedding wasn't coming up. I just want to look perfect, and Jeremy... well, he's..." Amy's voice trailed off. She looked like she was struggling to come up with the right words for what Jeremy was.

"Being a judgmental prick?" Carolyn didn't mince words, raising her eyebrows at Amy. Sam shot Carolyn a quelling look, not that Carolyn seemed to notice.

"He's concerned with her health," Noelle argued, frowning. "With as little as Amy is eating, it *is* worrying that she's gaining weight. Look, Amy, you haven't even touched your mozzarella sticks."

Picking up one of the sticks, Amy took a deliberate bite, but then she set it back down on her plate as she chewed. There was an odd expression on her face.

"Noelle is right. He's just concerned." Amy ducked her head.

Morgan looked around as everyone frowned at Amy. She wasn't sure why they were all frowning, but clearly something was wrong.

"Has he said anything that crosses the line from concern to being a judgmental prick?" Marissa asked, far more gently than Carolyn likely would have.

"No, no, I mean, not really. It's fine. He's concerned, and the stress of wedding planning is getting to him."

"What is he doing for the planning?" Morgan asked, interested. She was curious how Amy and Jeremy's wedding would be different from Cyrus and Anna's.

Amy's mouth opened.

Closed.

"Um."

"Well, I'm sure just the stress in general of knowing how much needs to be done for the wedding is getting to him," Noelle said quickly, shooting Morgan a dirty look.

Oops. Somehow, she'd made things awkward and uncomfortable even though she didn't mean to.

"Sorry," she said immediately, even though she didn't know exactly what she'd done wrong or why it was okay for Carolyn to call Jeremy a judgmental prick, but it wasn't okay to ask what he was doing for the wedding planning. "I was curious what you're doing for the wedding because Cyrus and Anna's was my first, and I wondered what might be different. I want to be a good bridesmaid."

"Well, we're looking at locations right now, and that'll help us decide on catering and things like that. We do have the guest list. Jeremy's mom got theirs to me yesterday, which was great because that's helping us decide on the location." Amy smiled, looking a little more relaxed now that the topic had shifted away from Jeremy to the actual wedding planning.

Morgan relaxed, too. She'd done the right thing.

"And I'm planning on going dress shopping next month, regardless of where my weight is, so I can at least get an idea of what I want. Plus, we need to pick out the bridesmaid dresses."

"Isn't that kind of early?" Morgan asked, surprised.

"Yeah, but they have to make the dresses, then sometimes they need alterations," Sam explained. "Well, for some dresses. Sometimes, you can get things right off the rack, but not always."

"I want you to each be able to choose a style you love." Amy beamed at them. "I want them to be floor length and sage green, but you can get whatever style you want that fits that."

"Sounds good to me," Marissa said, flipping her hair over her shoulder. "And thank you. I prefer that kind of set up. Not too many dress styles look good on *every* body type, and we're all very different."

That was a good point. Morgan liked the idea of being able to pick out her own dress, too. Certain fabrics really bothered her to wear, though she would have found a way to tolerate it for Amy's sake. Picking out her own should keep it from being a problem.

Before anyone could say anything, the front door opened, and Brian walked in. His eyes widened as he looked around at all the women in his home, then he grinned.

"Hello, ladies," he said, giving them all a nod. "Welcome home, Morgan." He waved at her before setting his keys on the table.

"Hi, Brian," they all chorused together, then started giggling.

Suddenly, Morgan was very glad all her friends were there because seeing Brian, a well of anger rose up inside her. Had he known that Asad had been told not to have sex with her last week? Had he been one of the people to make that decision for her?

It didn't seem impossible, considering he lived with her. Yes, she was here to help with the mortgage payments on the house—he needed the rent she gave him—but she knew the other Doms also considered him her protector. They asked him before scening with her, and they checked in with him after, asking her how she was doing, to see what he said as well. And he was constantly monitoring her.

Sometimes, Daddy Dom Brian acted an awful lot like a dad. Not her dad, of course, because her dad would never have given her the kind of freedom Brian did, but Sam had pointed out that he had kind of inserted himself into a 'father figure' slot, even though he was only a few years older than her. At the time, Morgan hadn't minded because she'd needed someone to cling to, someone to help her stand on her own two feet.

Now, though, she had to clench her jaw against demanding to know if he'd been a part of the decision to cock block her and Asad.

This wasn't the time, though. Not with her friends there.

"Hi," she managed to say, though she didn't think she did as good a job hiding her emotions as she'd hoped because the word came out a little choked, and everyone looked at her. A hot blush rose up in her cheeks, and she rocked on her seat, reigniting the sting from the welts Asad had left, which helped settle some of the turmoil inside her.

It wasn't just the pain; it was also the reminder of him.

She realized, it didn't matter what Brian and the other Doms wanted—she and Asad had done what they wanted. Some of the anger she'd felt fled in the face of her satisfaction.

She felt... rebellious.

"Sorry I forgot to let you know everyone was coming over," she said, looking around. "It just kind of happened. Do you want some pizza?"

"Sure, thanks." Brian smiled, his shoulders dropping back down. Noelle immediately scooted over, making room for him and smiling brightly as he grabbed a folding chair and put it between her and Sam.

"How are you doing, Brian?" Noelle asked, leaning toward him with interest as he served himself a few slices of pizza. She was sitting up straighter than before, focusing completely on him. Across the table, Carolyn and Marissa smirked at each other.

It wasn't the first time it seemed Noelle had a thing for Brian. Morgan had trouble imagining it, but unlike Brian and the other Doms, she certainly wasn't going to tell anyone who they could and couldn't have sex with.

Besides, it was nice to have the buffer between her and Brian while she got her emotions under control. Eventually, though, they were going to need to have a talk.

25

<u>*Morgan*</u>

"Are you upset with me?"

Apparently, her 'eventually' talk with Brian was happening her first night back, and she wasn't sure how she felt about that. She didn't *want* to be on the outs with him. She wasn't used to confrontation, though Mistress Julie had told her it would get easier the more she did it, especially with people who were safe.

People who wouldn't hurt her.

People who wouldn't reject her because she objected to something they'd done.

Brian was both of those. She was almost sure of it. There was always that little voice in the back of her head, though, the one that said she should never let her guard down because she couldn't be sure.

She'd confronted Asad about it, and she didn't live with him. She should be able to say something to Brian.

Squaring her shoulders, she turned around from the sink where she'd been doing the dishes. His eyes widened when she faced him.

"Oh, dear. I am in trouble." Sliding onto the bar stool on the other side of the counter, he rested his elbows on the granite. "What did I do?"

Now that she was here, she might as well face it head-on. She knew he wouldn't let it go. At heart, he was a fixer, which was probably why he'd been drawn to her in the first place. Well, now she was mad, and he needed to fix it. Morgan took a deep breath.

"Did you have anything to do with Master Asad being told he couldn't have sex with me this past week?" She fixed her gaze firmly on him. She wasn't always the best at reading expressions—she hadn't even been allowed to look Master Richard in the face—but she could immediately tell that yes, yes Brian had. There was no confusion, only guilt and the realization of being caught. "And you decided not to tell me?"

"No one told you?" There was the confusion that his previous expression had been missing. "I thought Lexie was going to tell you."

Morgan shook her head and crossed her arms over her chest, glaring at him.

"No one told me. I got there, thinking I was going to have a week of fun and hot sex, only to be told we'd been put on a sex moratorium, and no one had bothered to inform me." She glared harder. "I thought I was supposed to be able to make my own decisions about my life. That's what I was told. That you were all trying to get me to a point where I made my own choices, right?"

Brian stared at her helplessly, his arms moving to spread his hands out in front of him, palms up, in a gesture of penitence.

"I'm sorry, Morgan. Lexie was supposed to tell you."

Shaking her head again, Morgan let out a sigh of exasperation.

"Telling me isn't the problem. I mean, it's part of the problem that no one told me, but the real problem is that you all think you had the right to make that decision for us! It was none of your business! Not yours, and not Lexie's, and not Patrick's." She was practically shouting by the time she got to the end of her diatribe.

Now, it wasn't her head that was shaking; it was her whole body. She was trembling all over. Partly from anger and partly from fear, waiting for the retribution of daring to speak to him in such a manner. Her father would have already cut her off and slapped her across the face. The one time she'd dared raise her voice to him, he'd hit her so hard in the stomach, she'd lost her breath. Master Richard would have put her in the cage for a day if she'd tried such a thing.

Run, all her instincts screamed at her. *Run!*

But there was nowhere to run to.

"You're right." Brian took a deep breath. "You're right, Morgan. I'm sorry."

The sheer relief that flooded through her, the realization that nothing bad had happened, was too much to bear. Her knees crumpled beneath her, and she found herself on the floor, curled in a ball, sobbing.

"Morgan, sweetie, shhh, it's okay," Brian soothed, warm, firm hands pulling her onto his lap. "It's okay, sweetie, you did good. You did so well. I'm so proud of you. You were completely right. It's okay. I'm not mad. You did good, sweetie."

He kept murmuring the words of encouragement as she sobbed into his shoulder, crying hysterically without knowing why. All she knew was she couldn't stop. If he'd screamed at her, if he'd decided to punish her, if he'd lashed out at her—all of that she could have understood. That wouldn't have made her cry.

But his acceptance? His apology?

It broke something inside her, and she cried like a child, finally safe in someone's arms, able to release the torrent of emotions that had been bottled up inside her for so long. The whole time, Brian soothed her, rubbing her shoulder as he rocked her on his lap and holding her the way she'd wanted to be held so many times growing up.

Eventually, the emotions and tears were finally drained, leaving her soggy and empty. She was limp on his lap, whatever little energy she had left gone.

"I'm so sorry, sweetie. If I'd known a week without an orgasm would do this to you, I never would have agreed it was a good idea," Brian joked hesitantly.

Morgan snorted out a laugh, then her hand flew to her mouth and nose to cover them in shock. She'd *never* snorted before.

The giggles came then, almost as hysterical as the crying, but without the jagged edges that had cut into her insides. Brian laughed, too, hugging her tightly before releasing her and helping her to her feet. She still felt a little shaky, but she could stand.

"I really am sorry. I'll talk to everyone, and I'll find out what happened that Lexie didn't tell you."

Morgan shook her head again, wiping her tears away.

"No, I'll talk to Lexie. And Patrick." She needed to do it herself, or no one was ever going to believe that she could. She needed all of them to see that she could do things on her own if they were ever going to trust her to do things on her own.

Brian nodded slowly. She didn't know if he was actually going to listen or not, but either way, she was going to talk to Lexie and Patrick as if he wouldn't. As grateful as she was for all of their support, she wanted to live her life on her own terms.

Mistress Julie was going to be so proud of her.

Asad

Sleeping alone sucked.

That was a thought he'd never had before in his life, but here he was, rolling around over and over again, then hugging his pillow because... because he couldn't hug Morgan. Because he'd gotten *that* used to having her in bed with him.

Rolling over again, he reached for his phone and checked the time.

Quarter 'til midnight. He never had this kind of trouble getting to sleep. He laid down, he fell asleep. That was how his life was.

Until now.

He had to go to work in the morning. He needed to sleep. He should have been asleep an hour ago. While he might still stay up late on weekends, on weeknights he was responsible about getting his seven to eight hours.

Maybe he should invest in a teddy bear. Or a body pillow. 'Cause his little pillow that he was trying to snuggle with wasn't cutting it.

Or maybe he just needed to get over his shit and get used to not having something or someone to cuddle with because that wasn't who he was. He didn't do sleepovers, and he wasn't going to start. It had been a temporary situation, a tiny blip in his usual routine, and now it was time to get back to reality.

Rolling onto his back, phone still in his hand, he turned it on, not entirely sure what he was looking for. He ended up on the clock app, scrolling, and it took less than a minute for Morgan's current livestream to pop up on his feed, as if the algorithm knew what he really wanted.

She was smiling and tapping her nails against a piece of beeswax paper that was resting on her microphone. The sound was oddly soothing. Or maybe it was just that seeing her was oddly soothing. The comments coming up on the bottom of the screen were a little distracting, so he swiped them off so he could just watch her.

As always, her makeup was perfectly done, her hair falling in curls around her shoulders, pushed out of her face by the large blue and silver headphones she had on. They matched the dark blue shirt she was wearing. She looked good. Happy. A slight smile curved her lips as she looked at the camera. Even though he knew it wasn't true, it felt like she was looking directly at him.

Rolling onto his side, he put the phone down on the bed next to his pillow. It wasn't the best angle, but he could still see her while he lay there. A huge yawn cracked his jaw, his eyelids fluttering.

It was like now that he was trying to watch something, he was struggling to keep his eyes open.

Which was the point, right? He needed to sleep. Which meant he should close his eyes and stop watching Morgan.

A moment later, she stopped tapping on the beeswax and moved it to the side.

"Okay," she whispered, her voice so much lower and softer than normal. "Thank you all so much for the warm welcome back this evening. This week, I'm back to my usual schedule—yes, HappyGirl, I had a wonderful trip, thank you. Now, we're going to do a bit of reading from *Pride and Prejudice*. I'm picking back up where we left off, then I will see you all tomorrow night again. Don't forget, my schedule is Sunday, Tuesday, and Thursday nights, and I have my video channel for the other nights in-between. I'll be getting more content up on there this week as well."

The whispery quality of her voice and pacing of her words was almost hypnotic. Asad yawned again.

She laughed and responded to several more comments that must be going up, and for a moment he considered swiping them back to where he could see them, so they would make more sense to him, but then she said she was turning the comments off while she read. Picking up a book, she tapped on the cover, then traced the letters before opening it up and starting to read.

He'd read *Pride and Prejudice* in high school, but he didn't remember much of it, and she was picking it up in the middle. Not that it mattered. Her voice washed over him, soothing some of the jitters he'd been feeling. Yawning again, he hugged the pillow to him, sleepily watching as she whispered the story about Mr. Darcy and Elizabeth.

The fact he wasn't all that invested in the book and he knew how it ended probably helped. Each blink of his eyelids felt heavier and heavier. He didn't want to stop looking at Morgan, yet her whispers were making it impossible for him to keep his eyes open, which was the point.

He couldn't help but think about the fact he missed her, as her voice sent him off to sleep.

26

Asad

The end of the week and he was back at Stronghold, feeling... strange. It had been a strange week. Work had been the same as ever, that hadn't changed, but his nights definitely had. His mom had called him on Wednesday "just to chat." There was a cynical part of him that thought it was just because Cyrus and Anna were on their honeymoon and out of reach, but there was also the part of him that was surprised she'd called despite that.

After all, they'd just seen each other.

He'd had to make up a bunch of lies about Morgan when his mom had asked how things were going. He couldn't exactly say they broke up as soon as they got home, not without a lot of questions he didn't feel like dealing with right now. That and, for some reason, it felt disrespectful to break up with his fake girlfriend right after coming home from a family wedding.

So, he'd told her they'd both gotten right back to work, but things were good, which was mostly true. They had gotten back to work. He knew because he'd seen Morgan every night that she was live on social media, as well as the recorded content she'd been putting up. In fact, he hadn't been able to sleep without watching her this week.

When she was live, he fell asleep to that, when she wasn't, he turned on some recorded content and watched it until he passed out. The whole time, he hugged his pillow and tried not to think about the odd ache in his chest that persisted until he fell asleep.

"Hey, there! Welcome back," Law said, waving Asad over to where he was sitting with Connor and Iris. Iris leaned against him, her smile brightening when she saw Asad. Q and Sam were nowhere to be seen, so either they weren't there yet or were already scening.

"Nice to be back," Asad said, looking around the club. Nothing had changed since he'd been gone, yet he felt... different. There was a sense of anticipation he felt that was disappointed when he took in everyone and didn't see Morgan.

That's who he really wanted to see. Which he didn't realize until he was there and he didn't see her. Was she even coming tonight? She was here almost every night on the weekends, usually before he arrived. He'd assumed she'd be here tonight.

So, either she wasn't coming, she was running late, or she was off scening with someone else.

Which didn't bother him. It couldn't. Why would he care that she was scening with someone else? He didn't. Not at all.

He sure as hell wasn't going to ask where she was because he didn't need to listen to another lecture on magic pussy. He knew that's exactly what would happen if he indicated he wanted to see Morgan the weekend after spending a whole week with her.

"Are you all scening tonight?" he asked Law and Iris. He didn't know what he wanted to do. He hadn't really come to Stronghold with a plan, he rarely did, but in the back of his head, he'd been thinking he would probably run into Morgan there. Maybe do some of the things he'd been thinking about last week when they were in Pittsburgh and couldn't because they'd been in a hotel room.

But he didn't see Morgan.

It was probably best not to scene with her his first weekend back, anyway. Talk about giving all the 'magic vagina' believers ideas. He knew it wouldn't mean anything, but Iris would probably read all kinds of things into it and tell the other subs, and then he'd have *that* to deal with.

"Morgan's in the office with Patrick and Lexie," Iris said slyly, confirming his suspicion that she would read something into it if he'd asked about Morgan.

Right. Relief that Morgan wasn't scening with someone else flooded through him.

Okay, maybe there was something to the whole spending a week with a person and getting emotionally attached, but it was *not* because of magic pussy or because they'd had sex. It had been everything else. He'd spent more time with Morgan, romantic-type time, than he had with any other woman in years. It wasn't the sex; it had been the hand holding, the small kisses, and the sleeping together and all that shit.

Taking a break from her this weekend and finding someone else to scene with would remind his brain that he was *not* attached to anyone, and it would also send a message to Iris and the other subs.

See? I can spend a whole week with a woman and not end up attached. It's just sex.

Not that they knew he'd had sex with her, but something about the way Iris had jumped right into where Morgan currently was made him think she thought *something* had happened between him and Morgan. That or she was testing him either way.

"That's nice," he said mildly, as if he didn't really care. Which he didn't. At least, not much. He did wonder what she was telling them, but only because he didn't want to get in trouble. He looked over at the Lounge area where the unattached submissives hung out, waiting for a Dom to approach them. "I think I might find someone to scene with. It's been a while, if you know what I mean, since certain rules were laid down about my behavior last week."

"You mean the Persian Excursion is open for business again?" Iris snickered, her shoulders relaxing, as though she was relieved he wasn't concerned about Morgan. Maybe that's what she'd been fishing for—the down low on whether or not he'd followed the rules.

Well, as long as Morgan didn't spill the beans, it wasn't as if anyone would know. He would make sure of that.

"Hell, yeah." He grinned at them and stretched. Connor shook his head but didn't say anything, which was about par for the course.

"Have fun, then," Law said, also shaking his head.

Giving them a little salute, Asad turned and headed into the Lounge area, smiling at all the submissives who perked up as soon as they saw him. It didn't feel like a real smile, though. It felt fake.

Fake it 'til you make it.

He was just off kilter because... well, he wasn't sure why, but he was determined to get back in the saddle again.

<u>*Morgan*</u>

"We understand, and we're sorry," Lexie said contritely. The pixie-sized sub glanced at Master Patrick, who ran his hand over his bald head, also looking contrite. Well, as contrite as he ever did. He was also watching Morgan with sharp eyes, and she wasn't entirely sure what he was seeing. "I'm especially sorry that Master Brian and I didn't communicate better about who was going to talk to you and that you got blindsided."

"Thank you," Morgan said, pressing her hands together in her lap. She wasn't feeling panicked exactly, but facing the duo hadn't been easy. In fact, it had been one of the scariest things she'd done since leaving Master Richard. They owned both Stronghold and Marquis. They could have been upset at her lack of gratitude. They could have been mad that she was scolding them.

They could easily ban her access from kink activities, not just in the area but across the entire network of people they were connected to. Which were all across the country and some international clubs as well.

They didn't because they were good people, who truly wanted to help her and meant it when they said they wanted her to grow, which was also terrifying in its own way. She felt as if she was stepping into a whole new world all over again, but this time, without anyone to lean on.

That wasn't true, of course. If she needed someone, Master Patrick and Lexie would be there. Asad would be there. Naomi would be there. The friends she'd made would be there. Of course, there was a part of her afraid she was wrong, but she wanted to believe it. She was working on believing it.

So far, it was proving true.

"You're doing great, Morgan," Master Patrick said gently. "I know this wasn't easy, but I'm glad you came to talk to us." He smiled ruefully. "Sometimes, even with the best intentions, we make mistakes. I know I have in the past." He shared a look with Lexie, and his sub smirked at him. They had a total power exchange dynamic, but that didn't stop Lexie from being a brat when she wanted to. Something about the look they shared made Morgan feel like she was intruding on something private.

"Thank you for listening," she replied, suddenly antsy. She needed... something to help her spend some of the excess energy that was riding her. A scene maybe?

Master Asad's face flashed through her mind, but she didn't even know if he would be at Stronghold tonight.

"Of course. My office is always open to you." Master Patrick smiled at her. "Now, go back out on the floor and have some fun. I promise we won't dictate who you scene with. I'm sorry you had to go without last week."

Despite everyone's support when she confronted them, she'd still kept it a secret that she and Master Asad had broken the 'rule.' It wasn't entirely her secret, and she didn't want to go back on what she'd told Asad she would do. Fortunately, she didn't have to lie. Just like Brian, Master Patrick and Lexie had assumed they'd followed the rules. She let them.

"Thank you. I do think I need a scene."

Master Patrick nodded, as though she'd confirmed his thoughts. Which, since he thought she hadn't had a scene the entire week she was with Master Asad, made sense. She felt bad deceiving him, but she was protecting Master Asad, and that felt good. It was a very strange dichotomy.

When she stepped out onto the main floor, she stopped feeling so good.

The first thing she saw was Master Asad, but he wasn't at the bar. He was in the Lounge area, talking to other submissives. Cassidy, another submissive with a rough past, though she hadn't needed quite the same kind of rescue as Morgan. She'd been rescued by the Doms and subs of Stronghold when her abusive Dom had ignored her safeword during a scene at the club.

An odd flush of heat went through Morgan. It wasn't arousal. Her fists clenched at her side, and she sucked in a deep breath as an unhappy feeling twisted her stomach.

She didn't like seeing Master Asad talking to another submissive. She *really* didn't want him scening with another sub. She wanted him scening with her.

Cassidy wasn't even a masochist.

This must be what everyone had been worried about.

Taking a deep breath, Morgan tried to calm her rapidly beating heart. It was just an aberration. Once she got used to being back, she would be back to not caring who Master Asad—or anyone else— scened with. In the meantime, she needed a scene. That would help get her back on an even keel.

Considering her sudden rush of hurt and jealousy, it was probably better *not* to scene with Master Asad. If everyone was right, it had been having sex with him while they were on a trip that had caused her emotions to change in the first place. Therefore, having sex with someone else—or at least scening with someone else— should help put her back on an even keel.

Looking around, she didn't see anyone she particularly felt like scening with. And she didn't want a particularly painful scene. Not like she had wanted a few moments ago when she'd been thinking about Master Asad... before seeing him talking to Cassidy. She was suddenly feeling a little tender, and she wanted something more... cuddly.

Taking a deep breath, she made a beeline across the room to Master Connor.

He wasn't a sadist, but he was a very cuddly and comforting Dom. It also made sense if she was struggling with some unexpected feelings for Master Asad, scening with someone who was his exact opposite might help, like a palate cleanser. She'd scened with Master Connor in the past, and it hadn't been very satisfying, but she thought it might be exactly what she needed right now.

Something different.

"Hello, Master Connor. Hello, Master Law. Hello, Iris." She greeted each of them in turn. Iris' dark eyes widened, and she was looking at Morgan curiously as they all said hello back. Despite being friends with some subs who didn't particularly like Morgan, Iris had never been unfriendly. Right now, she looked very surprised.

Oh. Right. Submissives weren't supposed to approach Doms for a scene. Morgan was one of the few exceptions to the rule, something she didn't take advantage of often because she knew it was another way that set her apart from the other subs. They didn't like her having the privilege.

But sometimes, she needed a scene, or she would try to hurt herself instead, so Mistress Julie had decreed when Morgan needed a scene, she could request one. She wasn't the only submissive to have that exception, but they were few and far between.

Part of her wanted to run from Iris' gaze, but she needed the scene too badly. She knew if she went home right now, it wouldn't be good. There was too much energy, too much emotion bottled up inside her.

"Master Connor, can you scene with me?" The words came out in a rush as she avoided Iris' gaze, focusing on the big master. Amy had called him the teddy bear of the Dom world, and he kind of resembled a giant teddy bear. He was one of the tallest, biggest Doms in the place, scary for those who didn't know him, but a total gentle giant to those who did.

He blinked in surprise.

"Of course, if that's what you need."

"I do." Some relief trickled through her, but she still felt like she was fizzing under her skin, emotions bubbling and demanding to be let out.

Master Connor carefully slid out of his seat, getting to his feet, which was head and shoulders above her. He wrapped his arm around her shoulder, and she let out some of her tension on a sigh. The heavy weight of his arm helped her feel a little more grounded.

"Okay, Morgan, whatever you need." He appeared a little worried, but Law nodded at them. Morgan wasn't sure what the problem was, but at least Law was giving them the go-ahead.

She didn't look back at the Lounge as she and Master Connor headed down to the Dungeon, so she missed Master Asad's head snapping up to watch her and Master Connor walk away, his dark eyes boring a hole into her back.

27

———————

"Master Asad? Are you okay?" Cassidy leaned forward, looking at him with concern. He'd stopped to chat with her, even though she wasn't his type—not a masochist. In fact, she'd been abused by an abusive asshole masquerading as a sadist, which meant they would probably be terrible scene partners.

He wasn't sure why he'd stopped to talk to her instead of any of the number of submissives who would have been happy to give him what he needed from a scene.

Then he'd looked up and saw Morgan walking toward the Dungeon with Connor. The anger that had erupted inside him had frozen him in place, which was probably better than his impulse to jump up and run after them. Connor could easily pound him into the ground if he wanted to. And that wasn't how people conducted themselves in Stronghold.

It didn't even make sense to want to do that. Neither did the feeling of betrayal that his friend was going off with _his girl_.

Morgan _wasn't_ his girl.

Maybe he was feeling the residual responsibility of having been in charge of her for a whole week. That made more sense. It wasn't something he'd ever done before, not for that long, and he was just getting confused because he wasn't used to being responsible for someone else. He was having some trouble letting go, even though it was what he wanted.

"Master Asad?" Cassidy peered at him, brushing a lock of dark hair out of her face, and he realized he hadn't answered her yet.

She was very pretty. Very submissive. Very open to a scene, despite not being a masochist and also not expecting more than a single night. Yet... he didn't want to be here with her right now, and not because she wasn't a masochist—because she wasn't Morgan.

"Sorry, I'm a little distracted tonight... um... I just have to go and check on someone. Something."

"That's okay. Thank you for talking to me." She didn't seem upset that he was going to walk away. If anything, she seemed relieved. Probably because he was a sadist, but she hadn't wanted to tell him no. He made a mental note to tell Master Patrick. Someone needed to work with her on that.

Someone who wasn't him. That was the kind of work a more invested Dom would do. But he would let Master Patrick know. Cassidy shouldn't be afraid to turn down a Dom she didn't want to scene with.

Those were the thoughts swirling through his head as he headed down to the Dungeon, loosening his jaw because there was no reason to clench it or feel uptight. He was just going to check on Connor and Morgan because he still felt some lingering responsibility for her. They'd become close while she was his fake girlfriend. He just wanted to make sure she was okay since Connor wasn't the Dom he would have chosen to scene with her.

It didn't have anything to do with the unjustified feeling of possessiveness that had settled in his chest. It was just that Connor couldn't fulfill her needs the way she needed a Dom to.

Part of him wondered if she'd picked Connor because he was Asad's friend, and she was trying to make him jealous, but his brain dismissed the thought as soon as it occurred to him. Morgan wouldn't think to play that kind of game. If she wanted something, she would say so. She would also follow the rules, which meant not interrupting him while he was talking to Cassidy.

There was also the unspoken rule about submissives not approaching Doms, but every Dom in the club knew which subs were exceptions to that, and Morgan was among the few. Which meant she must have asked Connor for the scene. Connor wouldn't have approached her for one.

Why Connor?

That's what was bugging him. Connor wasn't a good match for a scene for her. They were completely mismatched. He couldn't give Morgan what she needed. Giving her the kind of pain she craved wouldn't just be hard for Connor, it would be mentally painful for him.

So, why had she chosen him?

The feeling that something was very wrong had gotten under his skin and wasn't going away.

When he reached the bottom of the stairs, he looked around. It only took him a moment to locate Connor—he was the biggest man in the room other than Jared, who was his equal. They were already on the far side of the room at a St. Andrew's cross.

Unclenching his jaw again, Asad strode through the Dungeon, ignoring the scenes that he was passing. Leather, whips, cries of pain and pleasure, all of it went by in a blur. He was too focused on where he was going. By the time he reached Connor and Morgan, Morgan had stripped off everything other than her thong and was stepping up to the St. Andrew's cross, placing her hands on the wood.

With her back to the Dungeon, she couldn't see him.

Asad came to a grinding halt and crossed his arms over his chest as he watched Connor get into place behind her, holding a flogger in his hand. Plain leather with thick strands, no knots, it was hardly the kind of implement that would give Morgan the satisfaction she needed. It didn't look like Connor was restraining her to the cross, either. She was just going to be holding on to it.

Not at all what she needed. Especially if she was in a place where she'd asked for a scene rather than just playing.

Gritting his teeth, he managed to keep from calling out as he glowered from the sidelines. Interrupting a scene was against the rules. Even if it had barely just started and wasn't going to be satisfying for either of the people involved. Several other members of the club drifted up to watch. Asad glanced at them. No one he was friends with. All of them appeared curious and anticipatory, just checking out another scene being performed in the Dungeon, nothing special to them.

Connor raised his arm and brought the flogger down on Morgan's upper back. Then her ass. Then her upper back again. His form was good, his aim was good, but there was no visible mark on her pale skin from the blows. Stepping forward, Connor put his hand on Morgan's shoulder, and they exchanged a few words. When Connor stepped back, he looked around, his expression troubled, as though appealing for help.

His gaze met Asad's, and his eyes widened.

Which was when Asad realized he not only had his arms crossed over his chest, but his jaw was clenched again, a muscle ticking in his cheek, and he was glaring at one of his best friends as if he wanted to murder him.

Shit.

He should go. He should leave Morgan to Connor. She wasn't actually his responsibility. He didn't need to be here.

Except Connor was walking toward him, appearing worried but also... relieved?

"Can you take over the scene?" Connor asked.

Asad stared at him. The urge to say yes and grab the flogger from him—so he could replace it with something rougher—and jump in was overwhelming. But Doms didn't just hand scenes over like that. Connor couldn't possibly be saying what it sounded like he was.

"What?"

"Can you take over the scene? I... she needs more than I can give her. She said she wanted to try something different, softer, but she's not actually happy with what I can do, and I don't think I can give her what she really wants."

Well, shit. Connor was saying exactly what Asad thought he was, and his expression had turned pleading. He might be one of the biggest, most intimidating guys in the club, but he was a complete softie on the inside. All the subs knew it. Connor knew it. Morgan knew it.

So, why had she chosen him?

He looked around Connor to see Morgan still holding her position. She didn't look over her shoulder to see what was going on. She just stood in place and waited for her Dom to return to her. The way a well-trained slave would because that's what she was. A lot of submissives wouldn't have been able to resist looking, or at least peeking, but not Morgan.

"We need to talk to her first," he said firmly. Morgan would have had some reason for choosing Connor, and he wasn't going to make the switch without asking her. Even if he knew he would be the better choice to scene with her.

Little warning bells were going off in his head, but he ignored them. Connor needed him. Morgan needed him. What other people might think wasn't part of the consideration. Neither was the fact that normally being 'needed' would make him run screaming into the night. This was different. If anyone asked him to explain why it was different, he would punch them.

It just was.

Connor nodded and turned. Asad's chest tightened, but he stepped up after his friend, both of them heading toward Morgan. He ignored the sighs of disappointment from the watching audience and the way they dispersed when they realized the scene wasn't going to be starting back up again. The fewer people witnessing, the better.

"Morgan." All he had to do was say her name, and something inside him reacted. He didn't have time to study the reaction, though, because Morgan was already looking over her shoulder at him, her green eyes widening in surprise.

"Master Asad?" There was a slight tremor in her voice, confusion threading through it. "What are you doing here?" She was looking at him as though he was the last person she'd expected to see, which he didn't understand, but it didn't really matter. He was here. That was what mattered.

"Morgan, I'm worried I'm not able to give you what you need in a scene," Connor said seriously, his deep voice almost mournful. It was clear he felt bad, even though it wasn't really his fault.

Asad hoped he wasn't getting a complex. Sometimes, he felt like Connor didn't even enjoy being a Dom, that he just came to the club because that's where his friends were.

Something for him to worry about later. Right now, his entire focus needed to be on the increasingly concerned-looking submissive, who was still clinging to the St. Andrew's cross as if it was her anchor in a storm. Shit. Maybe this was a mistake. Maybe she didn't want to scene with him again.

Disappointment and hurt hit him like a physical blow to his chest.

"Master Connor thought you might like to scene with me instead—"

"Yes."

She cut off what he'd been about to say, which was that they could find someone else for her to scene with. Instead, he ended up rocking back with surprise that she'd not only said she wanted to scene with him but that she'd actually interrupted him.

"I mean, if you want to, Sir." Two spots of color appeared high in her cheeks. Her break in protocol was over with as soon as it had begun.

"I'd be happy to scene with you if you'd like me to."

"I'd like that if you want to."

Connor's head moved with his gaze, going back and forth between them, his brow furrowing, and Asad realized how ridiculous they sounded. Like two kids on an elementary school playground trying to negotiate their first crush.

I like you. Do you like me?

I like you, too.

But do you like-like me?

Do you like-like me?

If you like-like me, I guess I like-like you.

Then I guess I like-like you, too.

Ah, fuck.

He *like-liked* Morgan.

The evidence was mounting to a point where he couldn't ignore or deny it, not now that she was in front of him, in the flesh. Something *had* happened between them last week, and he'd gotten emotionally involved. *Not* because of any magic vagina bullshit. Just because... just because of Morgan herself.

He had two choices—he could turn and run because he was the goddamn Persian Excursion, and he didn't *do* relationships, or he could nut up and accept that he'd fallen for Morgan and go from there.

When it came down to it, that really wasn't a choice.

28

Morgan

Master Asad was looking at her very oddly, but it sounded like he wanted to scene with her. And she didn't see Cassidy anywhere or any other submissive standing there like they were waiting on him.

He squared his shoulders, giving her a look she immediately recognized. The one that said he was in charge, that he was making a mental shift from Asad to _Master_ Asad, not just a Dom in the club but a Dom who was focused on _her_. Excitement thrummed through her, her anticipation heightening in a way that it hadn't when Master Connor had begun flogging her.

Not that he'd been flogging her very hard.

Master Connor was right; he wasn't a good match for her.

She'd been drawn to him for the wrong reasons.

Yes, he was the right Dom for a submissive who needed cuddling and comforting, which Morgan had wanted, but she needed more than that. She'd wanted him because he was the opposite of Asad. Because he wouldn't remind her of Asad. Because she didn't want something close to what she'd had with Asad. She'd wanted _Asad_. And if she couldn't have him, she now realized, she'd wanted the opposite of him.

Which was Connor.

"I'm taking over the scene," Master Asad said. He glanced at Connor. "Thank you for taking care of her."

"Of course."

"Thank you, Master Connor," Morgan echoed softly. "I'm sorry." She wasn't sure she could put into words why she was apologizing, but Master Connor seemed to understand. He smiled at her, putting his large palm on top of her head almost like a reassuring stroke, then moved away. For such a big man, he moved very quietly.

Then she was left with Master Asad, who was studying her with a dark, intense look she'd never seen before. He appeared to be contemplating something. Morgan dropped her head because looking at him over her shoulder while she held onto the cross was uncomfortable.

After a long moment, he finally spoke.

"Morgan, do you want a scene on the cross?"

"Um..." She lifted her head up. She hadn't really thought about it. That's what Master Connor had suggested, so that's what she'd prepared to do.

"Morgan." This time when she met his gaze, the intensity had solidified. "Run."

"What?" The question popped out of her mouth before she could think.

An utterly wicked smile curved the left side of his lips.

"Run, baby. Do your best not to let me catch you."

Oh. *Oh.*

Panic and excitement bubbled up inside her.

Master Asad took a step toward her, and Morgan bolted.

The haze of emotions was making it hard for her to think, especially when she glanced over her shoulder and saw him coming after her—he wasn't quite running, but the look of intense determination in his eye was scary as hell. She had absolutely no idea what he planned to do with her when he caught up, and the truth was, she didn't want to know.

It made everything more exciting.

Startled looks and a few cheers followed her as she scurried through the Dungeon with a Dom hot on her heels. Since she wasn't yelling 'red' and he wasn't yelling at anyone to catch her, everyone either moved out of their way or got in their way, according to their personalities.

She dodged around Master Connor, who had halted at the bottom of the stairs to see what happened, and he smirked down at her. Breathless, she rushed past, glancing over her shoulder at the top of the stairs just in time to see him move out of the way for Master Asad.

The big meanie.

She appeared at the top of the stairs of the main floor, and quite a few heads turned their way to look at her, more following the first as they realized there was something to look at—a completely naked sub standing there, out of breath and looking slightly panicked. She could see Master Brian, his eyes widening as he caught sight of her.

And Master Asad was still coming up behind her.

She was definitely not headed to the front of the room. Nope.

Not upstairs, either. That was a trap.

The gardens.

It was a nice enough night.

Darting to the left, she made the quick turn down the hall that led to the back of the club where the gardens were. Despite the industrial style of the building, the gardens behind it were extensive, filled with trees and large bushes, along with flowerbeds. There were small clearings with outdoor BDSM equipment for couples who wanted to play out there. Dungeon Monitors walked through them the same way they did the Dungeon and Stronghold's upper level.

It was perfectly safe.

Yet as Morgan rushed out the door and onto the garden path, she didn't feel safe.

She'd barely reached the line of hedge bushes that lined the garden when she heard the door behind her slam shut.

Master Asad.

Glancing over her shoulder, she saw him leaping down from the stairs. With a panicked squeak, she quickly turned down another path.

He wouldn't harm her, though he might hurt her, yet the adrenaline from being chased was making her pulse race. Her hair whipped around her when she reached another intersection, looking left and right before choosing to run right. How far was he behind her? Had he made a wrong turn?

She didn't know.

There was no way to tell.

The only thing she could hear was the sound of her breathing.

Turning into a clearing lit by little lights hanging from the trees, she paused. There was a padded bench in the center of the small space with no back, obviously meant for bending someone over it. Likely, it would make a very good spanking bench.

Morgan paused, pressing her hand to her chest to try to calm her pounding heart and ragged breath, straining to hear if anyone was approaching. Unsure of where Master Asad was behind her... if he was anywhere close to her.

Now that she was listening, she could hear a lot more people in the garden. Muffled moans. Some soft cries. Slaps of flesh against flesh. Which made it all the harder to hear someone stalking her through the pathways.

Holding her breath, she pressed her lips together.

Listening.

And shrieked as Master Asad rounded the corner, his gaze catching hers.

She darted for the other exit to the clearing, but he was there before she could reach it, appearing in front of her like a villain in a horror movie. Except she wasn't terrified so much as excited... although she shrieked as if she was in real danger.

Turning on a dime, she lurched forward, only to feel his hand catch her chin from behind, turning her back toward him. She fell face-first into his chest, which muffled her cry.

Oh my goodness.

She felt his growl as much as heard it.

"Going somewhere, baby?"

Tilting her head back, Morgan looked up at him. His face was shadowed by the dim lighting, but she could still see his dark eyes glittering at her.

"Um..."

Morgan tried to make a break for it again, but she found herself on her knees on the soft dirt a moment later, Asad's body surrounding her, his erection rubbing up against her ass. The leather of his pants was smooth against her skin, but she could still feel the prominent bulge pressing against her, and she whimpered. She wanted him so badly.

"Are you a naughty girl?" he asked, one hand still around her neck, the other moving to cup her breast. He squeezed, massaging the soft flesh, then pinched her nipple hard enough to make her gasp.

"No?" It came out as a question rather than a firm answer because she didn't know what her role was in this little scenario. She didn't think she'd been bad.

"Oh, no?" He pinched her nipple harder, twisting it, and her pussy spasmed in response. Arching her hips, she rubbed her backside against his groin, her swollen lips tingling as she clenched emptily. Asad's fingers fluttered against her throat, and he leaned forward, scraping his teeth against the back of her shoulder. "So you didn't try to scene with another man tonight?"

Morgan whimpered as his teeth bit into her flesh, sending a spurt of sheer ecstasy through her. Her elbows nearly buckled.

"I... I..." Her mind had gone blank. "I didn't know..."

She hadn't known it would be a problem. Hadn't thought he would care. Didn't know if he was being serious or if he was playing a role. The lines between fantasy and reality were blurring, and she didn't want to make a wrong turn or say the wrong thing.

Releasing her from his bite, though keeping his hold on her neck,

Master Asad pulled back and slapped her ass, hard. She cried out, shuddering as he spanked her again.

The hot sting rocked through her a moment before she felt his cock press against her pussy. She cried out as he thrust in, hard and fast.

It wasn't that anything he was doing was particularly painful, though he did keep spanking her as he began fucking her from behind, but the chase, the way her nipple still throbbed from his pinch, and the continuous smacks as he rode her from behind, were enough to satisfy her dark cravings. There was no gentleness to his thrusts. He was fucking her like a machine, pistoning into her from behind.

A moment later, his hands switched, so he could spank the other side of her ass. Instead of gripping her throat, his other hand went to her hair, wrapping the long strands around his hand and pulling her head back. Her scalp tingled and ached, pussy clenching around his cock as her ecstasy wound higher and higher within her.

Each slap of her ass made her clench around him, and she cried out as her orgasm crested.

As if he sensed her oncoming release, Master Asad suddenly stopped spanking her and shifted behind her. His fingers moved over her hip and dipped between her legs, seeking out her clit. They pinched the little nubbin, and Morgan screamed as the combination of pain and pleasure slammed into her, sending her orgasm over the edge, even as the pain swelled.

Tears slid from her eyes as his relentless grip turned her erotic bliss into inexpressible agony, his fingers rubbing back and forth, overwhelming her senses as he tormented her sensitive nub. Her elbows buckled, her lower body falling forward, and still he kept fucking her without losing a beat.

"Please!" She choked out the word, and shockingly, his fingers released her clit—only to give it a short, sharp smack. The sting on her swollen, sore nubbin made her scream again, her pussy convulsing around his thrusting cock.

With a low groan, he gripped her hip with the hand he'd been tormenting her with, and his grip on her hair tightened. The hard thrusts of his cock rocked her forward, then he buried himself in her with a guttural sound. Morgan shuddered, clenching, and felt the hot splash of liquid pulsing inside her, filling her.

He hadn't used a condom.

The feeling of him bare inside her, filling her with his cum, made her shudder with another, smaller orgasm, leaving her panting and weak before him.

"Fuck..." His low curse was followed by his lips pressing against the back of her shoulder, right where he'd bitten her before.

Morgan wasn't sure what to do next, so she held her position, waiting for some kind of cue from Master Asad. Her emotions were roiling as she tried to think of what it all might mean. She had no idea. There were endless possibilities, but her mind had gone completely blank.

"Fuck," he repeated, then he was pulling out of her. Morgan remained in position. She didn't know what else to do. A low chuckle, then she was pulled onto Asad's lap. He was still partially clothed, his pants around his thighs since he hadn't bothered to pull them all the way off before fucking her.

In the dim lighting, she blinked up at him, as surprised by the cuddling as she was by the interruption to her scene and the chase. She sat still on his lap. Waiting. Master Asad sighed. It was a very deep sigh.

"Morgan..." His voice trailed off almost as soon as he'd started speaking.

"Yes?" she asked after a moment. She felt a bit bruised but also incredibly satisfied. That had been wonderful. The only problem was that now she *really* didn't want him scening with other submissives. It had been hard enough walking away before. If she saw him with another submissive after this, it was going to hurt so much more. She didn't entirely understand what had changed—she just knew something had.

"I think I would like to... to try dating for real. If you're interested." He stumbled over his words, but his tone was distant. Nonchalant. But he didn't say things he didn't mean. He'd never made Morgan guess what he did or didn't want.

"I'm interested."

"Really?" The distance was gone from his tone. He reached up to cup her chin, turning her face toward him and tipping her chin back, so he could see her more clearly.

"Really."

"I'm probably going to be a terrible at it."

"Me, too." Morgan shrugged. "I had fun last week, though."

"I did, too. And I missed you this week."

"I missed you, too." So much so that she hadn't felt comfortable admitting it to anyone. Not to Mistress Julie during their weekly session and not to any of her friends. She hadn't wanted them to think Master Asad had led her on in any way because he hadn't. It had been a fake relationship... but some of her feelings had turned real.

"It's probably going to make a lot of people really unhappy."

"I don't care." She lifted her chin. "I get to make my own decisions. Even if they're bad ones."

"Are you saying that you already think I'm a bad decision?"

"I don't know, are you?" She giggled when he poked her in the side. She was being truthful, but she realized he'd been teasing when he asked the question.

Then he sighed.

"Probably. I haven't actually dated anyone in a really long time, but... I like you. A lot. I really don't like the idea of you scening with anyone else, and this is the best way to prevent that."

"I really didn't like seeing you with Cassidy," she admitted. "That's partly why I want to try too. I think it would hurt a lot to see you scene with someone else."

"Okay. Then we're on the same page." He smiled at her.

"Yeah." She smiled back at him.

"Now, we just have to go tell everyone."

Morgan's smile slipped just a little.

"Can we stay here like this a little longer?" she asked. For all her bravado about insisting that she get to make her own choices, she would like a little time to brace herself before having to actually do it.

"Sure, Red. As long as you need."

29

Morgan

If Asad hadn't been holding her hand, Morgan wasn't sure she would have been able to walk back into the club. Not because she was naked, with his cum dripping down her thigh, but because she was afraid of what might meet them inside. Yes, she'd told Master Patrick and Lexie and Master Brian that she got to make her own decisions, and they'd all taken it very well, but...

The fear remained.

At least part of her was encouraging that they would still understand and not give her and Master Asad a hard time.

Maybe they would all think that she and Master Asad were just reacting to not being allowed to have sex last week. That him chasing her through the club and into the gardens was pent-up need from following the rules. Though it wasn't like Master Asad was known for holding hands, but here he was holding hers.

Even if people didn't realize when they'd gone running out of the club, coming back in it would be very clear that something was different.

She realized she was gripping Master Asad's hand far too tightly as he opened the door for her, and they walked back inside. If he was feeling the same trepidation she was, he didn't show it. He walked in as confidently as he always did, which helped her a little.

Master Connor was waiting in the hallway that led to the back door, holding onto her clothes and leaning against the wall. He straightened as soon as he saw them, standing back up to his full height.

"Here, sweetheart," he said, holding out her corset and skirt to her. Glancing down at their conjoined hands, his eyebrows went up, but he didn't comment.

"Thank you." She took the clothing from him with her free hand and glanced nervously at Asad.

"Morgan and I are dating now." He announced it as though he didn't have a care in the world, as if it was no big deal. Maybe it wouldn't be. Master Connor took a moment, then nodded.

"Okay."

She let out a breath she hadn't known she was holding, some of her tension leaking away with it at the same time.

Maybe this wouldn't be so bad.

She was disabused of that notion as soon as they stepped out of the hallway and into the main room.

A small group of Doms was waiting for them on the other side, out of sight of the hallway, until they actually stepped through the doorway. Master Patrick stood at the front, his arms crossed over his chest, a slight frown on his face. His eyes scanned her and Asad for a second, and she was sure he saw everything.

The cum sliding down her leg when everyone knew Asad always wore condoms.

Their linked hands, which had started to feel natural after a week of doing it, now felt completely odd as it came under scrutiny.

The stubborn tilt to Asad's jaw as he lifted his chin up in challenge against the group of Doms staring at them.

Right next to Master Patrick was Brian, also with his arms crossed over his chest, also frowning. Morgan narrowed her eyes at him, and he avoided her gaze. She decided to take a page from Asad's book and rip the Band-Aid off, but as she opened her mouth, Asad was already letting go of her hand and stepping forward.

"Let's go talk in your office," he said to Master Patrick.

Morgan's mouth dropped open.

"Hey!" She was saying it to Asad, but everyone looked at her in surprise, and she flushed. Turning back, Asad smiled at her.

"Go get dressed, baby. Then you can come join us if you want." He turned all the way around, pulling her against him reassuringly. "They need to hear from me that I'm serious about you. It has nothing to do with you making your own decisions, I promise."

Looking up at him, Morgan nodded. That made sense. She couldn't turn off their protective natures any more than she could become a dominant herself.

"Come on." Sam appeared at her elbow, sliding her arm through Morgan's. "You owe us updates, girlfriend!"

Her friends surrounded her—Noelle, Marissa, Carolyn, Amy—walking her through the club like an escort. Or maybe to protect her. Everyone was staring at either her or the group of Doms trailing Asad and Master Patrick to the office.

"What was that?" Amy asked as soon as they got into the locker room. "You went down to the Dungeon with Master Connor, and the next thing we know, Master Asad is chasing you out into the gardens! And then Master Connor basically stood guard at the hallway and wouldn't let anyone through!" Her eyes were sparkling from the excitement.

"Holy shit, is that cum?" Noelle asked, sounding shocked as she stared at Morgan's legs.

"Um, yes."

"He didn't use a condom?" Marissa and Carolyn chorused in the exact same tone at the exact same time.

This was getting almost farcical.

"No. I think he forgot." She said the words but wasn't sure she believed them. Master Asad *never* forgot a condom—with anyone. On the other hand, the only other option was that he'd chosen not to wear one. She wasn't sure she could believe that, either.

He knew she was on birth control, but still. He was practically infamous for wearing a condom, no matter what. So, if he hadn't... what did it mean? She didn't think it meant he was ready to have a baby with her or anything. Maybe that he trusted her?

"You think *Master Asad* forgot a condom?" Noelle's voice dripped with disbelief. Okay, so she wasn't the only one to find that highly unlikely.

"I don't know what he was thinking. It all just kind of happened." She ducked into one of the stalls to clean herself up before putting on her clothes. She didn't think Master Asad would expect her to walk around with his cum dripping down her leg, and he hadn't told her *not* to... She didn't know if she could talk to her friends, much less the other Doms, while feeling confident if it was still there.

"So, what is going on with you two?" Amy asked through the door.

Sighing, Morgan came back out, holding her corset so someone could help her get back into it while she told them. Not just about tonight but about everything. The rules that the Doms had laid down for her and Asad—the fact that they'd ignored him. The way she'd missed him this past week. How seeing him talking to Cassidy had made her feel.

His confession that he didn't want her scening with anyone else, either.

"Wow, coming from Master Asad, that's practically a confession of love," Sam joked.

"Aren't you worried this is all happening a little fast?" Noelle asked, frowning at Sam before focusing on Morgan. "Just two weeks ago he's the Persian Excursion. You spend one week with each other in a fake relationship, and now all of a sudden, he wants to be your boyfriend?"

"Should I be worried?" Morgan looked around. She hadn't been worried—at least not about how Asad felt about her—until Noelle brought it up. It wasn't as though she had a lot of experience with relationships. Maybe it was too fast, but he'd seemed to think it was okay.

"He interrupted your scene with Master Connor, had sex without a condom, said he doesn't want you scening with anyone else, and is now facing down the other Doms to explain that you two are dating," Amy said, patting Morgan's shoulder. "Even if it's fast, I think it's pretty safe to say he's serious. He wouldn't be doing any of that if he wasn't. Not everyone moves as slowly as Jeremy and I have."

"You're right. I just don't want Morgan getting hurt," Noelle said, dropping her hands from where they'd been planted on her hips. "He just doesn't seem like the relationship kind of guy."

He hadn't. At least, not until last week.

"He was a really good fake boyfriend," she said, reaching into her corset to lift her boobs up a little as Sam tightened the laces. The corset was specially made for women with large breasts, but it could still flatten them if she didn't lift them higher than they normally sat.

"Well, if he was a good fake boyfriend in front of his family, it probably means he'll be a pretty good boyfriend, at least to start," Marissa said. She was sitting on one of the benches, listening intently with a small smile of amusement on her face. "Whether or not he'll be able to keep it up... who knows. Nothing wrong with jumping in to find out, though."

"The Persian Excursion is closing for business," Carolyn said thoughtfully. "Who would have guessed?"

"It's the magic vagina," Sam said with a smirk. They all looked at her, and Noelle frowned, looking around in confusion.

"What's the magic vagina?"

---

*A*sad

Following Patrick to the main office, Asad tried to feel like he wasn't walking into a trial or something. It did help that Connor was with him, and Law and Q joined the little march as it passed by them. When they got to the office, they stood on the side of the desk with him, while Patrick, Brian, Kincaid, Andrew, Adam, and Jared went on the other.

It felt almost farcical as he sat down in the chair across from Patrick, the two groups of Doms arrayed behind them like they were crime bosses with their men. Maybe he should stand up and start snapping and dancing.

"So... you and Morgan. I'm guessing you didn't follow the rules last week." Patrick pinned Asad to the chair with his gaze, his expression stern. Behind him, the other Doms reacted in various ways. Andrew smirked before covering his mouth and trying to look more serious again. Brian closed his eyes and looked like he was silently counting to ten.

"That's none of your business. Morgan gets to make her own decisions about her life, and she doesn't have to share them with anyone she doesn't want to." He leveled his own look at Patrick before flicking his glance up to the Doms behind him.

His statement didn't seem to have much effect on the stoic Adam, but Brian didn't meet his gaze, and Jared appeared thoughtful now rather than glaring. Kincaid actually nodded in agreement with Asad, and he felt himself marginally relax.

"You're right. On both counts. On the other hand, you did agree to the rules before you left, and you broke that agreement, which was your decision and not Morgan's." Patrick lifted his eyebrows, the scar that ran through one of them making his expression even more intimidating.

"It was a bad rule. It kept me from empowering her to make her own decisions." He really had intended to keep it, but what Morgan needed trumped what Patrick or anyone else wanted, and he wasn't going to apologize for that.

Before anyone could say anything else, the door to the office opened and Mistresses Olivia and Julie breezed in, Lexie trotting on their heels. The two Dominatrixes shifted to the side as they came in the door to let Lexie in, but they didn't move to one side of Patrick's desk or the other. Instead, they stayed off to the side, right next to the door. Mistress Olivia leaned against the filing cabinet there, and Mistress Julie smiled as she stood next to her.

Ignoring her master's glare, Lexie went and disappeared behind the desk, kneeling on the cushion that was kept there for her. Patrick closed his eyes and pinched the bridge of his nose before opening them and focusing on Olivia and Julie.

"Do you need something?" he asked in a tightly controlled voice.

"Not yet." Olivia smiled sunnily at him, her grey eyes flashing. "We'll let you know."

Mistress Julie just smiled.

Patrick shifted uncomfortably in his chair but refocused on Asad.

"Okay, well." He cleared his throat. "I guess the question now is, what are your intentions with Morgan?"

At that, the tension in the room—which had dissipated at the entrance of the Dommes and Lexie—ramped right back up. Now, every eye in the room was on Asad, for good reason. He knew even though his friends would back him up, they were protective of Morgan, too. Rightfully so.

"I'm going to date her. We're going to see what happens. You know, the way things normally happen when you're dating someone."

"How would you know? You don't date." Adam raised a blonde eyebrow at him. "You've always avoided dating. Or even scening too often with another submissive."

"So did he." Asad pointed at Andrew, who shrugged. "So did Mitch. Look at them now. I can't promise I know where things are going with Morgan, but she and I deserve the chance to find out without a bunch of people hovering over us. I *can* tell you I would never deliberately harm her, and that includes emotionally. The only hurt I want to give her is the fun, sexual kind. And I will never cheat on her. If things don't work out, they don't work out, and I'll end things as respectfully and compassionately as I can if the problem is on my end. Then I'll come get one of you to be there to support her. That's all I can promise."

"That sounds reasonable." Everyone's head whipped to the side to look at Mistress Julie. She smiled back at them serenely. Next to her, Olivia smiled as well. Somehow, it was way scarier than anyone's glare. "That's all anyone can really ask of you. And I think it's exactly what Morgan needs."

Patrick cleared his throat again.

"Right. That's all we needed to hear... I think. And if you do need support, we're here, Julie is here, and I know Morgan's friends will be there to support her." A muscle ticked in Patrick's cheek, and Jared's head fell back as he stared up at the ceiling for a moment. Probably because his ex was among Morgan's friends. "We just want what is best for her."

"We all do," Asad said.

A little niggle of doubt crawled into his chest. How could he really be what was best for her? Best sex, sure, but best boyfriend? This whole thing was probably fucked before he even tried.

Someone's hand landed on his shoulder, and he jumped, looking up in surprise. Mistress Julie smiled at him, a real smile that was far more reassuring than her earlier one.

"Morgan told me she had a wonderful time with you last week," she said, giving his shoulder a little squeeze. "She said having you as her fake boyfriend made her want a real one. Just keep that up, and you'll do great."

And just like that, his whole perspective shifted again.

Maybe he wouldn't be as bad at it as he thought.

30

———

Asad

It felt like every single eye was on him when he came out of Patrick's office. Gritting his teeth, he pretended to ignore it, heading over to the bar area with his friends while the rest of the Doms scattered. Patrick and Lexie had stayed in the office, but everyone else had come back out into the main room with them.

"Come on," Q murmured, tilting his head and leading the way over to a table where Iris, Domi, and Rae were waiting. All three of them perked up at the sight of the Doms, like they knew the answers to all their questions were coming.

Asad sighed inwardly. He wasn't sure he wanted the third degree from them as well. It might be unavoidable, though. At the very least, they were going to want to know everything that was going on.

As soon as he reached the table, all the questions tumbled out.

"What happened?"

"What's going on with you and Morgan?"

"Are you in trouble?"

"Are the Mistresses going to punish you?"

"Seriously?" he asked Rae, who had shot the final question at him. "You think they bring in the Dominatrixes to handle naughty Doms or something?"

"It's not the worst idea," Connor said, sliding into his own seat next to Rae.

She shrugged at Asad. She was looking a little... off. A little sad, maybe.

"No, thank you," Asad replied dryly. "And no, I'm not in trouble, and no one is punishing me. The other Masters wanted to talk a little about me and Morgan now that we're dating."

"You are?" Domi looked as shocked as the other two subs, but that didn't stop her from asking. Oddly, Rae looked a bit cheerier at the news than she had before or at least less sad. "Like, you're *dating-dating*?"

"Yes."

"Exclusively?"

"Yes."

"Oh my God. She magic vaginaed you!" Domi pointed at him as she squealed loudly enough that if everyone around them hadn't already been listening to their conversation, they probably would be now.

"That is not a thing!"

All three subs exchanged a look that made it clear they not only thought it was a thing, they also thought it had happened to him. Asad groaned and looked around, trying to find some kind of escape from this ridiculousness.

"What happened to Law?"

The other Dom had been right behind them, and he needed some more Domly backup.

"Talking to Mistress Julie," Iris said easily, nodding in the direction behind Asad. He turned to look and saw Law frowning, his arms crossed over his chest, while Mistress Julie was shaking her head at him. "She got a delivery of chocolate-covered strawberries at the office today, and Law is freaking out again. He's been waiting all day to talk to her."

Connor rolled his eyes while Rae and Domi giggled. None of

them seemed disturbed by the secret admirer who kept sending gifts to Mistress Julie at Marquis, but it was driving Law up the wall not to know who was sending them. Asad was also unbothered but not as entertained by Law's reactions as the subs were.

Not that it mattered. Just past Law and Julie, the door to the women's locker room opened, and Morgan's friends started coming out, followed by Morgan herself. She looked up, and from across the entire room, their eyes met. It was something out of a cheesy movie, yet it made his heart beat a little faster.

Just keep it up, and you'll be fine.

Mistress Julie's advice echoed in his head.

If this was last week and he was with his family, and Morgan had just come out of the bathroom at the end of the night, what would he do? He'd take her back to the hotel room and have sex. Okay, barring that, he would go over to her and see what she wanted to do.

That seemed like a solid plan.

"In case I don't come back, have a good night, everyone," he said, peeling away from the table before any of them could protest, ask him anymore questions, or make references to magic genitalia again. Several shouted goodbyes followed him as he made his way over to Morgan.

Passing by him, Sam pointed two fingers at her eyes and then both of those fingers at him, letting him know that she was keeping her eye on him. Inwardly, he sighed. It was probably going to be a bit before everyone trusted him with Morgan. At least his friends had had his back, even if they were a little uncertain. Both Carolyn and Marissa smiled at him as they passed, turning away from where Sam was headed to go into the Lounge area rather than following her to the bar table. Noelle followed them, but instead of a smile, she gave him a hard glare, which he ignored.

Of all their opinions, he cared about hers the least. Maybe because he knew Morgan did, too. Whatever problem Noelle had with him was not his concern.

He looked right over her to Morgan, who was smiling up at him, though she looked a little nervous.

"Hey, Red," he said, smiling as he reached for her. Her shoulders relaxed, her hand sliding into his, fingers curling around each other. "Wanna get out of here?"

He had no desire to be here with everyone watching them.

"Yes, Sir." She leaned into him, looking at him as though he was the only person in the room. "Together?"

"Hell, yeah. My place?" Because Brian would be at hers.

Morgan nodded.

Asad wanted some privacy. He wanted to be able to talk to her without worrying about interruptions. And... well, he wanted some goddamn sleep, which he was pretty sure would be best with her in his bed, either in his arms or wrapped around him like the big spoon she seemed to enjoy being. The position didn't matter as long as she was with him.

"Yes, please, Sir."

Ignoring everyone else, Asad whisked her away into the night. On their way out, the submissive behind the desk gave him a narrow-eyed look as she handed Morgan's purse over. As soon as they'd turned around to leave, he could hear her picking up the phone. The gossip train was already at work.

Morgan

She was going home with Asad. To his home. As his real girlfriend. Well, his date. Was she his girlfriend? Maybe it was too soon to put that kind of label on things. But they had agreed to date and be exclusive, and that was close enough that she felt like a girlfriend.

She was his *girlfriend*. She felt giddy. Similar to how she'd felt when Jason had first started paying attention to her but different. She was no longer a teenager who didn't understand what was happening. She was an adult who chose to be here, with the full knowledge of relationships and sex and all that. And while the Doms of Stronghold might take on a father figure role with her sometimes, especially Brian, none of them were like her actual father. Thankfully.

They knew exactly what was going on with her and Asad, and they'd stepped back and let her make her own decision about it.

Which made her feel giddy. And really good.

"Do you have your car here?" Asad asked as they walked out to the parking lot, pausing when they reached the curb.

"No, Brian drove us."

"Okay." He squeezed her hand. "We can go to my place, and I can give you a ride home later tonight or tomorrow morning. We'll play it by ear."

She nodded. Whatever he wanted to do was fine with her. Was that okay? Or should she know what she wanted to do?

Before she could decide, her phone rang with Freddy's ringtone. Somehow, she wasn't surprised. In fact, it almost felt like she'd been waiting for that to happen. He was always protective of her, as he was with all the submissives, and he was also a friend. She wouldn't be surprised if Trish at the front desk had been calling him over at Marquis where he was working tonight as soon as she'd seen Morgan and Asad leaving together.

"I need to get this, it's Freddy," she said apologetically. Asad just chuckled and nodded, opening the car door for her as she picked up the phone. "Hello?"

"Hey, gorgeous, just wanted to check in and see what's going on." Freddy's tone was warm, but he spoke briskly. Probably because he wasn't supposed to be taking personal calls, especially since Mistress Olivia was here at Stronghold right now, which meant he was in charge at Marquis.

"I'm going home with Master Asad. We're dating now." She glanced over at Asad as he sat down in the car, his shoulders shaking with silent laughter. She wasn't sure what he found funny, but seeing his happiness made her smile.

"O-kay... I thought nothing happened between you two last week?" His voice lifted in question.

Morgan hesitated because she hadn't actually said that. He'd assumed like everyone else, yet she wasn't sure if she should keep trying to lie or if she should tell the truth. When she didn't answer immediately, Freddy sighed.

"I see. You tell him he'd better be good to you, or he's going to have to answer to me."

"You'd have to get in line, Freddy," Asad said, not bothering to pretend he couldn't hear the conversation. "I'm pretty sure it will be out the door." He didn't sound bothered by the fact.

"I'll be the first in it, and there won't be anything left for anyone else!" Freddy's voice was raised to make sure Asad could hear him. Morgan pulled the phone away from her ear, wincing.

"Or everyone could accept that I can make my own decisions, regardless of how they turn out." She glared at the phone, even though Freddy couldn't see her.

"Maybe she'll break *my* heart. Did you ever think of that, Freddy?" Asad asked before Freddy could respond. "Yet no one's threatening her."

There was a long moment of silence. Morgan frowned at him. She certainly didn't plan on breaking his heart. Then again, she supposed no one ever did. Asad winked at her. Ah. He was giving Freddy a hard time.

Freddy sighed again.

"You both make very good points. Take care of each other, okay? Your friends will be there for you. But seriously, Asad, the Persian Excursion better be closed."

"Well, not closed so much as going private... exclusively available to one special rider." Asad chuckled, coming to a stop at a red light. He didn't let go of Morgan's thigh. Instead, he reached over with the hand that had been on the wheel to pluck the phone out of hers. "Say goodnight, Freddy."

"Goodnight, Freddy," Morgan echoed.

"Good night, you two. Morgan, we'll talk later? Maybe at lunch tomorrow?"

"Okay. I'll see you then."

Asad shook his head as she hung up the phone.

"It's a good thing I know that you're both subs and that Freddy is dedicated to Mistress Camille, or I'd be worried about you making a date right in front of me," he teased.

"I'm pretty sure it's the dates you don't know about that are the problem in that scenario," Morgan replied. After all, if he knew about them, then they weren't really dates. If she was hiding them, that would be the problem.

"Okay, well, don't do any of those, for sure." He glanced at her in the darkness, the passing streetlights revealing a pensive expression on his face before he had to refocus on the road. "I really want to give this a real go. Like dating exclusively. I want us to be like we were in Pittsburgh."

Morgan covered his hand on her thigh with her own, giving it a little squeeze.

"That's what I want, too."

"Good." He flipped his hand around, so it was no longer palm against her thigh, lacing her fingers through his. "Just so long as we're on the same page."

31

———————

Morgan

"It's like the fake relationship, but better because it's real." Morgan couldn't keep the silly smile off her lips as she answered Mistress Julie's question about how things had been going the past few days. The first few days of being Asad's girlfriend. She'd overheard him calling her that when talking to a co-worker on the phone, and she was still giddy about it.

She felt giddy all the time now, like happy butterflies had taken up permanent residence in her stomach.

"Is there anything different?" Mistress Julie asked, looking Morgan over. Sitting comfortably in her chair, wearing a pantsuit and her hair pulled back into a neat bun, the Dominatrix therapist looked professional and put together. Morgan was... not. She had on her makeup, but she'd only had time to throw her hair into a messy bun before running out the door to get to her appointment, wearing yoga pants and one of Asad's t-shirts because they were the only clean clothes she'd had at his place.

"I'm becoming more comfortable going out of the house in very casual clothing," she said ruefully, tugging at the hem of the t-shirt. She was sure that was what Mistress Julie was noticing. Going by the size and that it was a Star Wars t-shirt, it was pretty clear it wasn't hers. Though Asad had shown her the first movie last night, and she'd liked it, graphic t-shirts weren't really her thing, even in her downtime.

"That's one thing. Are you okay with that, or was it out of necessity?"

Morgan hesitated a moment before answering.

"Both. It was out of necessity, but I don't feel uncomfortable." She tugged on the hem of the shirt again. "It's not something I'd ever choose for myself, but I do like wearing Asad's clothes when I'm not going *out* out." And he seemed to like seeing her in them. Something about her walking around in his clothes turned him on. She often didn't get to wear them long unless they'd already had sex. "I think I would be uncomfortable if I was going out to eat at a restaurant or with my friends."

"That's good to know. How is everything going with them? Is everyone being supportive?" Mistress Julie's eyes twinkled with amusement. "Or at least accepting?"

"Accepting." Morgan sighed. "Sometimes, I wish there was more support."

"It's only been a few days," Mistress Julie pointed out. "You'll get more acceptance as people see that things are going well and start to relax. They're not used to you being in a relationship, and they're definitely not used to seeing Asad in a relationship."

"Right." It felt natural to her, as if it had been going on for far longer, but she needed to remember that no one else had seen what they'd been like in Pittsburgh. For all of them, it had only been a matter of days, and they were getting a very incomplete picture. "My friends feel cautious but mostly supportive. Except Noelle. She keeps telling me to be careful and doesn't think I should trust Asad's turnaround."

"How does that make you feel?"

"Annoyed." Morgan knew that question would be coming as soon as she mentioned Noelle, so she'd already thought a lot about it. "I talked to Amy about it, and she said she thinks Noelle is just worried about me, and that sometimes she can be a little overbearing without realizing it."

"What do you think?"

"I think Amy likes to think the best of everyone. I understand what she's saying, but I don't understand why Noelle would be that worried or why she can't accept my decisions. We haven't been friends that long, and she's not as close to me as the others are." They all accepted her decisions. Carolyn was the most supportive, acting as if she'd achieved some kind of accomplishment. Other than Noelle, Sam was the most cautious, but she wasn't constantly bringing it up the way Noelle was.

"Have you asked Noelle about it?"

"No. Do you think I should? I don't think she likes direct questions." That was another reason Morgan couldn't entirely relax around Noelle. Carolyn and Marissa found her bluntness entertaining, Sam encouraged her to say what she meant, and Amy thought she was wonderful just the way she was. Noelle always acted like there was some deeper meaning behind what Morgan said or something she wasn't saying, which Morgan didn't understand. Why bother saying something she didn't mean?

"I think it matters what you want to do."

She should have expected that answer. Mistress Julie smiled when Morgan sighed again.

"I don't know what I want to do about Noelle. I just try not to spend too much time with her. Which I think will be harder as Amy's wedding gets closer. I'm excited about being a bridesmaid, so I think that will help. We'll be able to talk about wedding things instead of Asad or my relationship."

"That should help, having a neutral conversation topic. How are things going with that?" Mistress Julie shifted in her chair, uncrossing and recrossing her legs, settling into a new comfortable position.

Morgan found herself doing the same, mimicking her and only noticing it once she was doing it. Well, her foot had been starting to fall asleep, anyway.

"Good." She tugged at the hem of her shirt again. "Amy got her results back from the doctor. Her thyroid isn't working the way it's supposed to, so she just started medication. She said she's already feeling like she has more energy, and she's hoping it'll mean she starts losing weight again."

Raising her eyebrows, Mistress Julie cocked her head at Morgan. "You sound like you don't approve."

"It's not that... it's just, she doesn't seem that unhappy with the way she looks. I think if her fiancé wasn't pressuring her, she wouldn't be so worried about it. But I don't think it's my place to say that." Morgan grimaced. Sometimes, it felt like there were more things she wasn't supposed to talk about than there were things she could talk about.

"Probably not. People can be very protective of their relationships. Especially once they've committed to someone, as you're finding out." Mistress Julie smiled as Morgan frowned.

"Do you think there's something bad about Asad that I'm not seeing?"

"Do you?"

She considered it for a moment before shaking her head.

"I don't know. I don't think he's perfect, if that's what you mean."

"Good enough." Mistress Julie chuckled. "If the two of you ever want to come in together, please know that he's welcome to join you."

"Thank you. Isn't couple's counseling something you do when you're having problems though?"

"It can be. Or it can be something you do to help prevent problems." Mistress Julie's smile faded a little. "Usually, by the time a couple comes in for counseling, it's a last-ditch effort. Those rarely work out because they've already basically given up, and usually there's a lot of work to be done to save things."

That made sense. Maybe she'd ask Asad if he wanted to come with her next time. It couldn't hurt to ask.

Asad

Damn, Morgan looked good in his clothes.

He would never have guessed he was a possessive person, especially since he'd never wanted a relationship, but seeing Morgan walking around in his shirt just flat out did something for him.

"I'm right here," Brian growled at him from where he was sitting at the kitchen counter. Morgan and Asad were on the couch while she uploaded some recordings to her various channels, scheduling them for release. She looked up in confusion.

"I'm not doing anything," Asad said innocently.

"You're thinking about it, though."

"Sorry, Daddy." He chuckled as Brian growled again, his countenance darkening. Next to him, Morgan stifled a giggle and shot him a look.

"You don't have to antagonize him, you know."

"You could always distract me." He leaned closer to her, his smile widening, his hand moving along the back of the couch. The soft t-shirt she was wearing didn't show off any of her body, and it was the sexiest fucking thing he'd ever seen on her. He wanted to peel it off and—

"Still right here."

Sighing as he straightened back up again, Asad shook his head.

"You know we're scening at Stronghold tonight, right? You can't cockblock me there." He smirked at Brian, who glowered at him. It wasn't a real glower, though. Asad felt he was slowly winning the other man over when it came to Morgan, which made him feel good. They were just giving each other a hard time in a half-joking, half-serious manner that happened when two Doms were head-butting over something or someone.

"Is that a challenge?" Brian grinned at him. Yeah, he wouldn't be giving Asad a hard time like this if he had a real problem.

"No, no, it is not." Morgan looked up from her computer again, glaring across the room at Brian. "I will be very upset if you block his cock. I like his cock. I want it inside me."

Brian groaned, scrubbing his hands over his face like he was trying to wash the words off. Asad cracked up. He loved it when Morgan got simultaneously sassy and blunt.

"Don't worry, Red, no one's going to keep my cock away from you." He'd thought about taking her to Marquis, but he wanted to scene again at Stronghold. Publicly. Everyone needed to get used to seeing them together.

They needed to get used to being together around their friends.

It had been easier than he'd thought it would be to be Morgan's boyfriend during the week. Despite his reputation at the club, he really didn't spend that much time pursuing anyone outside of it. Last night, he and Morgan had gone to Marquis' bar to hang out and spend some time with Freddy and Mistress Camille. It had basically been a double date and surprisingly fun. By the end of the night, Freddy had gone from wary to fully supportive.

That's what had made him realize it was better to keep showing up where people were and letting them see him and Morgan together rather than trying to hide away until they got used to the idea. It also made him feel as though maybe he wasn't so bad at this boyfriend thing if Freddy approved after one evening with them.

Brian's phone dinged, and he looked down at it. The air around him immediately changed as he frowned at it.

"What's wrong?" Asad asked.

Morgan was still tapping away at the keys in front of her, back to fully focusing on her work.

"Cassidy got a weird note in her mail, telling her to 'watch out.' She told Kincaid, who passed it along to Patrick, who is passing it along to the other Doms. It might be nothing, but..."

"But it might be something." Asad frowned, too. Poor Cassidy. She'd gotten away from her nightmare ex, thanks to Iris and Law, and she'd just started to relax. "Do you think it's her ex? The time limit for Law to press charges against him just ran out, right?"

That was how they'd kept Douchebag Dom—Iris' nickname for him—away from Cassidy for the past year. They hadn't been sure they'd be able to make charges stick for any amount of time, and they hadn't wanted him going after Cassidy or blaming her for anything that happened to him.

Law had hoped the threat of charges being brought against him would be enough to keep him in line and eventually forget about Cassidy and move on with his life. They *had* blackballed him from any BDSM clubs in the area to keep him away from any other vulnerable submissives, and Asad was pretty sure that someone had been tasked with keeping an eye on him, though he wasn't sure who. Kincaid maybe.

"Right," Brian said grimly. "We can't be sure it's him. It's not really a threat... it's just concerning, especially because it's anonymous."

"Who else could it be?" Morgan asked, looking up from her computer. "Has she been having trouble with anyone else?"

"I don't know, and Patrick didn't say. I'll talk to Kincaid later if I can catch him. He's been busy with the job change."

"Job change?" Asad echoed. He was clearly out of touch with the gossip... which was fair since he was usually the last to know things. Apparently, having a girlfriend wasn't going to change that since Morgan was also not in the middle of the gossip train.

"Oh, yeah, he's leaving the police department and going to work for a security firm that's opening up a branch down here," Brian said.

"The same firm Drew works for," Morgan chimed in, still looking at her computer.

Okay, scratch that. Apparently, his girlfriend *did* know the gossip. She just hadn't been sharing it. Well, at least now he had a good reason to punish her during their scene tonight. That was always fun.

32

Morgan

Being Asad's girlfriend was fun, and it didn't seem like he was getting tired of her, which had been her main concern the first few weeks they were dating. After all, that was what everyone else was worried about—that he couldn't commit. During her last session with Mistress Julie, the Domme had made the comment that maybe he'd just never _wanted_ to.

But he did want to with her.

Whenever they went to Stronghold, he didn't seem to be interested in any other submissives—though a few had tried flirting with him at first. None of her friends, of course. Asad had been polite, but it was as though there was a wall there that hadn't been there before, and only Morgan was allowed on the other side of the wall.

They occasionally watched scenes together, but it didn't seem as though he wished he was scening with anyone else. He was endlessly, sadistically creative with their scenes.

He invited her to spend time with him and his friends, which was a bit awkward the first time Domi and Rae were there, but Sam and Iris helped bridge the gap between them. It didn't hurt that they were very close to another submissive named Avery, who was very nice and whom Morgan hadn't really interacted with until now.

Asad also spent time with her and her friends. Q was there a lot, which didn't hurt since now he had someone to talk to other than Jeremy and Carolyn's husband, Chuck. Neither of them was very talkative, and Q had been struggling to try to make friends with them. Now, he didn't have to, which made Sam more relaxed and happier, too.

It was all going really, really well until their one-month anniversary. Which wasn't really an anniversary as far as she knew, but Asad had pointed it out and was excited about it, which made her excited about it. But when he got up to go to work that day, she struggled to open her eyes. She was so tired. And achy.

She felt his kiss on her forehead and his whispered goodbye, then she fell back asleep.

She didn't feel any better when she woke up.

With a groan, she made herself get out of bed and stumble out to the kitchen. Brian was out there, to her surprise.

"Why are you here?" she grumbled, rubbing her eyes. Her throat felt scratchy and so sore, it was hard to even grumble. Brian frowned at her.

"I'm going on that work trip today, remember? I don't leave for another hour."

Oh, right.

No, she hadn't remembered. She'd forgotten. Asad had been all excited about Brian being gone for a week because it meant they could fuck all over the house if they wanted to. They'd already had sex in every room of Asad's apartment, and he wanted to do it at her place now.

Ugh, her brain felt foggy, like her thoughts were coming more slowly than usual.

"Sweetie, you don't look so good," Brian said with concern, coming around the side of the counter. He set his mug of coffee down on it as he passed by.

"I'm fine."

She couldn't be sick. Not today. It was her one-monthversary, and Asad was taking her to dinner and a show at Marquis. He'd even gotten one of the rooms for them to stay in. She was not going to ruin that for him by being sick.

Brian stepped in front of her, blocking her movement and bringing a hand up to her forehead. Morgan tried to duck, but the movement made her dizzy. He caught her, cursing under his breath, and put his hand on her forehead before making a hissing sound.

"You're burning up, Morgan. We're going to the doctor."

"No!" Morgan stumbled away from him. "I'm not sick. I'm fine. I just need to eat something." She managed to straighten up and get to the fridge by sheer force of will. She could feel herself swaying, not that she was going to admit it. Nope. She had all day to get better, even if she wasn't feeling that well.

"Morgan, sit down!" Brian barked out the order, and Morgan's knees buckled immediately, her butt hitting the floor so fast, she cried out in surprise. "Shit." A moment later, he was scooping her up and carrying her into the living room.

"You used your Daddy Dom voice on me," she said accusingly.

"Damn right, I did. Now, you're going to sit right here and not move an inch." He put her down sideways on the couch and stood over her, glaring down at her with an expression that meant business. Morgan huffed, an odd feeling curling inside her. She wasn't sure what she felt, but she was close to bursting into tears.

"I need to eat something."

"I'm going to make you some soup, and in the meantime I'm going to call Mitch to get over here and check you out. It's his day off, so I know he's around."

Morgan huffed again, but she didn't protest. Brian had gone into full overprotective Daddy Dom mode. Hopefully, Mitch would be able to check her out and pronounce her as fine. Then Brian would leave for his trip, and she could rest up and be better for Asad this evening. Crossing her arms over her chest, she leaned against the back of the couch, her head and knees resting on it, and sighed.

Her throat really did hurt a lot.

She shivered.

A moment later, something heavy and warm covered her, and she opened her eyes to see Brian already walking back to the kitchen after having dropped one of their throw blankets over her. It felt good being curled up under it. Also, strange. She felt she was supposed to be up and doing something, but she could hear pans clattering in the kitchen as he started to get the soup ready, then his phone beeping with incoming texts.

"Mitch will be here soon."

"Okay." Morgan sighed, and it turned into a yawn. There was no point arguing with a bossy Daddy Dom once he hit Daddy mode, and she knew it. Mitch wasn't as strict, even though he was a sadist. He was a lot like Asad in that way. Maybe he could give her something to help her feel better and get through the night.

There was no way she was disappointing Asad.

---

*A*SAD

> Brian: Morgan's sick—she's running a fever and she won't go to the doctor. Mitch is coming over to check her out. I have to leave in an hour for my trip.

Asad stared at the text, his mind completely blank. His thoughts were whirling so fast that none of them made sense. He couldn't focus on anything but the words on the screen.

"Asad? Everything okay?" Duke, the manager of the company whose project he was currently on, was looking at him with concern.

"Um. Yeah. I mean, no. I... I have to go."

"Okay." Duke's blue eyes looked more concerned than ever.

"I'll be back tomorrow, but I just... I have to go."

"Sure, man, take the afternoon. It's no problem."

"Thanks." He managed to nod, his jaw clenched so hard, he could feel his teeth grinding together as he turned and walked out of the plant. Power walked, basically. Everything was going by in a blur as the words beat a mental drum in his head.

Morgan's sick. Morgan's sick. Morgan's sick.

By the time he slid into the front seat of his car, his heart was beating so fast, he could feel it in his throat, and his palms were sweaty enough to slide on his steering wheel. Shit. He had to get himself together. He needed to get home to Morgan, he needed to make sure she was okay, he needed...

He needed to stop panicking.

I need fucking therapy.

Mistress Julie.

He hadn't gone with Morgan yet, but she'd told him about Mistress Julie's offer. Grabbing his phone, he quickly found the Domme's number and crossed his fingers she'd be able to pick up. The phone rang once. Twice.

"Hello?"

His voice caught in his throat. He couldn't respond. He felt like he was choking.

"Hello? Asad?"

"Morgan's sick." That's what he meant to say, but it came out more like a croak.

"What?"

Somehow, he managed to get a hold of himself and actually form the words in a voice that was understandable.

"Morgan's sick. Brian just texted me that Morgan's sick, and I'm... fuck, I don't know what I'm doing."

"Okay, hold on, I'm going to switch you to video chat. I'm out at lunch with Olivia and Camille. Is it okay if they can hear you? Or I can walk outside."

"It's fine if they hear." He didn't really care. Maybe they would have some advice. He needed to get to Morgan, but he couldn't fucking think, much less move. He was sitting in his car, and he hadn't even started it. He was frozen. He needed someone to smack him into movement.

If one Dominatrix couldn't do it, maybe three would.

The phone beeped at him to accept the switch to video call, and he made his muscles move, holding the phone away from him as he switched over. Which was the first time he'd gotten to see his face. He looked ashy under his normally tanned skin, his eyes wide and blank, and sweat beaded his forehead.

Oh. It was hot in the car.

Fuck, he really should start the car. He turned the key in the ignition. Starting it didn't mean driving it. He needed to drive to get to Morgan, but he just couldn't make himself move.

Julie appeared on screen, and her eyes widened as she got a good look at him before a neutral expression swept over her face, wiping it all away.

"Hi, Asad, so Morgan's sick? Do you know with what?"

"No. Brian texted me. He said she has a fever, and Mitch is on his way to see her. But Brian's leaving for a trip, and I… I need to go over there. I need to take care of her." He practically choked on the words, his emotions rising again, so intertwined that he wasn't sure what he was feeling, only that he was feeling too much. Far too much. It felt as if he was going to explode at any moment. He wanted to scream, but his throat was clogged.

"Asad. Look at me. Focus on me. Focus on my voice. Okay, good. Now, take a deep breath in. Hold it. Deep breath out." Julie smiled at him as his breath came out in a whoosh. He felt his shoulders relax. "Now another one… deep breath in, deep breath out. Good. Now, Morgan told me a little about your brother and your family; she said you gave her permission to. I want you to say out loud… Morgan doesn't have cancer."

Dumb. That was his first thought. It was dumb because he knew Morgan didn't have cancer.

If it's so dumb, why don't you just do it? His brain prodded him.

"Morgan—" His throat choked him off again. Dammit. It was a simple sentence. It was true. Brian hadn't texted him because Morgan had gotten some kind of dire diagnosis. He'd texted him because she wasn't feeling well. She had a fever. Brian had Mitch coming to check on her. If he was really worried about something, if it was serious, he'd be taking her to the doctor or the hospital.

"Morgan doesn't have cancer."

The tight squeeze on his chest suddenly released, and he slumped in his seat.

"Aw, sweetie," Camille was peering over Julie's shoulder. "Do you want me to send Freddy over to check on her?"

"No. No." He shook his head. "I'm going to go check on her. I just... I think I panicked."

"I think you did, too." Julie smiled at him. "I'm glad you're going to check on her. I should warn you, I think you're going to have a bit of a fight on your hands to take care of her."

"What?" Asad stared blankly at the three women looking back at him.

"Morgan's not used to being taken care of," Olivia chimed in. "She tends to fight it. You might have to get bossy with her. But her former... hmmm. Well, let's just say that was completely on her own any time she wasn't feeling well prior to this. She doesn't feel comfortable being taken care of."

And Asad didn't feel comfortable taking care of people because it reminded him of his brother. He'd spent a lot of childhood doing sick days with his brother, both in and out of the hospital.

He groaned.

"I... I really, really like Morgan, but sometimes, I think we're the worst match-up in history," he confessed. He wasn't sure if the Dommes were following his thoughts, but they didn't seem confused.

"Or one of the best. You challenge each other, and you're in a good position to grow together. You also make her really happy, and that's what matters the most." Julie smiled at him.

That was good to hear. And they did challenge each other. This felt like a massive challenge.

"I feel like a shitty boyfriend because there's a part of me that doesn't want to go home and take care of her." There. He'd said it out loud.

None of the women seemed particularly horrified at the confession, which took some of the wind out of his sails. Hadn't they heard him?

"Is it that you don't want to take care of her or that you don't want to face the fact that sometimes people you care about get sick?"

"Ouch." He rubbed the spot on his chest where it felt like Julie had just punched him. That one had hit like a physical blow.

"Suck it up, Asad," Olivia said, leaning in. "The Persian Excursion can't be all smooth sailing. Sometimes, things are going to get a little bumpy. Then you have to decide—are you bailing or are you going to captain the fucking ship? You get to control where you're going. You just have to make the decision, then follow through."

Right. That made sense. Decision and follow through.

"I'm going to Morgan's to check on her and spend the afternoon with her... oh, um, can someone cancel our reservation for Marquis tonight?" Damn. He'd almost forgotten they were supposed to be going out. She was going to be disappointed, but he'd make it up to her, eventually. "If she has a fever, we're obviously staying in."

"No problem," Olivia, manager of Marquis, said. Her grey eyes softened as she studied him through the screen. "You just go take care of your girl."

"Let us know if you need anything else. Freddy and I are free this evening," Camille chimed in.

Julie smiled at him. "You can do this, Asad. And please, feel free to come talk to me any time."

"I might just have to do that. Thank you. I'll... keep you updated."

"You'd better." Olivia winked at him, then they cut the phone off.

Asad took a deep breath... then another. He put the car in drive. It was time to go take care of his sick girlfriend.

He could do this.

33

———

Morgan

Curled up on the couch, Morgan was already feeling better, other than having Mitch and Brian hovering over her.

"Don't you need to go?" she asked Brian. His hour was more than up.

Brian looked at Mitch. Mitch looked back at Brian. Despite the difference in their appearances—Brian with his brown hair and hazel eyes, dressed in a suit, Mitch with blond hair and blue eyes wearing a tank top and sweatpants—they looked remarkably similar in that moment. Morgan frowned at both of them.

"I can't stay. I have to get back to pick up Ana," Mitch said apologetically. Ana was his soon-to-be stepdaughter once he and Domi got married. Morgan had never met the little girl, but she'd heard about her.

"Fuck," Brian muttered under his breath.

"I'm fine," Morgan repeated for the eleventh time. "You can go. I'm feeling much better. My throat doesn't hurt as much, and my fever has gone down."

"That's because Mitch gave you stuff to help with both. That doesn't mean it's going to last. I don't want to leave you here on your own while you're feeling like this," Brian huffed, pinching the bridge of his nose and closing his eyes, which was what he often did when he was thinking hard.

That meant he would be missing work, or very late, because of Morgan. As touched as she was by their dedication to taking care of her, she also felt like an unwanted burden. She was making life harder for him, which was the exact opposite of what she wanted.

She also needed both of them to leave because she doubted they'd let her go on her date with Asad when they were convinced she was in no shape to be moving from the couch. She'd done a lot more while feeling much worse. She'd taken care of herself while feeling much worse. Richard hadn't tolerated sickness, and whenever she'd gotten *really* sick, he'd put her in another room until she was better.

All this hovering was making her uncomfortable.

"Kincaid's out. He's got too much going on. Maybe Zach?" Mitch scrubbed his hand against the back of his neck.

Morgan sighed again.

The doorbell rang.

"I've got it," Brian said as she sat up straight, pointing a threatening finger at her. "Don't you dare move."

If he had his way, she'd be stuck on the couch forever, but she didn't move. She was already making things harder for him. She didn't want to make him mad on top of that. Hands on his hips, Mitch was looking down at her, but not as if he was really seeing her, more like he was doing some kind of calculation in his head.

"Hey, what are you doing here?" Brian asked in surprise from the doorway, causing Morgan and Mitch to look up. She peered over the back of the couch, but the door was blocking her view of whoever was there.

"You texted me that Morgan was sick... where else would I be?" Asad pushed past Brian, his arms filled with grocery bags. Morgan's mouth dropped open as her heart sank.

Dammit! Brian had told on her.

Now she'd made his life harder, *and* Asad was going to be disappointed. Morgan moaned and dropped her head against her knees.

Suddenly, she had three Doms crowding around her, asking what was wrong. She hugged her legs, hiding her face and trying to stifle her sniffle because she didn't know how to tell them that *they* were what was wrong.

"Just go!" Those were the only two words she could get out, directed at Brian.

"Is she talking to me?" Asad sounded bewildered and hurt, and Morgan's breath caught in her throat. Thankfully, Brian knew exactly who she'd been talking to.

"No, she's talking to me, I'm supposed to be headed out on a work trip, and I was supposed to leave about fifteen minutes ago, but..."

"Then go. I've got this." Strong arms suddenly wrapped around her, pulling her back onto a lap. She recognized the smell of Asad's cologne the moment he pulled her against him, subtle but spicy and incredibly comforting at that moment. "I'll text you updates."

"I... okay." Brian took a deep breath. "Okay. Mitch can't stay either."

"That's fine. Like I said, I've got this." Asad stroked her arm, tucking her head under his chin as a little shiver went through her. She wasn't sure if it was from the fever or because she was trying so hard not to cry. She'd ruined their night, and he was being so nice about it.

"Alright. Keep me updated. Bye, Morgan. I hope you're feeling better soon. Listen to Master Asad."

She felt herself being shifted on Asad's lap so Brian could drop a kiss on the top of her head.

"Bye," she managed to choke out, though she didn't lift her head. She wanted to crawl under the blanket and never come out. Unfortunately, she doubted that was an option. She would call Brian later and talk to him and apologize for making him so late. And then chew him out for texting Asad.

She heard the front door opening and closing again because Brian was in such a rush now that he was so late. Closing her eyes, she did her best not to cry while Mitch updated Asad on her symptoms, what he'd already done, and when she could have more medicine. Asad asked some questions, stroking her arm the whole time.

At least he didn't seem angry that she was sick and had ruined their night... but maybe he figured she'd be feeling better with the medicine, and they could still go do it.

"I didn't see any spots in her throat, so I'm not too worried about strep, but keep an eye on it, especially if her fever keeps coming back," Mitch instructed. Most of the time he was a fun, funny guy who never stopped smiling, a lot like Asad, but right now, he was in Nurse Mitch mode and was all business. "If she's still running a fever over 101 degrees tomorrow morning, without the fever reducer, take her in to the doctor."

"Got it. Thank you." Asad's arms tightened around her.

"No problem. Let me know if you need anything else." Another soft kiss on her head. "Bye, Morgan."

"Bye."

Then it was just her and Asad. Morgan slumped in his arms, everything that had been holding her together draining away in a moment.

"Hey, Red, how are you feeling?" he asked, shifting her on his lap again, pushing her away enough that she could tell he was trying to get a good look at her.

"I'm sorry!" she blurted out as he met her gaze. He was wearing his work clothes, and she was in one of his t-shirts and a pair of yoga pants.

"Sorry?"

"I'm sorry Brian texted you. I'm fine, I really am. I just need to take it easy this afternoon, then we can go to Marquis and—"

"Baby, I already canceled our reservation tonight." He was shaking his head as he cut her off. "We're not going anywhere until you feel better."

She was the worst girlfriend ever. Morgan couldn't hold back the tears any longer.

<u>ASAD</u>

Things he'd always thought would make him run:
Commitment
Taking care of someone who wasn't feeling well
Crying

Yet here he was, holding his sick girlfriend on his lap while she cried, and he didn't feel like running. All he wanted to do was make her feel better. She wasn't some vague idea in his head or some made-up placeholder with no real personality—she was Morgan. He didn't want to be anywhere but here, holding her and taking care of her.

Something settled inside him with that realization. This was where he belonged. No matter what happened with her or if she was only a little sick or really sick, this was where he was choosing to be because this was where he wanted to be. He wanted her to rely on him, and he wanted to be there for her. He wanted everything he'd rejected for so long... as long as it was with her.

"Baby, Red, what's wrong?" he asked, smoothing her hair back and cuddling her close again. He'd noticed she was calmer when she was against his chest, being held tightly. He could feel how warm she was, warmer than usual, which must be the remnants of the fever.

She might just be crying because she was tired, sick, and a little overwhelmed, but after talking to Julie, he thought it might also be a bit more than that. From the looks of it, she'd been struggling with having Mitch and Brian take care of her. She definitely hadn't expected him to show up, any more than Mitch and Brian had, even though Brian had been the one to text him.

Asad would be insulted if he hadn't spent years carefully cultivating his reputation as someone who wouldn't be there.

Once he'd appeared, neither Mitch nor Brian had balked at leaving Morgan in his care. Brian had looked relieved and grateful as he'd done the handoff, which was more than Asad had expected.

There had been no warning looks, just the request to be kept updated, which is what they would have done from anyone.

"I'm sorry I ruined our night! And made you leave work! And made Brian late! And—"

"Hey, hey, this is not your fault, got it?" He hugged her tighter, rocking her slightly. "You can't help when you get sick. Brian didn't mind delaying leaving any more than I minded leaving work—those are things we both chose to do, nobody made us. We're still going to celebrate our one-monthversary, we're just going to celebrate it a little differently than we planned."

"We are?" She sniffled, though thankfully, her tears had slowed.

"Yes, we're going to celebrate it here. I'll make us dinner, we'll watch some movies, and snuggle on the couch, then I'll reschedule our night at Marquis for when you're feeling better. It's not a big deal."

"It's not?"

"I mean, it is, but it isn't." One of the reasons he'd wanted to do the one-monthversary thing, even though it was very high school, was because he knew it was the kind of experience Morgan hadn't had during her teenage years. His high school experience hadn't been entirely typical, either, but at least he'd had some of those milestones. He'd been excited about doing it for her, but they'd just move it.

"I think it's a big deal because a month is a great start, but having to cancel or move the Marquis night isn't a big deal because the important thing is that we're acknowledging that we're together and we want to keep being together. Right?"

"Right."

"Good. So, I need to put away the stuff I brought over, some of it needs to be refrigerated, then we'll figure out what movie we're going to watch first. We can celebrate this being the first time I get to take care of you being sick, and we'll celebrate again the first time I get sick and you take care of me."

That got a little giggle from her, and Asad smiled. Come to think of it, being taken care of the next time he was sick definitely didn't sound bad. He hadn't had that since he was much younger. One thing about his parents, the slightest hint of illness on his part had meant a lot of care and pampering until he was feeling better. He'd always tried to get better as soon as possible and sometimes downplayed how he was feeling, so they didn't have to worry about him *and* Cyrus, but that hadn't stopped his mom from going overboard every time he was sick.

"Does that mean we're going to celebrate the first time we do everything?" she asked, moving on his lap so she could look at him. Her eyes were still puffy, and her nose was pink and a little swollen, but she looked beautiful to him.

"Absolutely." He tapped his finger against her nose. "Now, I'm going to go get this party started."

"I'll help."

"No." He put some authority into his voice, pulling her back down onto his lap as she started to get up and shifting her to the side instead, so her butt was firmly planted on the couch. "You will sit right there, rest, and work on feeling better. Think about what movie you want to watch."

Morgan huffed, crossing her arms over her chest and looking so miserable at being denied, he almost wanted to give in, but she was going to need to get used to being taken care of. He was good at it, even if he'd been out of practice for a while. It was time to tap back into that side of himself.

"I'm going to choose a chick flick," she said, glaring up at him.

It was hard not to smile when she looked like an angry little doll. Especially since he had a feeling she was getting her threat from the stereotypes she'd bought into. All the movies they'd watched together so far had been his choice, movies from pop culture she'd never seen, and there had been a distinctly nerdy bent to the choices, so she probably thought she was making an effective threat.

"You do that."

Joke would be on her. Asad loved chick flicks.

34

Asad

Even though she was feeling better, leaving Morgan in the morning wasn't easy. Her fever was down to under one hundred degrees when she woke up, which meant it was down without the effects of the medicine since she'd fallen asleep around eight the evening before, halfway through *Princess Diaries 2*, which they were going to have to rewatch eventually because she'd missed most of the best stuff. She really enjoyed the first one and what she'd managed to stay awake for most of the second one.

"Call me if you need anything."

"Mm-hmm." The sleepy murmur didn't reassure him that she was truly awake, much less processing what he was telling her. Maybe he should write it down. That wasn't a bad idea.

"And take your temperature every two hours and text me a picture of it."

"Mm-hmm."

Yeah, he was definitely writing the instructions down. Quickly finding a pad of paper and a pen, he did that and left it on her nightstand, dropping a kiss on her forehead before leaving. She sighed happily in her sleep.

She would be fine.

It was still hard walking out the door. He made himself feel a little better by texting Brian and Mitch an update.

Even though it was hard to leave, he knew Morgan would be happy to know she was trusted to be on her own. It was a delicate balance, making sure she was taken care of while also making sure she didn't feel like a burden or like she was disappointing anyone. They'd talked through some of that last night, between the movies, but she would probably need reassurance again, eventually.

So would he. Once she was feeling better, they would be making an appointment to see Mistress Julie together, and he would do a few on his own. He was feeling more even-keeled now, but he knew he still had work to do. He wasn't magically fixed just because he'd gotten over this one hurdle.

As he got into his car, his phone rang. His mom. Sighing, he started the car and turned on the Bluetooth.

"Hello?"

"Good morning, honey. How is Morgan?"

When his mom had called yesterday before dinner, he'd told her that he couldn't talk because Morgan was sick. After a few minutes of advice, which he'd already gotten from Mitch, she'd finally gotten off the phone with him. It didn't surprise him that she wanted a morning update.

"Good, she's much better," he said, pulling out of the driveway. "Her fever is down. I don't know if her throat is any better yet because she was still mostly asleep when I left."

"Oh, that's good. You two had a restful night?"

"Yeah, watched some movies and fed her soup for dinner. It wasn't the one-monthversary that she wanted, but she seemed happy."

"The what?"

His brain stalled out.

Rewound.

Ah, fuck.

This is what he got for talking to his mom when he was distracted by driving. Things just slipped out.

"Um. Well." He sighed. Might as well confess. It was easier than trying to come up with a lie. "Yesterday was our one-month anniversary."

"But..." His mom's voice trailed off and he could practically hear her doing the math in her head and coming up with a negative number.

"Yeah, we weren't really together when I brought her to the wedding. She was a friend who came with me and pretended to be my girlfriend."

Asad braced himself for the full blast of his mother's reaction.

What he got was a long sigh.

"Your father is going to be so upset. He just lost a hundred dollars to Mason."

Wait, what?

"What?" The first part of that sentence had made sense to him, then it took a sharp left turn in the second half. "What do you mean he lost a hundred dollars to Mason?"

"Mason told us that Morgan was your fake girlfriend. Your father and I thought that was ridiculous. It was obvious you had real feelings for her. Which, I guess we were right about that, so maybe the bet was really a draw since she's your real girlfriend now..." his mother mused.

He shook his head, trying to make it make sense.

"Mason told you that he thought my relationship with Morgan was fake, and you made a *bet* on it?"

"Yes." Her amused tone was nearly as disconcerting as the revelation itself. Though his relationship with his parents had improved by leaps and bounds over the past couple weeks, he hadn't realized she'd actually find him lying to her and bringing a fake girlfriend to his brother's wedding *funny*. He sure as hell thought he'd done a better job fooling Mason than he apparently had.

He couldn't believe they'd made a *bet* about it. He was so getting Mason back for that. Mason didn't know that *he* knew Mason belonged to the Outlands. He wasn't sure what he could do with that information yet, but he'd figure something out.

"Does Cyrus know about the bet?"

"Of course not, honey. He's been on his honeymoon." The amusement hadn't left his mother's voice. "Do you want to tell him or should I?"

"I'll tell him," Asad said gruffly. He didn't need his mom playing telephone between him and Cyrus. Especially since he really was trying to have a better relationship with both his parents and his brother. Cyrus would want to hear it from him. Plus, he probably owed his brother an apology for bringing a fake girlfriend to his wedding, even if Morgan was his real girlfriend now. He pulled into the parking lot.

"I'm at work now, Mom. I've got to go."

"Okay, sweetie. Well, I'm glad to hear that Morgan's doing better this morning. Keep me updated."

"Will do. Love you, Mom, bye."

"Love you, too. Tell Morgan we're so happy she's your real girlfriend. Bye, honey."

Shaking his head, Asad hung up the phone. Sometimes, he felt like his entire world had turned upside down the week of Cyrus' wedding. In a good way, overall, even if it was a little weird at times.

Morgan

It took a whole day before she was feeling better enough to record more content and another three days before she convinced Asad she could eat something other than soup. Her fever was gone, and so was her sore throat. She was back to recording content.

Everything was back to normal... except that she still wasn't getting laid.

"You should tell him it's bothering you," Sam advised. She and Amy had come over to hang out with Morgan for some girl time. Marisa was traveling, Carolyn had plans with her husband, and Noelle had a date with Master Damian, who had apparently broken up with Rae a few weeks ago. Some juicy gossip that she'd missed because she'd been preoccupied with getting ready for the trip with Asad. It did explain why Brian had been so cheerful right before she'd left for Pittsburgh, though she didn't know why he hadn't shared the gossip with her.

"Or just seduce him," Amy suggested from her perch next to Sam. They were sitting on the opposite side of the counter, each sipping a glass of wine while Morgan made dinner. "Holy crap, Morgan, that smells so good. Are you sure that's healthy?"

Morgan laughed. "Absolutely."

She was making them salmon with quinoa with red lentil dahl and a spinach salad on the side. It was delicious and fit right into Amy's diet, though a little time-consuming to make since she was making the dahl from scratch. Even though Amy's new medication had halted her weight gain, and she'd dropped a few pounds back toward where she had been, she didn't seem to be able to lose any more than that. She'd come asking Morgan for recipes, and Morgan had been happy to help out, though she worried about what would happen if they didn't help the way Amy hoped.

"Amy has a point. You could just be naked when he gets home. I mean, obviously not right now since we're here, but maybe tomorrow. Or... are you two going to Stronghold?" Sam took a sip of her wine, tilting her head as she watched Morgan turn to stir the pot.

"I don't think so. He hasn't mentioned going anywhere." Morgan sighed. "Well, other than rescheduling our night at Marquis for our two-monthversary." Which was almost an entire month from now.

"Okay, but that's really freaking cute," Amy said, grinning. "Not only that he wants to celebrate your monthversaries, but it's a good sign that he's already planning a month ahead. He went from being totally uncommitted to one hundred percent on board and planning for the future."

"Magic vagina," Sam whispered, furtively glancing over her shoulder as if making sure Asad wasn't there to pop up and yell at her. They all cracked up.

That was a good point, though. Morgan hadn't thought about it that way. She'd mostly been disappointed that he'd moved it so far away, but really it wasn't that far away in the grand scheme of things, and it did show he was planning for a future with her. She did have one question, though.

"So, the month anniversary thing isn't silly? Noelle thought it was weird." She'd liked it right up until last night when Noelle had called, and they'd chatted for a bit. She'd told her about the move, and Noelle's scorn had been so obvious, Morgan couldn't miss it, even over the phone.

"No, it's adorable. Don't listen to Noelle." Sam scowled, and something about what she said had Amy sitting up straight and looking at her with surprise.

"Did something happen between you and Noelle," she asked.

"No, I mean, not really. Sort of." Sam sighed, tapping her fingers on the counter next to her wine glass. Morgan just kept focusing on the food, although she was listening, because she didn't know what to say. "We were hanging out yesterday afternoon just talking about, like, stuff. Q and me. Things going on at the club. Her date tonight. And then out of nowhere, she asks me if I've been talking behind her back with Iris."

"What?" Amy let out a small gasp.

"Yeah, exactly. It was in the middle of a totally normal conversation, and she asked it really aggressively. I was so stunned, I couldn't say anything back right away. I just sat there, trying to process the change in topic, then she got mad at me and said she *knew* it. And I was like, knew what? She said the fact I couldn't answer that I hadn't done anything like that right away meant that I had." Sam threw her hands up in the air. "I told her I was just caught completely off guard, and obviously, I hadn't been talking about her with Iris—her name has only come up once or twice because I mention I've hung out with her, and Iris doesn't say a *thing* when she's mentioned. I'm not sure she believed me, though."

"I wonder if that's why she called me last night," Morgan said thoughtfully. "It was really weird that she did, and she did ask if I'd talked to you lately."

"Does she not call you often?" Amy asked, frowning.

"No." Morgan hesitated then figured it couldn't hurt to be honest. Sam had just done the same thing. "That was the first time she's ever called me. Normally, we just talk on the group text or in person. I didn't think she likes me very much."

"That's so weird. She calls me a lot." Amy shook her head. "She hasn't asked me anything about either of you, though. Mostly we talk about my exercise routine and the wedding. She's been super helpful. Although I think Marissa is getting a little annoyed with her because she keeps trying to do things that Marissa feels are her job as my maid of honor."

"Because she is," Sam muttered, avoiding Amy's look and taking another sip of her wine.

"She's trying to *help* Marissa since she's out of town a lot," Amy stressed.

"Then maybe she should wait till Marissa asks her to do something instead of only talking to you instead of Marissa," Sam retorted.

Morgan paused, nervously watching them both. Were they fighting? It kind of seemed like they were fighting.

But Amy didn't take offense; she just sighed.

"You're right. I've told Noelle as much, and she says she will, but then..." Amy shrugged. "I think maybe sometimes she just gets really excited, so she forgets. It's hard to be mad at her. She's really been there for me recently, especially with helping keep me motivated to go work out. And she's helped get Jeremy to ease up on putting the pressure on me."

"She has?" Sam looked at Amy again, this time seemingly surprised.

"Yeah, they've become pretty good friends. She's been over a lot and spending more time with us, and they really hit it off. I think she just wants to make the wedding perfect for me and him, sometimes she just goes about it in the wrong way." Amy rubbed at an invisible spot on the counter, sighing again. "I'm excited about the wedding, don't get me wrong, but I can't wait until it's over and Jeremy and I can just be married. I didn't think wedding planning would be so stressful."

"Well, it didn't help that he was harping on you about your weight gain, which you literally couldn't help," Sam said, leaning over to wrap her arm around Amy's shoulder. "I'm glad to hear Noelle helped get him to back off, although I would have thought finding out it was a medical reason and that you have medication would have done that."

"It did help, but I think he thought the medication was going to be an immediate fix or help me lose weight really fast." Amy shook her head. "Obviously, that's not what's happening. But it's okay. I've told him I really am happy with how I look. If this is what I look like for the wedding, I'll be thrilled. I don't care that it's more than I was a year ago. I feel good now that I have my energy back, and I like my new curves. And he does like the new boobs." She giggled, looking down at her chest and giving a little shimmy to make them shake. Morgan giggled, too, and Sam outright laughed.

"Okay, good. I'm glad she helped there. I just... yesterday was weird." Sam scrunched her nose, making a face.

"I can only imagine. I would have reacted the same way," Amy reassured her. "I just wish everything could calm down. The wedding stress is getting to me. Marissa and Noelle sniping at each other is getting to me. And I could really use a scene with Zach, but there's something going on with him and Kincaid, and I don't want to do anything to make things harder for them." She ran a hand through her hair, raking it back from her face in frustration.

"You could scene with Asad if you need to," Morgan offered. "I'm sure he'd be willing if I explain, and I don't mind." They'd agreed to be exclusive, but Amy only scened platonically. Like Morgan, she was a masochist who needed the pain. Something her fiancé was understanding about, even though he couldn't provide it. That's why he was happy to let her scene with Zach, who was in a happy monogamous relationship with his boyfriend. At least, it was usually happy. Maybe Morgan should reach out and talk to them. They were her friends, too, and she'd barely seen them other than a glimpse or two at the club since getting back from Pittsburgh.

"You are the best friend," Amy beamed at her. "I appreciate it, although hopefully, it won't come to that. I'm going to give it another week, then I'll bring it up to Zach. Hopefully, he and Kincaid will be over whatever issue they're having right now."

"Let's hope so. They seem really good for each other. I want everyone to get their happily-ever-after." Sam smiled.

Was Asad a happily-ever-after? A month ago, the idea would have been laughable, but right now, Morgan really felt like he might be.

Though he was going to need to start putting out again if that was going to remain true.

35

—————

Asad

A two-monthversary wouldn't be a big deal to most people, but it was to him and Morgan. It had been a really good two months, too. He was a regular fixture at her and Brian's place. As much as he would have liked to spend all their time at his place, he didn't have the studio setup she needed for recording her ASMR or doing lives. So, on nights when she went live, he would sleep over at her place, hanging out with Brian or entertaining himself while she was doing her thing. That meant three nights a week, he and Brian were hanging out.

It usually wasn't just them. Mitch, Kincaid, and Zach came over regularly to hang out with Brian on those nights as well, so Asad got to know all of them a little better. They were protective of Morgan, but the longer he and Morgan were together—and the more they saw of him—the more they all relaxed.

Though Brian did ask them to keep sex to Morgan's room when he came home from his trip a day early, despite Asad's reassurances that she had recovered from being ill. He'd walked in on them not long after Asad had come to the house to find her wearing a frilly maid costume, complete with a feather duster and no underwear.

She'd proved to him that she was feeling all the way better, even though they'd had to take their antics back to her room after the interruption. It hadn't ended their night at all. In fact, he'd taken the opportunity to tie her down to the bed and dust her, teasing her with the feathers until she was begging for him to fuck her. As scenes went, it had been pretty light, but she *had* just recovered from being sick.

Tonight, however, there was going to be nothing holding him back, and Asad had *plans*.

Tonight was the night he was going to tell Morgan he was in love with her. He didn't know how it had happened, and he worried it might be too fast, but at some point a few weeks ago, he'd been watching one of her live feeds, and the emotion had hit him in the gut out of nowhere.

He loved her. He'd fallen in love with her. He wanted a future with her.

No, he wasn't going to propose immediately, but he wanted to tell her, and he wanted to make it special. But he also wanted to make it very him.

So, he had plans for tonight.

First, though, was dinner and the show. Tonight, Master Michael and Ellie were performing. Master Michael had been working on his Shibari techniques lately, and they were going to do a suspension scene with some knife play. Since Master Michael was a sadist and Ellie was a masochist, Morgan was particularly excited.

Asad was going to enjoy himself, too. Before they left the house, he'd dressed Morgan the way he wanted her. Little rubber rings hugged her nipples, tightly enough to keep them erect and pulsing, giving them some extra sensitivity, but not so tight that he had to worry about her circulation. The waist cincher she was wearing kept her breasts completely bare, so he'd covered her up with a coat before they left, knowing that every move she made would make her nipples rub against the fabric.

Then he'd bent her over her bed and inserted a silicone plug in her ass, preparing her for his plans later that evening. He also filled her pussy with a U-shaped vibrator that nestled against her body, one part of it right up against her clit. She had to sit with her hips tilted forward to stay comfortable, so her weight wasn't resting on the toy, but she didn't seem bothered by it.

Especially since the vibrator was remote controlled, and Asad had the control. He could turn it on inside her, turn on the suction that was right over her clit, or both.

"Do you think they'll be starting soon?" she asked, bouncing slightly in her seat, which made her breasts bounce enticingly above the waist cincher. Asad reached over to pinch a pert nipple between his fingers, making her moan and arch her back. His cock throbbed at the sound.

"Yes," he answered, just as the lights started to dim.

Letting go of her nipple, he reached around her body, pulling her in closer to him, so he could touch her as much as he wanted during the show. The lights went out. The second floor of Marquis was set up as a circular room with booths lining the walls and a round stage in the center where the performances were held.

Each booth could fit up to six to eight people and had two curtains that could be drawn across the booth's opening for various levels of privacy. The first curtain was sheer, and when the stage lights were on, would keep anyone from being able to see what was happening inside the booth. That was for voyeurs who didn't want to accidentally become exhibitionists or who desired a modicum of privacy. The second curtain was heavy velvet and would turn the booth into a kinky little cocoon.

Obviously, they wanted to watch the show, and neither of them cared about being watched, so they were leaving the curtains completely open. Once the stage lights were fully on, they could no longer see into the booth across from them, so it was still mostly private. And the people on either side of them certainly couldn't see them since the walls of the booth swent all the way up to the ceiling.

Marquis had been designed for a myriad of possibilities. After the show, he'd be taking Morgan back to the Dungeon room, though he'd asked for a few modifications when he'd made the reservation. The

Dungeon could also serve very well as a medical scene room, and Freddy had been happy to make the arrangements for him.

Master Michael and Ellie walked into the room. She already had some ropes wrapped around her, the ends hanging loosely down her legs. More ropes descended from the ceiling as they stepped onto the stage. Petite and curvy with her long black hair hanging down her back, Ellie looked utterly delectable in her rope outfit.

Maybe he should work on some Shibari so he could dress Morgan up with ropes. Definitely something to consider for the future.

As the show started, he leaned in and began to toy with Morgan's nipple and the remote in his pocket. Not that he was going to let her cum. No, he needed to get her prepared. He needed her as wet as possible for what he wanted to do with her.

Her low moan as they watched Master Michael insert a hook plug into Ellie's ass before attaching the rope on it to her hair made him feel like it wasn't going to be that difficult.

---

*M*ORGAN

By the time the show was over, Morgan was a slippery mass of seething need. Her aching nipples were throbbing in the confines of the rings, sensitive to every stroke, pinch, and twist from Master Asad's fingers. Her pussy juices had soaked through her thong, and the tops of her thighs slid against each other, thanks to the leaking cream. Her pussy lips felt swollen, throbbing between her legs as she walked, and that bit of stimulation teased her clit, which was already highly sensitive, thanks to the vibrator that had been tormenting it.

The vibrator had gone completely silent during the last ten minutes of the show when Master Asad had realized she was too close to orgasm. Following him out of the dining room into the hallway leading to the hotel rooms, she was barely aware of the others doing the same thing. Her entire focus was centered on him and the pulsing desire in her core.

"In here." He opened up the door to the Dungeon room. She hadn't known what room they were going to. He'd been so secretive, taking care of picking up her bags and bringing them to check in so her evening would be a surprise. Grinning at her, he swept his arm out like he was showing off the door and encouraging her to walk through it. Not that she needed encouragement.

Though she did grind to a halt as soon as she stepped inside because this wasn't the Dungeon she was used to. During classes, she'd spent plenty of time in this room, which had been rearranged. The general décor was still the same, but in the center of the room, there was now a padded doctor's table complete with stirrups—the kinky BDSM version of it, at least, with all the rings and straps for restraints—and a gleaming silver cart beside it with a tray resting on top. The only things on the tray were a huge bottle of lube and a pair of thin medical gloves.

"What's this?" she asked, then squealed when pain exploded on her buttocks. Asad had given her a short, sharp, harsh swat to get her moving forward again.

"Your second monthversary present." Asad grinned. "I looked over the form you filled out when you joined Stronghold, about things you wanted to try, your soft and hard limits, and I discovered there was only one thing listed as 'want to try' that I know you haven't done yet. So, that's what we're doing tonight."

Oh God.

Morgan's gaze dropped down to his hands as her thighs automatically pressed together in defense. When she'd filled out the form, she'd been curious about the idea, especially since it wasn't something Richard or Jason had ever tried to do with her.

"You're going to fist me?" Her voice came out in a high squeak.

"Yes, I am. I'm going to fist you until you cum, then we'll see where the night takes us from there." Turning her to face the table, his fingers stroked down her upper spine, from between her shoulders to the top of her waist cincher, and suddenly it felt like she didn't have enough air to breathe.

That sounded incredibly hot and also terrifying. He didn't have small hands. When she'd been fantasizing about it while filling out the form, she'd pictured someone with small hands... like, her size hands.

"Don't worry, Red, I've got you." His soft murmur in her ear helped her take another breath.

It was Master Asad. He would never harm her. And she had a safeword. If she needed to use it, she could, and he wouldn't think any less of her. Heck, he'd probably applaud her for using it since her *not* using it was the bigger concern. She trusted him completely.

She could do this.

And she wanted to.

Now she knew why he'd been teasing her so relentlessly. He wanted her pussy soft, supple, and ready to be stretched. That was as important as the lube, and the more turned on she was, the easier it would be.

A soft kiss pressed against her shoulder, then he patted her ass, right where he'd swatted her but much more gently this time. She felt a tug at the laces of her waist cincher as he began to loosen them.

"We need to get this off first. Once you're naked, I want you up on the table, heels in the stirrups."

Mouth dry, she knew there was only one answer possible.

"Yes, Sir," she whispered.

36

Morgan

Naked, feet in the stirrups of the chair, butt resting on the edge of the table with her legs spread wide apart, Morgan squirmed as the vibrator hummed away inside her. Master Asad had decided not to remove the toy or the little rings on her nipples. The erect buds were standing at attention, dark pink against the black bands at their base. She'd been surprised he wasn't clamping them until she realized it was likely because he wanted all of her focus to be on the hand stretching open her pussy.

Which was not reassuring.

Neither was the sound of the glove snapping.

She lifted her head, scowling at him over the length of her naked body. Naked other than the gloves he'd just put on, he grinned back at her.

"You made that sound on purpose," she accused. The chains of the restraints on her wrists rattled as she jerked on them. "It's not a necessary part of putting on the gloves."

He laughed, his grin widening. "Correct, but it is fun."

Picking up the lube, he squirted a generous amount onto his right palm, then put the bottle down so he could begin rubbing it all over his hand. Morgan's breath hitched in her throat. Her pussy spasmed, and she moaned, shuddering as her body clenched around the vibrator.

The low humming level wasn't going to get her off, especially since he hadn't turned on the clit suction and restrained her legs far enough apart that she couldn't squeeze it closer to her body. Instead, it was another long, massive tease while he prepared to fist her.

She shuddered again.

Then moaned when she felt him tug on the base of the vibrator, sliding it out of her soaked pussy with a wet sound that made him hum with approval. She could hear the soft thud as it was placed on the tray beside him.

"Good girl." The plug followed a moment later before also being deposited on the tray, leaving her feeling so empty... but not for long. Slick fingers pressed at her pussy, stroking then pushing in easily, thanks to the lube and her own arousal. "Now, do your best to relax."

Easy for him to say.

Actually, it wasn't that difficult as he began fingering her, using his other hand to make slow circles with his thumb around her swollen clit while his palm pressed down on her mound to hold her in place. He started with two fingers and quickly added a third once he realized there was no resistance.

It felt so good.

So full.

The pressure on her mound increased her pleasure, though her swollen clit was aching to actually be touched.

"More, please," she begged. She needed to get off. The long tease was driving her wild. Every part of her skin felt more acutely sensitive the longer it went on—her poor clit felt as if it was going to explode, and her nipples were throbbing on her chest in time with the thrusts of his fingers.

"Well, if you insist." His dark, sadistic chuckle as he began to push four fingers into her sent shivers up her spine. "Does it hurt yet, baby?"

"Yes and no." She moaned as he moved his hand a little more

roughly, sinking all four digits in up to the knuckles. "Oh fuck... Sir..."

"That's it, Red. Take my hand. This part might be a little more difficult."

Morgan whined, her hips trying to move upward as more of his hand began to slide inside her. She couldn't see his hand, but she knew how it was done. His thumb would be folding into his palm, making his hand into a kind of spear that he was now trying to push the thickest part of into her body. With his other hand pressing down on her mound, she couldn't move away or even lift her hips as he began pushing in.

She was so wet, she could hear the squishing sounds as she was stretched open, the slippery lube and her juices combining to help ease his passage. Not that it made it easy. Morgan whimpered, shuddering, yanking at the cuffs around her wrists as she tried to writhe in place.

"That's it, baby, you're doing so good," Asad crooned, his dark eyes glowing with approval. "Just a little more."

Her cry when he pushed his whole hand inside her echoed around the room. The knuckles and thumb had been the hardest part, and now she was so full, she could barely breathe.

"Oh fuck... oh fuck..."

"That's it, good girl. It's so fucking hot, seeing my hand inside you up to the wrist. Now I'm going to make a fist. It might feel weird."

"Fuck!"

Weird wasn't the word for it. Morgan didn't have the words to describe the sensations as his fingers moved inside her, curling into a fist. It felt like a ripple in her stomach, utterly foreign, not entirely pleasant, yet not painful, either. Then he was there, impossibly thick, filling her entire channel... and he began to move.

"Oh!" She uttered a short scream as his arm pulled back, then pushed forward, deeper inside her. It was too much. Her thoughts short-circuited. It hurt and felt good at the same time. It was heaven and hell and everything in-between. Her muscles spasmed around the moving fist and arm.

"That's it, baby. You've got my whole hand inside you. Fuck, that's so hot."

Master Asad's praise was even hotter. She couldn't respond. She couldn't think. She could barely breathe.

"Such a good girl. I love you, Morgan."

The words didn't fully register, then she lost all semblance of sense as he began to rub his thumb against her clit as he fucked her with his fist. Ecstasy exploded through her, throwing her into the air and sending her into freefall as she screamed from the sheer, overwhelming exhilaration.

Her body felt as though it was levitating, lifting into the air from the force of her climax. She couldn't breathe, couldn't think, couldn't do anything but drown in the sensations crashing over her until her vision went dark.

───────

*A*SAD

He would admit to slight panic when Morgan went still for a moment. Thankfully, she hitched her breath and opened her eyes a moment later. Pleasure overload. He'd seen it before, though never when he had his whole hand inside someone.

"Good girl," he murmured, carefully unclenching his fist, so he could slide his hand free. It took several long moments to complete the process, and she shuddered as he pulled his hand away, her body going limp with relief at the absence. Her pussy gaped open, and the sight was so fucking hot, he wrapped his fingers around his cock.

The glove felt a little odd, but knowing that he was holding himself in the fist that had just been inside her was such a fucking turn-on. He was so pent up, it only took a few strokes of his hand before he was groaning and spraying his cum over her lower body.

"Fuck..."

That hadn't been his intention, but he'd gotten himself too worked up. And there was something so satisfying about seeing his cum decorating her skin, another way of claiming her as his own. If nothing else, he felt sure she was never going to forget this night.

"Fuck," she agreed with a soft sigh, her eyelashes fluttering. "That was… intense."

"But good?" he couldn't help asking, running his hands over her legs and giving her muscles a little massage on his way to release her ankles from the restraints.

"*Very* good. I don't know that I'd want to do it very often, though." Morgan shivered.

Moving around the table, he rolled the rings off of her nipples and uncuffed her wrists before pulling her into his arms, as if she was the heroine on the cover of an old school romance novel, so he could carry her to the bath.

"As a special occasion treat, it's a good choice."

"Noted." But she wasn't saying anything about what he really wanted to know. "Um. So. Did you hear me? When I said I loved you."

She looked at him in surprise. Maybe she hadn't heard him.

"Yes, but I didn't think it counted."

"Why wouldn't it count?" He frowned as he shouldered open the door to the bedroom, turning to the side so he could carry her through without banging her head on the frame.

"I don't think it counts if you say it while you're having sex. Sometimes, it just slips out or something, and the guy doesn't actually mean it, so it doesn't count."

Ah, okay. He saw where she was coming from, and that was a thing that people really did say. For good reason. However…

"I had my hand inside you, not my dick. It counts. That's when I intended to say it."

"It is? Why?" Morgan blinked owlishly at him.

He shrugged as they went into the bathroom. Setting her down next to the tub gave him a minute to think, but the truth was, he wasn't sure. He'd been thinking that it was an intimate moment, a way to show her how much he appreciated her trust, trying to be emotionally vulnerable while she was so physically vulnerable…

All of that sounded really silly now and not like anything he wanted to say out loud. He stared at the water as it poured into the tub.

"Asad." Morgan touched his arm. "I love you, too."

Green eyes met his, and he felt the tension in his shoulders melt away.

"Sorry I kinda fucked it up the first time. I'll do better the second." Leaning over, he pressed a kiss to her lips. When he pulled back, she was smiling.

"I think it was perfect for the first time... for our first time. Because we're not perfect. We're a little messy and a little different, but we're in it together. And that's what matters."

He liked that.

Good thing she felt that way, too, because the second time he said it was when he was balls deep in her ass thirty minutes later, and he was pretty sure that wasn't actually the perfect time, either.

But it was perfect for them.

EPILOGUE

Living with a happy couple while being unhappily single was a form of torture. Not that they were there all the time. Sometimes, he ended up walking around a completely empty house, knowing they were off somewhere else, being happy.

It wasn't that he begrudged them that. He wanted Morgan to be happy. Asad made her happy. They were ridiculously cute together, too.

The club's biggest playboy had turned into the club's most devoted and slavishly sweet boyfriend—though doing so definitely hadn't curbed any of his sadistic tendencies. Talk about the 'magic vagina' effect.

Too bad he didn't have a magic penis.

The woman he really wanted had had no problem turning him away after their night together.

"You okay back there?" Asad asked, glancing in the rearview mirror to look at Brian in the backseat. "You look like you're constipated or something."

Morgan turned around to look at Brian, a frown on her pretty face as she looked him over.

"I'm fine," he said to them both, making a shooing motion at her to turn back around. Rolling her eyes, she obeyed. Asad really was good for her. A few months ago, there was no way she would have rolled her eyes at him for giving her an order. Definitely not where he could see, and probably not even when he couldn't. "Just worried about how much of my furniture you're going to have sex on before I get back from this trip."

"All of it," Asad said immediately, making Morgan giggle.

Now it was Brian's turn to roll his eyes. Not that he actually cared. He just liked to give Asad a hard time, just like Asad did to him. It was how they showed each other love.

"At least leave the stuff in my room alone."

"Hey, your poor bed probably misses someone having sex in it."

Brian rolled his eyes, making a disgusted noise, but the sad truth was that Asad was right about how long it had been since he'd had anyone in that bed with him. Or any bed. He'd done a few scenes at Stronghold, the kink club he was a member of, but none of them had led to anything more.

Which sucked because he wanted to be in a relationship.

It was really unfortunate that the one woman he really wanted didn't want anything to do with him. Despite that, he didn't seem to be able to find anyone else he wanted to date.

"We won't have sex in your room, I promise," Morgan said, making Asad groan in protest because Morgan always followed through on her word. Thankfully, he didn't have to listen to Asad's complaining—which was really just foreplay for them—for too long before they pulled in front of the airport.

"Thanks for the ride. Take care of yourselves... and I'm charging you for any stains I find on the couch when I get back," Brian said, leaning forward to wrap his arms around Morgan from behind in a hug goodbye. She hugged his hands to her chest, just above her breasts. Asad reached out for a fist bump.

"Have a good trip!"

Right. A good trip.

He would be the only single guy on a jack-and-jill wedding party weekend, and the only single woman attending was Rae—aka, the woman he desperately wanted but who wanted nothing to do with him because of who he was... a Daddy Dom. Even though she was absolutely a babygirl at heart, she wouldn't admit it.

He pasted a grin on his face for Morgan's benefit, waving to her through the window before walking back to the popped trunk to get his bag.

On the upside, at least Rae and Master Damian had broken up a couple months back, so Brian didn't have to go on this trip with both of them while he was on his own. So, things could be worse, but they still didn't feel good. He was going to do his best to focus on making sure Mitch and Domi had an incredible week, fulfill his best man duties, and ignore his impossible attraction to the maid of honor.

For a whole week in paradise at a kinky island retreat while they were surrounded by happy couples, and their attraction to each other remained undying.

Piece of cake.

MASTER BRIAN AND RAE WILL RETURN IN HIDDEN AWAY, BOOK 7 OF THE Masters of Marquis series!

The End

ABOUT THE AUTHOR

Golden Angel is a USA Today best-selling author of heart and bottom warming romance.

She is happily married, old enough to know better but still too young to care, and a big fan of happily-ever-afters, strong heroes and heroines, and sizzling chemistry.

When she's not writing, she can often be found on the couch reading, in front of her sewing machine making a new cosplay, hanging out with her friends, or wandering the Maryland Renaissance Fair.

www.goldenangelromance.com

BB bookbub.com/authors/golden-angel
g goodreads.com/goldeniangel
f facebook.com/GoldenAngelAuthor
O instagram.com/goldeniangel

OTHER BOOKS BY GOLDEN ANGEL

Contemporary BDSM Romance

Venus Rising Series (MFM Romance)

The Venus School

Venus Aspiring

Venus Desiring

Venus Transcendent

Venus Wedding

Venus Rising Box Set

Stronghold Doms Series

The Sassy Submissive

Taming the Tease

Mastering Lexie

Pieces of Stronghold

Breaking the Chain

Bound to the Past

Stripping the Sub

Tempting the Domme

Hardcore Vanilla

Steamy Stocking Stuffers

A Sassy Christmas

Entering Stronghold Box Set

Nights at Stronghold Box Set

Stronghold: Closing Time Box Set

Masters of Marquis Series

Bondage Buddies

Master Chef

Law & Disorder

Switch Play

Legally Bound

Shallow Submission

Hidden Away

Giant Tamer

Third Wheel

Dungeons & Doms Series

Dungeon Master

Dungeon Daddy

Dungeon Showdown

Daddies Everywhere

Chef Daddy

Foosball Daddies

Taco Daddy

Little Villain

Historical Spanking Romance

Domestic Discipline Quartet

Birching His Bride

Dealing With Discipline

Punishing His Ward

Claiming His Wife

The Domestic Discipline Quartet Box Set

Bridal Discipline Series

Philip's Rules

Gabrielle's Discipline

Lydia's Penance

Benedict's Commands

Arabella's Taming

Pride and Punishment Box Set

Commands and Consequences Box Set

Deception and Discipline

A Season for Treason

A Season for Scandal

A Season for Smugglers

A Season for Spies

Desire and Discipline

A Season for Bliss

Bridgewater Brides

Their Harlot Bride

Standalone

Marriage Training

The Duke's Pursuit

Rogue Booty

Sci-fi Romance

Tsenturion Masters Series with Lee Savino

Alien Captive

Alien Tribute

Alien Abduction

Standalone

Mated on Hades

Shifter Romance

Big Bad Bunnies Series

Chasing His Bunny

Chasing His Squirrel

Chasing His Puma

Chasing His Polar Bear

Chasing His Honey Badger

Chasing Her Lion

Night of the Wild Stags

Chasing Tail Box Set

Chasing Tail... Again Box Set